The Diary of Alice James

Edited with an Introduction by

Leon Edel

PENGUIN BOOKS

Penguin Books Ltd, Harmondsworth,
Middlesex, England
Penguin Books, 625 Madison Avenue,
New York, New York 10022, U.S.A.
Penguin Books Australia Ltd, Ringwood,
Victoria, Australia
Penguin Books Canada Limited, 2801 John Street,
Markham, Ontario, Canada L3R 1B4
Penguin Books (N.Z.) Ltd, 182–190 Wairau Road,
Auckland 10, New Zealand

First published in the United States of America
under the title *Alice James: Her Brothers—Her Journal* by
Dodd, Mead & Company, Inc., 1934
This edition first published in the United States of America by
Dodd, Mead & Company, Inc., 1964
Published in The Penguin American Library 1982

LIBRARY OF CONGRESS CATALOGING IN PUBLICATION DATA
James, Alice, 1848–1892.
The diary of Alice James.
(The Penguin American library)
Reprint. Originally published: New York:
Dodd, Mead, 1964.
1. James, Alice, 1848–1892. 2. James, William, 1842–1910.
3. James, Henry, 1843–1916. 4. James family.
5. United States—Biography. I. Edel, Leon, 1907–
II. Title.
CT275.J29A3 1982 973.8′092′2 [B] 81-13906
ISBN 0 14 039.011 1 AACR2

Printed in the United States of America by
George Banta Co., Inc., Harrisonburg, Virginia
Set in Linotype Caslon Old Face

THE PENGUIN AMERICAN LIBRARY

EDITOR: JOHN SEELYE

THE DIARY OF ALICE JAMES

Leon Edel was Citizens Professor of English (now Emeritus) at the University of Hawaii from 1970 until 1978 and earlier was Henry James Professor of English and American Letters, a chair created for him, at New York University. He is a member of the American Academy of Arts and Letters and of the American Academy of Arts and Sciences and a Fellow of the Royal Society of Literature. He has been president of P.E.N. (American Center) and of the U.S. Authors Guild and secretary of the National Institute of Arts and Letters. Mr. Edel has written or edited more than thirty volumes, including the five-volume *Life of Henry James*, which won the Pulitzer Prize and the National Book Award and which many critics over the years have called the greatest biography in English since Boswell. He has also edited four volumes of Henry James's letters. Leon Edel's most recent work was *Bloomsbury: A House of Lions*.

Contents

Preface

❧

THE DIARY of Alice James, invalid sister of the psychologist William and of the novelist Henry, represents her modest claim on posterity beside the works of her famous brothers. She kept the record of her sickroom world in two closely-written scribblers during the final months of her abbreviated life, and bequeathed them to her loyal friend and companion, Katharine Peabody Loring, who had cared for her during the better part of a decade. Miss Loring brought the diary back to her home in Beverly, Massachussets, where she edited the manuscript by straightening its punctuation a little, altering an occasional word, deleting some passages, and introducing half-a-dozen footnotes. She then (in 1894) had four copies printed, one for each of the three surviving James brothers, and one for herself. It was her intention, if they approved, to publish the book. Alice had asked during the last six weeks of her life to have the diary typewritten, and "though she never said so, I understand that she would like to have it published."

Years later Miss Loring wrote that William James "never thanked me for his copy, simply acknowledged the receipt of it and certainly never made any suggestion as to its being read or not." Henry James urged Miss Loring to refrain from publishing the diary, and destroyed his privately printed copy. His reasons were expressed with unmistakable clarity in a series of letters to his brother. He was "terribly scared and disconcerted —I mean alarmed—by the sight of so many private names and allusions in print." Alice had never told him she kept a diary;

and he had gossiped freely to her about London society and his daily life, often exaggerating in order to enliven the sickroom. He did not mind Alice's having written down so much of this talk—but it was quite another matter to give it the permanence of print. Miss Loring should have "sunk a few names," he said, and used initials (she actually did in a few instances). "When I see that *I* say that Augustine Birrell has a self-satisfied smirk after he speaks—and see that Katharine felt no prompting to exercise a discretion about the name, I feel very unhappy and wonder at the strangeness of destiny."

Henry James's immediate fear was that the youngest brother, Robertson, or his children, would through carelessness or indiscretion make the diary known. "I seem to see them showing it about Concord—and talking about it—with the fearful American newspaper lying in wait for every whisper, every echo." And the novelist added: "I bow my head to fate, I am prepared for the worst." The worst never occurred. Miss Loring respected Henry's wishes, even to not conveying a copy to Robertson. Almost half a century after Alice's death she presented the manuscript to Robertson's daughter, the late Mrs. Mary James Vaux, of Bryn Mawr. She did this, she said, out of friendship and because Robertson's children were "the only grandchildren who have ever taken any interest in me, or have asked me about my relations with the James family."

Mrs. Vaux had long felt that some memorial should be created for the less-known members of the James family: her own father, the gifted Robertson, who had never used his gifts, and his older brother, Garth Wilkinson James, generous spendthrift who died in his fortieth year. Thus the diary finally reached book form in 1934 not as Alice's "letter to the world," but as part of a volume devoted also to Wilky and Robertson. It bore the title *Alice James: Her Brothers—Her Journal*. Alice remained posthumously—as she had been all her life—the mere younger sister; her claim to attention was still as an appendage to brothers.

Mrs. Vaux entrusted the editing of the volume to Anna Robeson Burr. Mrs. Burr wrote an 82-page introduction devoted to the younger brothers. *Their* claim upon posterity, ironically, was largely derived from their kinship to William and Henry and Alice—although they had, like so many of their fellow-citizens, been ardent Abolitionists, had fought bravely in the Civil War and been broken by it. Wilky and Robertson had then, with more idealism than practical business sense, tried to run a plantation in the post-bellum South, and finally ended up working in the Midwest. They were honorable citizens in the American republic; but in that special republic of which they were "natives"—the James family—life had bestowed a kind of honorable second-class citizenship upon them. It was their uncommon fate to have genius for brotherhood and to experience (as Stanislaus Joyce was to feel in another century) the glow of the family pride in the achieving and creative brothers. Small wonder that Robertson fancied he was a foundling, and that Garth Wilkinson, badly wounded in the assault on Fort Wagner in 1863, found no career and died young.

Mrs. Burr showed less respect for the text than Miss Loring. In her preface she said that "the journal is printed here as written"; however, she excised French passages and certain others where the text could not be understood without explanation. She robbed the diary of much of its point by omitting Alice's clippings from the English papers, "because they concern events long past, relating often to minor Parliamentary debates and English local politics, but also because they dilute the rich flow of her own observation and feeling." This necessitated cutting out some of the allusions to the clippings. Thus truncated, the "journal" was given to the world. What Mrs. Burr was glossing over was the fact that the clippings served Alice more often than not as vivid text for some of her sharp comments on English manners; and the "minor Parliamentary debates" were still part and parcel of the Irish Home Rule issue which gave so much life—and acerbity—to the otherwise monotonous invalidical existence. Far from "diluting'" Alice's journal, they are integral to it.

In publishing the full text of the diary for the first time, I have worked from photo copies of both the original manuscript and Miss Loring's privately printed version. From this it is clear that Mrs. Burr did not base her text on the manuscript, but on the privately printed version. Some of the clippings are missing in the original manuscript, having long ago dropped away from the pages to which they were pasted. For the text of these, I have relied upon the Loring edition, where they were reproduced in full. There has been some harmonizing of Alice's idiosyncratic punctuation and some of the abbreviations have been spelled out as an aid to the reader. In all other respects, however, the diary now conforms to the original manuscript. I am indebted to the late Mrs. Vaux, who first showed me the manuscript and who some years ago expressed the hope that I would bring out a new edition. Her son, Professor Henry James Vaux of Berkeley, California, gave me valuable assistance and I wish particularly to thank him and his daughter, Alice James Vaux, the present owner of the manuscript, for permitting it to be microfilmed. I am indebted, in the editing of this diary, to Donald G. Brien, a friend of many years; to William A. Jackson, director of the Houghton Library, and the librarian, Miss Carolyn E. Jakeman; and not least, to my former student, Dr. Gloria Glikin of Brooklyn College, who assisted me in the collation of the Loring edition with the manuscript and patiently searched the English newspapers and helped with the annotation. Finally I wish to express my thanks to Mr. John James of Cambridge and the President and Fellows of Harvard University for continued access to the James family papers in the Houghton Library. I am grateful to Mr. Rupert Hart-Davis for help with certain of the footnotes.

Almost a century has elapsed since Alice James wrote her diary. The annotation accordingly has been designed to place the writer's allusions in their proper historical context and to identify—especially for a new generation—some of the persons mentioned in the text. For those interested in the bibliographical side of my task, the manuscript of the diary is contained, as I have said, in two ordinary English scribblers. The first consists of some 232 numbered pages unruled (some pages carry duplicate numbers), 4½ by 7 inches, and the second 6¼ by 7¾ inches, containing 201 pages ruled of which 71 are in Alice James's hand and the remainder are written by Katharine Loring. One other handwriting appears, though rarely, that of her nurse, Emily Bradford. The diarist began on page one, on the right-hand leaf at the front of each book, and continued on each successive right-hand leaf until the back of the book was reached. Then she turned it upside down; the blank pages were now on the right, and these were duly filled. Accordingly, when the diary is opened the text on the right-hand page is in the proper position, but that on the left is upside down.

Alice James also used the first scribbler for a time as a commonplace book. Some pages are blank in the second book, and into half a dozen of these has been copied a letter from the elder Henry James to Emerson (containing a description of Hawthorne) and a portion of a letter from William James of 1885, apparently written to Alice. The father's letter was published in 1936 in Ralph Barton Perry's *Thought and Character of William James* (I, 88-90).

The four-copy edition has the following title page:

The Diary/ of / Alice James / Four Copies Printed./ Cambridge:/ John Wilson and Son. / University Press./ 1894

The Bancroft Library at Berkeley in California has the copy probably never given to Robertson James, but given by William James's son, Henry, to his sister Mary Margaret Porter. It is inscribed "Henry James [3rd] from Katharine P. Loring, October 1923." The third copy is in the Barrett collection, Alderman Library, University of Virginia, and on its title page, in Miss Loring's handwriting, is the following notation: "One copy destroyed by Author's brother Henry; one belongs to Katharine P. Loring; Two copies to Henry James (3) of which he placed one in the Harvard University Library." With the known destruction of Henry James's copy, this must be considered one of the rarest of nineteenth-century privately printed books in the United States.

Although I have told much of the story of Alice James's relationship to her brother in my *Life of Henry James*, the material is dispersed in various relevant chapters of the second and third parts, *The Conquest of London* and *The Middle Years*. The editing of her diary has afforded me the opportunity of unifying this material, and I have done so in the biographical essay which serves here as introduction. I have, however, used certain documents which were irrelevant in the other volumes. The correspondence of Alice James with members of her family is in the Houghton Library at Harvard, as are some of her letters to members of the Norton family. Some of Henry James's letters to Miss Loring are at Harvard; others are in the library at Beverly; some are in the National Library of Scotland. Others are in the Barrett Collection at the University of Virginia. I am indebted to C. Waller Barrett for access to these before they were added to the collection. The Vaux papers contained letters from various members of the James family to Robertson James. In this preface I have used a letter now at Harvard written by Miss Loring to William James's daughter, Mrs. Bruce Porter, on June 6, 1934, justifying publication of the diary. Lilla Cabot Perry's description of the household at 20 Quincy Street is contained in a letter to Van Wyck Brooks which he published in the third volume of his reminiscences, *From the Shadow of the Mountain*, in 1961. Other accounts of Alice James can be found in Henry James's autobiographies, Ralph Barton Perry, *The Thought and Character of William James*, and F. O. Matthiessen, *The James Family*. Mr. Augustus P. Loring of Boston kindly allowed me to quote from the unpublished Loring material. I wish finally to thank Jean Strouse, author of the admirable full-length *Alice James: A Biography* (1980), for helping me correct various slips and printer's errors she encountered in the diary during her extensive researches.

I have retold Alice James's life not as a part of her brothers' lives, as in these volumes, but as a life possessing its particular logic and its own—in this case distinctly muted—drama. The diary itself helps to complete the portrait.

L.E.

Introduction:
A Portrait of Alice James

ALICE JAMES began to keep a commonplace book at the
end of her second year in England. She had crossed the
Atlantic in November 1884, and the first entries are dated
"*December 1886.*" Into this book she copied verses, aphorisms,
passages from novels, sentences culled from her wide and ever-
curious readings. We encounter at the outset lines from the
Rubáiyát—"the wine of life keeps oozing drop by drop, the
leaves of life keep falling one by one." On the next page she
sets down Hamlet's "I do not set my life at a pin's fee."
Carlyle's "Everlasting Yea" follows—her father might have
written it—"There is in a man a HIGHER than Love of Happiness: he can do without Happiness, and instead thereof find
Blessedness," and immediately after this she copies (in the
French in which she read *War and Peace*) Tolstoy's account of
Prince Andrei at Austerlitz—the vivid moment when the
wounded Prince, falling backward, discovers above him the blue
immensity of the heavens and experiences, in the very midst of
battle, a sense of exquisite peace. The pages of the commonplace book are filled with the words of famous writers. They
seem to speak for Alice. In 1887 she is quoting Howells and
Loti, La Bruyère, Flaubert, Edgar Quinet, George Sand, and
again Tolstoy. In the following year Renan, Maupassant, her
brothers William and Henry, Auguste Comte, George Eliot.
But when she writes down the year 1889 it is to announce, in
effect, that she will henceforth deal with her life in her own
words: "I think that if I get into the habit of writing a bit about

what happens, or rather doesn't happen, I may lose a little of the sense of loneliness and desolation which abides with me."

She kept her diary faithfully thereafter, save on days when she was too ill; and she persisted even when she lost the strength to write. During the last months of her terminal illness, she dictated. Apparently the diary came to be much more than a substitute for loneliness and desolation. On one of the pages she set down words from Cotton Mather, "so the character of his daily conversation was a trembling walk with God." In a certain sense Alice's diary, with its mixture of stoicism and doubt, its laughter at death—and its fear of death—its renunciation and its protest, represented her particular and frequent "trembling walk with God."

I

Alice James was born in New York City on August 7, 1848, the fifth and last child of Henry and Mary James. The father, who came from Albany, was a man of leisure in a country where leisure was almost unknown; while his fellow-Americans were pushing farther westward in their conquest of the continent, the elder Henry James dreamed of Utopias and of a Swedenborgian Heaven on Earth. With a comfortable income inherited from his Irish immigrant father, and a large house at 58 West Fourteenth Street, he provided his four boys and his daughter with a wide, far-ranging, but deeply troubled childhood. There were long stays in Europe, *pensions*, experimental private schools, a train of tutors and governesses. The elder Henry was a dreamer in his library and a maker of paradoxes on the lecture platform. A friend of Emerson, Carlyle, Thackeray, and most of the Boston Brahmins, he limped through life (he had lost a leg in a boyhood accident), cheerfully and gregariously, but also, his children were to feel, with a certain ineffectuality and vagueness. His wife, a plain, unimaginative woman (considerably transfigured in the imaginative prose of her novelist-son), provided the practical down-to-earth management required in a household otherwise volatile. Her children in later years spoke of her "self-effacement." This masked a strong will and a vigorous guiding hand. Not the least of the family's paradoxes thus was a father who was in reality maternal, and a mother inclined to be gubernatorial, as Henry James implied and Alice's recollections in her diary suggest.

Alice grew up in a family circle almost entirely masculine, save for the hovering figures of her mother and her mother's sister, Catherine Walsh, the "Aunt Kate" of the family. Five men, the father and the two older sons (who were half-a-dozen years older than Alice), and the younger brothers of her own age, Garth and Robertson, dominated her early years. Her elder brothers cultivated a courtliness with her that was really a form of self-display and teasing, and her younger brothers, when they did not ignore her, heaped the usual petty indignities small boys have in reserve for baby sisters—"the anguish," Alice remembers (recalling a childhood outing), "greater even than usual of Wilky's and Bob's heels grinding into my shins." The "greater even than usual" sums up chapters of childhood history. Even the great Thackeray teased, when he joined the family at dinner in Paris. From his towering height he looked down on the eight-year-old Alice, in her pretty frock, and in a high, shocked voice said, "Crinoline—I was suspecting it! So young and so depraved!"

Alice may not have known what the word "depraved" meant, but she knew she was the butt of laughter—as she was in countless family episodes. She found ways of defending herself; her mother's letters record that she often effectively "sassed" her father and brothers. A family friend in Newport later spoke of the "unhappy" James children, fighting "like cats and dogs"; and if Alice was not in the thick of the battles, she constantly sought to raise her feminine voice among the stronger male voices around her, which means she learned how to be aggressive, like them, with words.

Alice's education seems to have been as casual as that of her

brothers: a modicum of home-learning; French taught by th
same governess who taught her brother Henry; certain strug
gles with arithmetic, when the family was in Geneva and th
boys had been farmed out to various schools. "Our Alice i
still under discipline," writes the father to a friend, "prepar
ing to fulfil some high destiny or other in the future by reduc
ing decimal fractions to their least possible rate of subsistence."
The European experiences of the young William and Henry
which played so large a role in their development, touched
Alice much less, perhaps because she was only seven when the
family went abroad in 1855. The Jameses were constantly on
the move; and later the sons and daughter complained they
had had an "hotel" childhood. They were swept from Geneva
to London, London to Paris, Paris to Boulogne-sur-Mer, a
sweep across the Atlantic for a brief stay in Newport, and, jus
as they were restoring their American roots, a sweep eastward
again to schools and *pensions* in Geneva and later in Germany
Small wonder that Alice, in adult life, warned William agains
repeating the same pattern with his children. "What enrich-
ment of mind and memory can children have without continuity
and if they are torn up by the roots every little while as we
were? Of all things don't make the mistake which brought
about our rootless and accidental childhood." Europe should be
left for his children "until they are old enough to have the
Grand Emotion, undiluted by vague memories."

On the eve of the Civil War the Jameses finally ended their
wanderings and settled in Newport. Here Alice passed the early
years of adolescence. Her younger brothers disappeared from
her life; they became soldiers—but then they had always disappeared to play games not for girls. Her older brothers remained at home, but went through a long period of self-
absorption and invalidism, suffering deeply from the fratricidal
war. Alice was much alone. She describes in her diary how she
took gloomy walks around Newport, "absorbing into the bone

that the better part is to clothe oneself in neutral tints, walk by still waters and possess one's soul in silence." That was "woman's place" in the genteel society of her time; but neutrality was impossible: there remained in Alice the long-formed need to assert herself. The old articulateness could not, in reality, be silenced. "The only thing which survives," she concluded, "is the resistance we bring to life, and not the strain life brings to us."

Alice brought a full measure of defense rather than resistance. Increasingly it took the form of a struggle between body and mind. When she was fifteen there were attacks of "neuralgia" and William James writes in a letter that he hopes Alice is "back at school instead of languishing and lolling about the house." At this school Alice remembered a struggle between doing her lessons and "shrieking or wiggling through the most impossible sensations of upheaval."

By the time the family moved to Cambridge at the end of the Civil War the upheavals took serious form. When a conversation proved too exciting, Alice had a fainting spell. At the moment of falling asleep she experienced terror. And the house in Cambridge provided a melancholy environment. In one of his letters Henry speaks of their home as being "as lively as an inner sepulchre." And the backward glance of an eyewitness, Lilla Cabot Perry, who married a boyhood friend of the Jameses, is eloquent. Recalling various households in Cambridge, she speaks of "the poky banality of the James house, ruled by Mrs. James, where Henry James's father used to limp in and out and never seemed really to 'belong' to his wife or Miss Walsh [Aunt Kate], large florid stupid-seeming ladies, or to his clever but coldly self-absorbed daughter, who was his youngest child. . . . Henry James's mother (even to my own perception as a child) was the very incarnation of *banality* and his aunt, Miss Walsh, who lived with them, not much better. His father always seemed to me genial and delightful . . . but he seemed to me out of place in that stiff stupid house in Cambridge."

We must allow for possible limitations of a Cabot-eye view of the James household in Cambridge, so at variance with most of the pictures offered by the Jameses themselves. There is much in it, however, that corresponds to the content of the mother's letters to her children. The truth was that 20 Quincy Street harbored during the late 1860's three disturbed young adults, the two older brothers and Alice, with her illnesses which set the stage for her invalidism. Her breakdowns, particularly that of 1868, when she was in her twentieth year, are documented in letters written by her parents to the youngest son, Robertson, who was living in the Midwest. She had "violent turns of hysteria." "Alice," the father wrote, "is half the time, indeed much more than half, on the verge of insanity and suicide." During this period she had violent impulses to "knock off the head of the benignant pater." The controlling of such impulses imposed upon her a burden which she described with insight: that of being "doctor, nurse and straitjacket, all in one." And by being ill, she rendered herself powerless to execute the violence. At the same time she could hold those around her in bondage. "Father is bearing Alice's calls upon him in a most miraculous way," the mother writes. Alice demanded indeed that he be at her bedside day and night. During certain of these hours she told him of her wish to commit suicide. Was it a sin? she asked. The elder Henry coped with this in a shrewd but self-exalting way. He did not see that Alice needed some expression of being wanted and loved. He did not think suicide was a sin. It might be, he said, if a person did this as a consequence of drink or opium and "the utter degradation of his faculties." But it was absurd to believe it sinful if Alice wished release from her suffering. He gave her his fatherly permission to end her life whenever it pleased her, beseeching her only to "do it in a perfectly gentle way in order not to distress her friends."

In subsequent conversations Alice rationalized that her assertive and attention-getting inquiry had had a deeper purpose—that it had been a way of asserting her freedom. She told the elder Henry that "now she could perceive it to be her *right* to dispose of her own body when life had become intolerable, she could never do it." And although later Alice told her father she was still "strongly tempted," she never took the final step that would have brought her an earlier peace. She lived to pursue her career as a patient and to exact the love she had failed to receive when young.

To his youngest son the father wrote: "Never have I had such deep tranquil joy in thinking of the Divine name revealed in Christ as in these profoundly trying experiences with Alice. I certainly never before saw such a believer in the truth of a better world as she is, when her suffering is most acute; and when she comes out of it I never saw one so fitted by her grace and playfulness of wit to adorn this life. But I really think she is gradually getting better, though she is opposed to doing so herself, and evidently desires to go into the spiritual world at once, if it were possible." His optimism reveals his failure in empathy and his characteristic egotism. He "spiritualized" his children.

Between illnesses there were forays into activity. For a while she attempted charitable work in Boston and New York. She belonged to a sewing circle and went to parties. She indulged, when she could, in the minor sociabilities of Quincy and Kirkland streets in Cambridge. In 1872 she traveled abroad with her brother Henry and their aunt Kate. All the remedies of the time were attempted: massage, visits to specialists in Manhattan for ice and electric therapy, special "blistering" baths, sojourns in the "Adams Nervine Asylum" near Boston—but they proved ineffective. She was to speak in her diary of "the ignorant asininity of the medical profession in its treatment of nervous disorders" and of "these doctors who tell you that you will die or *recover*." To which she grimly added she had been at these alternatives since she was nineteen, "and I am neither dead nor recovered."

The doctors diagnosed her illnesses as "rheumatic gout," or "spinal neurosis." When she had palpitations they spoke of "cardiac complications" and "nervous hyperaesthesia." They seemed to find Alice's heart strong and most of the treatments prescribed seem to have been for "nerves." We may speculate that at least some part of her condition was the common one of Victorian restrictions on women. Elizabeth Barrett offers a record of an analogous kind of bedridden life and of her escape from it. But no Robert Browning came to carry Alice off to some Italy of her own. What we get instead, in the diary, is a sense of early frustration, that of a strong-limbed active girl who never found an opportunity to indulge in activity. In our time she would have played tennis, or gone water skiing or followed various forms of outdoor life. In earlier New England she wore long dresses, and sat decorously at dull teas—and had her periodic prostrations.

Years later Henry James was to understand this. He was to write to Mary James Vaux, his niece, that "in our family group girls seem scarcely to have had a chance." And he concluded, having been the closest witness of her final decline, that Alice's "tragic health was, in a manner, the only solution for her of the practical problem of life."

In the early 1880's Alice James demonstrated that she could meet responsibilities with courage, strength, and resolution. Her mother's death in 1882 found her active in ministering to her father. They sold the Quincy Street house and moved into a smaller residence in Boston, in Mount Vernon Street. Here, during the greater part of a year, "haunted by the terror that I should fail him, as I watched the poor old man fade, day by day," she nursed her father and presided over the household. She and her aunt Kate were with him during his last hours; the sons were away, and when Henry arrived after rushing across the December seas, the funeral had already taken place. Her father left her ample means; and to her $3,500 a year Henry added his share of the Syracuse rents, $1,200 a year, since he was earning much more by his pen. Henry remained with Alice in the house on Beacon Hill for several months. The bachelor son and the spinster daughter seem to have found much peace and harmony in being together. The novelist slept in his father's room and settled the family affairs. Alice kept house. "My sister and I make an harmonious little *ménage*, and I feel a good deal as if I were married," the novelist wrote to his London publisher. They had always felt an intimate kinship that transcended ties of family, a strong emotional compatibility reaching back to their early years. The novelist now could replace the father in his relation to Alice, and his bestowing of his income on her was in itself a fatherly act. He felt for her a peculiar and intense affection, such as he was to describe in some notes for a story he never wrote—"two lives, two beings and *one* experience," an intensity of feeling "in relation to the *past*, the parents, the beloved mother, the beloved father—of those who have suffered before them and *for* them and whose blood is in their veins." The brother and sister of James's unwritten tale were to experience "the pain of sympathy," and "a deep, participating devotion of one to the other. . . . The brother suffers, has the experience, and the effect of the experience, is carried along by fate, etc., and the sister understands, perceives, shares, with every pulse of her being." When the novelist set down these quasi-incestuous feelings, Alice had been dead three years; but some part of his emotion seemed to go back to this period of their life together, during a winter and a summer in Boston.

Henry remained with Alice for the better part of a year and then returned to London to resume his own life. Alice seemed well established and comfortable in Mount Vernon Street. Although their aunt Kate lived in New York, she could be relied upon to visit her niece regularly. William James and his family

were easily accessible in Cambridge. And Alice had a new
friend. Henry James had seen her sufficiently to recognize the
beginning for his sister of a close and, as it proved, an abiding
attachment.

II

Katharine Peabody Loring and Alice James met during 1873.
Alice was then twenty-five and Miss Loring twenty-four. The
frail Alice had been promptly attracted to the energetic young
woman from Beverly, Massachusetts, who was identified with
various social and charitable enterprises in Boston. To a friend
(Sara Darwin) she described her as having "all the mere brute
superiority which distinguishes man from woman combined
with all the distinctively feminine virtues. There is nothing she
cannot do from hewing wood and drawing water to driving
runaway horses and educating all the women in North America." Miss Loring, shortly after their meeting, took Alice with
her to New Hampshire. To the astonishment of the James
family Alice went willingly instead of begging off, as was her
custom, from any new experience. "I hope her experiment has
been happy to the end—if the end has come, as I trust not,"
Henry James wrote to his mother. He added, "I trust she built
a monument somewhere of forest leaves (or rather of New
Hampshire granite) to the divine Miss Loring, who appears to
unite the wisdom of the serpent with the gentleness of the
dove."

To Alice, her brother expressed delight in Miss Loring's
"strength of wind and limb, to say nothing of her nobler qualities." During the summer of 1881 Alice and Miss Loring
traveled abroad, visiting England and Scotland. Henry saw
them briefly and was delighted with "the precious Miss Loring," who wore high collars, with pince-nez attached to a ribbon, and was a distinctive Bostonian bluestocking. He wrote to
his mother that she was "the most perfect" companion Alice

could have found; "Alice seems so extraordinarily fond of Miss Loring that a third person is rather a superfluous appendage." During his two visits to America (1881–1882 and 1882–1883) he became better acquainted with his sister's friend. She seemed to know how to cope with Alice's nervousness; she was a good nurse; she attended her with loving attention. Sometimes she took her under her own roof at Beverly to care for her during her prostrations. But Miss Loring could not give all her time to her Cambridge friend. She had a sickly sister, Louisa, to care for as well. And in 1884 she took Louisa to Europe in the hope that this change would effect a cure.

Left behind, Alice seems to have been seized by a kind of inner panic. In her diary she speaks of "these ghastly days" and of longing "to flee in to the firemen next door and escape from the 'Alone, Alone' that echoed through the house, rustled down the stairs, whispered from the walls, and confronted me like a material presence." Beyond a normal need for friendship, the little girl lurking in Alice out of earlier years craved undivided attention as well as the center of the stage. Alice issued an appeal to Miss Loring, who generously recrossed the Atlantic to escort Alice abroad; the latter would visit her brother Henry in London while Katharine was occupied with Louisa. Louisa, in this way, became Alice's rival for Katharine's attention. Alice sailed with no thought of remaining abroad: nevertheless it proved a decisive step.

It was November; the sea was calm; yet Alice never left her cabin. She had one of her nervous attacks shortly after the ship sailed and Miss Loring spent the voyage attending her two invalids. Henry James, boarding the vessel at Liverpool, when it was still out in the stream, was astonished at Alice's feebleness. Two stout sailors carried her ashore and she spent a week recuperating in a Liverpool hotel, attended by a maid Henry had brought along and a nurse. Then the novelist took her to London. Miss Loring, meanwhile, had taken her sister—whose health was much less precarious than Alice's—to Bournemouth. By the time Henry had installed Alice in lodgings off Piccadilly, near his own rooms, the situation seemed clear to him. Alice was bitterly jealous of Miss Loring's sister, Louisa: she wanted to have Katharine to herself. And something else became increasingly clear. "I may be wrong in the matter," the novelist reported to his brother, "but it rather strikes me as an effect that Katharine Loring has upon her—that as soon as they get together Alice takes to her bed. This was the case as soon as Katharine came to London to see her (she had been up before) and she has now been recumbent (as a consequence of her little four-hour journey) ever since she reached Bournemouth." The British doctors gave Alice a thorough examination. Their verdict coincided with that of their American confreres. They could find no sign of organic illness and they too ended by treating her as neurasthenic.

The trip to Europe proved beneficial for Louisa Loring. As she recovered, Katharine was increasingly free to be with Alice. When she was not, Henry James, reinforced by servants and a nurse, took charge. Whatever her ailments, if any, it became clear to the novelist that his sister was involved in an inextricable human relationship which had to take its own course. As he explained to his aunt Kate (many months had by this time elapsed and Louisa had been pronounced cured): "Katharine comes back to Alice for a permanency. Her being with her may be interrupted by absences, but evidently it is the beginning of a living-together, for the rest of such time as Alice's life may last." There was evidently, said Henry, "a kind of definite understanding between them." He added, "we must accept it with gratitude." He observed that also "there is about as much possibility of Alice's giving Katharine up as of giving her legs to be sawed off." Alice had told him that "if she could have Katharine *quietly* and *uninterruptedly* for a year 'to relieve her of all responsibility' she would get well." James could only say to this, "Amen! She will get well, or she won't, but, either way, t lies between themselves." He could hardly cease his career as novelist and set himself up as his sister's nurse. When his aunt Kate offered to come to England to help, he urged her not to; Alice "would then have *five* people under contribution, really, to take care of her, and she has quite enough now." Miss Loring, on her side, told Henry it was her desire "quite as strongly as Alice's, to be with her to the end." Henry James observed to his aunt that "a devotion so perfect and so generous" as Miss Loring's was "a gift of providence so rare and little-to-be-looked-for in this hard world that to brush it aside would be almost an act of impiety. Not to take it would be to get something much worse." What this meant to Alice may be judged from a brief allusion in a letter to William James of 1891. "This year has been the happiest I have ever known, surrounded by such affection and devotion, but I won't enter into details, as I see the blush mantle the elderly cheek of my scribe." In Miss Loring Alice had found not only a companion, but a friend whom she could love. If Alice was too ill to be an active lesbian she was nevertheless finding fulfillment by being chronically ill. There was a distinctive underlying sexuality in the relation: but it would probably be equally true to say the relationship was symbiotic, and involved a double power-play. Alice got a sense of power in manipulating her friend; and her friend felt powerful in controlling Alice's life. Both found gratification in their roles. This became the central subject of Henry James's novel *The Bostonians*, which he wrote as he was observing the power-drama in his own family.

The novelist discovered, on his side, that he was tied by a kind of delicate moral bondage to his sister's sickbed, very much as his father had been before him. He kept in close touch with her when he traveled on the Continent; he could go only when Miss Loring was fully available; and on at least two occasions he rushed back to London in answer to urgent telegraphic summons. Alice never recrossed the Atlantic. She feared the voyage; and she was never again sufficiently strong. She

lived periodically in London, and part of the time at Leaming
ton. When she was better, she held a semblance of a salon, re
ceiving, while on her couch, certain of her brother's friends—
Mr. Lowell, Mrs. Humphry Ward, Mrs. Matthew Arnold
the aged Fanny Kemble who, in spite of a bad heart, came puff
ing up the stairs to pay her a call. After a longish residence in
Leamington, she settled in Kensington and finally in a little
house at 41 Argyll Road, on Campden Hill. She began to keep
her diary in May of 1889. It tells the remainder of her story
Little more than a year before the end the doctors finally dis
covered an organic symptom. Alice developed cancer of the
breast.

III

How she faced this final verdict of the hitherto baffled doctors
is told in the diary; and between the lines we can read Alice's
confusion of feeling—relief that the eternal ambiguity of her
life was to be ended, awe and fear before the unknown, "the
great mortuary moment," as she characteristically put it. When
William received word of the definitive diagnosis, he wrote a
gentle and consoling letter to his sister (on July 6, 1891) that
did not altogether conceal his deep anxiety. Alice would now
know, he said, "a finite length of days, and then goodbye to
neurasthenia and neuralgia and headache, and weariness and
palpitation and disgust all at one stroke—I should think you
would be reconciled to the prospect with all its pluses and
minuses!" He went on to speak of immortality and the "ex-
plosion of liberated force and life" that would come "when that
which is *you* passes out of the body." It might seem odd, he
said, "for me to talk to you in this cool way about your end; but
my dear little sister, if one has things present to one's mind . . .
why not speak them out?"

Alice's reply, dated July 30, 1891, had in it some of the
same coolness—at least on the surface. She would have felt
wounded and misunderstood, she said, if William had "walked

round and not up to my demise." Her letter is of a piece with her diary:

It is the most supremely interesting moment in life, the only one in fact when living seems life, and I count it the greatest good fortune to have these few months so full of interest and instruction in the knowledge of my approaching death. It is as simple in one's own person as any fact of nature, the fall of a leaf or the blooming of a rose, and I have a delicious consciousness, ever present, of wide spaces close at hand, and whisperings of release in the air.

Like Tolstoy's Prince Andrei she was now looking at the blue immensity of the sky. She told William he greatly exaggerated the tragic element "in my commonplace little journey."

You must also remember that a woman, by nature, needs much less to feed upon than a man, a few emotions and she is satisfied; so when I am gone, pray don't think of me simply as a creature who might have been something else, had neurotic science been born. Notwithstanding the poverty of my outside experience, I have always had a significance for myself, and every chance to stumble along my straight and narrow little path, and to worship at the feet of my Deity, and what more can a human soul ask for?

William speaking both as a doctor and a psychologist advised Alice to accept all possible relief from pain. "Take all the morphia (or other forms of opium if that disagrees) you want, and don't be afraid of becoming an opium drunkard. What was opium created for except for such times as this?" Alice, however, did not take well to drugs; and William, who had seen the great Charcot use hypnotism at Salpetrière, advised Alice to resort to this when sedation did not help. Dr. Lloyd Tuckey, an eminent British alienist, was summoned and he taught Miss Loring to use a modified hypnosis, on the theory that Alice should not be put wholly to sleep in this way. This induced a calming of the nerves, and she was able to drop off "without the sensations of terror which have accompanied that process for so many years."

What is striking in the diary is the quantity of cheerfulness in Alice's dying. She follows with great excitement her brother's first nights in the provinces and in London when he dramatizes *The American*. He brings her his anecdotes regularly; and Alice occupies herself with "the grim shoving of the hours behind me." She came to recognize that her diary was "an outlet to that geyser of emotions, sensations, speculations, and reflections which ferments perpetually within my poor old carcass for its sins."

The end came with great rapidity on March 6, 1892, and there is preserved among the family papers Henry's minute account of the last painful hours written for his brother William, with all the precision and power habitual to the novelist's pen. Alice had a troubled dream just before her death. She saw certain of her dead friends in a boat, on a stormy sea, beckoning to her as the boat moved into the shadows. She dictated her journal to within a few hours of her death and took the trouble to rephrase a sentence that bothered her. Before she lost consciousness she dictated a cable to her brother and his family in Cambridge, "Tenderest love to all. Farewell. Am going soon." Katharine and Henry sought to create an intense stillness in the house in which she lay; and before sinking into her last sleep she told Henry that "she *couldn't* oh she COULDN'T, and begged it mightn't be exacted of her, live *another* day." If she wished for death, she nevertheless died reluctantly. She remained unconscious for twenty-four hours. It was the next afternoon—a Sunday—that Alice's breathing finally ceased while her brother was raising the blind to let a little more light into the room. Three days later Katharine and Henry accompanied her body to Woking, where cremation took place. The ashes were taken back by Miss Loring to America and were laid in the family plot in Cambridge Cemetery.

The claim of life against the claim of death—this is the assertion of every page of Alice's diary. Even when her strength

ailed her, she brought a resistance to death that was all the
tronger for her having decided long before that she would not
ake her own life. In her final entry she says she had "almost
sked for Katharine's lethal dose," but added, "one steps hesi-
atingly along such unaccustomed ways and endures from sec-
nd to second." The need to endure beyond the grave was
eflected in her worries, even in the final hours, about her prose.
This prose had in it many echoes from her father—his quickness
o seize on the paradoxical and the contradictory, his double-
lay between man's glory as a creature of God and man's mun-
dane stupidity. However much she might be exhausted and
depressed, Alice's aggressive intellectual strength, her ability to
xclaim and to complain—literally to fight disability and the
cruelty of her fate—revealed itself in all that she set down. Life
s reduced in the diary largely to the simple existential fact—as
t was for her. "He didn't fear Death, but he feared dying,"
he had written in her commonplace book, long before the doc-
ors gave her the final verdict. Yet she chose the act of dying
ather than the immediacy of death even as she had chosen illness, and to this act she addressed herself in her pages.

For the rest she had her string of daily facts, her comments
on British manners, the crass egotism of the gentry, the misery
of the masses, the heroic qualities she saw in Parnell. Her
expatriation aided her. One cannot imagine her keeping quite
this kind of diary in Mount Vernon Street: she needed something alien on which to discharge her anger. Her British surroundings made her even more American than she was. Only
an American, living abroad, could ridicule "the British constitution of things" quite as pointedly as Alice does—the monarchy
and "its tinsel capacity," the "boneless church," the "hysterical
legislation over a dog with a broken leg whilst Society is engaged making bags of 4,000 pheasants or gloating over foxes
torn to pieces by a pack of hounds!" The docility of classes
enslaved by respectability, whatever the "good form" of the
moment may be; and finally the supine masses—

the passivity with which the working man allows himself to be
patted and legislated out of all independence; thus the profound
ineradicables in the bone and sinew conviction that outlying regions
are their preserves, that they alone of human races massacre savages
out of pure virtue. It would ill-become an American to reflect upon
the treatment of aboriginal races; but I never heard it suggested that
our hideous dealings with the Indians was brotherly love masquerading under the disguise of pure cussedness.

That was the bite in Alice's prose, as she looked at the British
world through the newspapers: and doubtless there was within
it an unpleasant, overly aggressive side, which her brother caught
when he was creating Rosie, the little working-class invalid, in
The Princess Casamassima. Alice could seize on one of her
brother's amusing anecdotes, say his remarks about some individual, and spend a full page tearing the poor man to pieces.
Life had to answer for a great deal to her; and when she could
discharge her resentments nowhere else she attached them to
a mere bit of gossip, a humble paragraph in the *Standard* or
the *Times.* She possessed a vigorous and often belligerent democratic feeling. "She was really an Irishwoman!" Henry exclaimed as he read her, "transplanted, transfigured—but none
the less fundamentally natural—in spite of her so much larger
and finer than Irish intelligence. She felt the Home Rule question absolutely as only an Irishwoman (not anglicized) could.
It was a tremendous emotion with her—inexplicable in any
other way—but perfectly explicable by 'atavism.' What a pity
she wasn't born there—and had her health for it. She would
have been . . . a national glory!"

Henry's tribute to Alice's diary was contained in a long letter
written to his brother from Rome on May 28, 1894. The first
part expressed his concern at the printing of four copies by
Katharine Loring (one for each of the brothers and one for
herself), her failure to disguise names and persons, the danger
this represented to his privacy and the privacy of others. Then,
turning away from his misgivings, he launched into an appre-

ciation of his sister's power as a writer, and here there were few reservations, save in his feeling quite accurately that the diary reflected Alice's confined state. As he put it, "she simplified too much, shut up in her sick room, exercised her wondrous vigour of judgment on too small a scrap of what really surrounded her." He felt her opinion of the English might have been modified "if she had *lived* with them more—seen more of the men, etc. But doubtless it is fortunate for the fun and humour of the thing that it wasn't modified—as surely the critical emotion (about them), the essence of much of their nature, was never more beautifully expressed."

As regards the life, the power, the temper, the humour and beauty and expressiveness of the Diary in itself—these things were partly "discounted" to me in advance by so much of Alice's talk during her last years—and my constant association with her—which led me often to reflect about her extraordinary force of mind and character, her whole way of taking life—and death—in very much the manner in which the book does. I find in its pages, for instance, many things I heard her say. None the less I have been immensely impressed with the thing as a revelation of a moral and personal picture. It is heroic in its individuality, its independence—its face-to-face with the universe for-and-by herself—and the beauty and eloquence with which she often expresses this, let alone the rich irony and humour, constitute (I wholly agree with you) a new claim for the family renown. This last element—her style, her power to write—are indeed to me a delight—for I never had many letters from her. Also it brings back to me all sorts of things I am glad to keep—I mean things that happened, hours, occasions, conversations—brings them back with a strange, living richness. But it also puts before me what I was tremendously conscious of in her lifetime—that the extraordinary intensity of her will and personality really would have made the equal, the reciprocal life of a "well" person—in the usual world— almost impossible to her—so that her disastrous, her tragic health was in a manner the only solution for her of the practical problem of life—as it suppressed the element of equality, reciprocity, etc.

As for her allusions to H.—they fill me with tears and cover me

with blushes. What I should LIKE to do *en temps et lieu* would be
should no catastrophe meanwhile occur—or even if it should!—to
edit the volume with a few eliminations of text and dissimulation
of names, give it to the world and then carefully burn with fire ou
own four copies.

Alice would have agreed with her brother's view that she had
been exposed to too little of the world, for she speaks of "my
centimeter of observation" and "the poverty of my outside ex
perience." Henry's eloquent appraisal expresses the essence of
his sister's life and the strength and weakness of the book she
left to the world. His is the testimony of an artist as well as of
a brother—one who, next to Miss Loring, had been the most
intimate witness of his sister's decline and her painful end, in
her restricted alien world. That world did not know her; she
remained an intensely private memory in the lives of her dis
tinguished brothers and her few surviving friends. It was only
years after they had all disappeared from the scene that the
contents of the diary became known.

Alice James's record is a particular page of personal history
in an otherwise obscure life, as well as a page in the annals of a
family of intellectuals. There are few such documents in Ameri
can or English literature. Its "facts," as Henry James warned
us, are suspect; it is filled with gossip and exaggeration; it
seems to be, at times, little more than a series of exclamations.
Yet it is an intensely human document. One thinks of Marie
Bashkirtseff's journal—the young Russian woman who died of
tuberculosis at a much earlier age than Alice. She, however,
had been out in the world and had led a precarious life as a
painter: she had "lived" in a way that Alice never could. Yet
one analogy is possible, for what is to be found in both these
nineteenth-century diaries—although they are worlds apart—is
the spirit that moved the diarists: their supreme need to per
petuate themselves and the intensity of this need. Alice's diary
was her way of conquering time, as Proust might say: it was
also her way of asking for a hearing beyond the grave. Not her

pages, but the spirit residing in them gives the diary its unique
place in literature and testifies to its continuing appeal, not least
as a document of "literary psychology."

In 1905, when Henry James revisited America after an absence of twenty years, he walked one evening to the Cambridge
Cemetery. He had taken this walk long before, and particularly
on the last day of 1882, when he had gone out in bright sunshine and deep snow to visit the newly cut grave of his father.
This time he went in the dusk of late November. He noted that
the western sky had turned into "That terrible, deadly, pure
polar pink that shows behind American winter woods." The
moon had come up, white and young, and was reflected in
the white face of the empty Stadium which framed one of the
boundaries of Soldiers' Field across the Charles. He stood on
the little hillock—"that unspeakable group of graves"—and it
seemed to him suddenly that he knew why he had come back to
his native land. It was for this private reunion, this recovery of
old feeling—"it was the moment; it was the hour; it was the
blessed flood of emotion that broke out at the touch of one's
sudden *vision* and carried me away." Soldiers' Field stared at
him through the clear twilight, from across the river. Everything was here, as he had known it long before—"the recognition, stillness, the strangeness, the pity and the sanctity and the
terror, the breath-catching passion and the divine relief of
tears." Alice, too, long ago had invoked the favorite paternal
adjective *divine*—when she had prayed for a "divine cessation."
And Henry invoked it a few sentences later, when he spoke of
the lines from Dante which William had found and inscribed
on Alice's urn—William's "divine gift to us, and to *her*"—*ed
essa da martiro e da essilio venne a questa pace.* The long exile
and the suffering had led to this final peace; and the line from
Dante took Henry "so at the throat by its penetrating *rightness*,
that it was as if one sank down on one's knees in a kind of
anguish of gratitude before something for which one had waited

with a long, deep *ache*." And in the later time, after Henry
James's ashes had, in turn, been committed to a grave beside
his sister's, Alice's diary could be placed beside the series of
family memorials the novelist had brought into being—beside
A Small Boy and Others and *Notes of a Son and Brother*. The
diary, more modest and more personal than these soaring and
beautiful works, implied without insistence that it too—the
thoughtful notes of a daughter and a sister—had its place on
the brotherly bookshelf, and on that of the James family.

—Leon Edel

The Diary

Leamington

1889-1890

I THINK that if I get into the habit of writing a bit about what happens, or rather doesn't happen, I may lose a little of the sense of loneliness and desolation which abides with me. My circumstances allowing of nothing but the ejaculation of one-syllabled reflections, a written monologue by that most interesting being, *myself*, may have its yet to be discovered consolations. I shall at least have it all my own way and it may bring relief as an outlet to that geyser of emotions, sensations, speculations and reflections which ferments perpetually within my poor old carcass for its sins; so here goes, my first Journal!

June 1st, Saturday

I received today the prettiest letter from Henrietta Child.[1] As delicate, quaint and flowing as Helen's. How exceptional they are. They give forth a sound as unlike that of this tin-pan generation as if they had just stepped out of Miss Austen. À propos, Mrs. Sidgwick[2] has just sent me a sketch of Lyme Regis and the veritable Cobb off which dear, sweet Louisa Musgrove jumped.[3] Think of my being so mentally clumsy as

---

[1] Henrietta Child, the youngest of the three daughters of Professor and Mrs. Francis J. Child of Cambridge, Massachusetts, old friends of the James family.

[2] Mrs. Henry Sidgwick (1845–1936), wife of the Cambridge (England) philosopher, and principal of Newham College for women in Cambridge from 1892 to 1910.

[3] An allusion to Jane Austen's *Persuasion* (1818) in which Miss Musgrove, jumping from the pier, falls to the ground instead of into Captain Wentworth's arms, and is injured.

not to have seen her ghost of my own motion! The sketch i
of the feeblest, altho' it is rather shocking to say so for Mrs
S. gave it with great modesty—but then I didn't ask her for it
and I am impatient for the moment when the knitting of a
good stocking will be thought as "worthy work" as the painting
of a flimsy sketch. Miss C.[4] said "Isn't it wrong, Miss, to have
the sky cloudy! because I've always been told that the sky in
a picture should be perfectly clear, they say it is very 'ard to
do." I asked Nurse if she thought Mr. Goodwin's sketch better
"Oh, yes, you can see the stones in his!" Their only standard
pictorial is the number of recognizable objects.

June 2nd, Sunday

Last night I thought that I would write to-day to Mrs. Kellogg
and ask her to get me, when in Paris, a photo of the adorable
Jules Lemaître.[5] The post this A.M. brings the *Paris Illustré*
with a group of the contributors to the *Journal des Débats* and
there *he* is just in the middle of 'em! But, my dear Jules, how
cruel of you to look like that! How can you? why, you aren't
ugly, delightfully ugly, as you ought to be, but you look simply
common! ! and veritably as a writer in *La Nouvelle Revue*
says, suggestive, by some strange irony of fate, of Georges
Ohnet![6] "Le vaste visage" of Renan by happy fortune, is close
to you, "décidément il me hante"—even when exhorting Sarah
Bernhardt to die—" . . . puis, un beau soir, mourez sur la scène
subitement, dans un grand cri tragique car la vieillesse serait
trop dure pour vous. Et si vous avez le temps de vous reconnaître avant de vous enfoncer dans l'éternelle nuit bénissez,
comme M. Renan,[7] l'obscure Cause première."

[4] Apparently Miss Clarke, Alice James's landlady in Leamington.
[5] Jules Lemaître (1853–1914), French critic and dramatist.
[6] Georges Ohnet (1848–1918), French author of a series of best-selling,
snobbishly sentimental novels.
[7] Ernest Renan (1823–1892) French historian, Hebrew scholar, philologist,
and critic.

June 3rd

H.[8] writes that Grandmother Walsh's[9] portrait has come without a scratch—"and is delightful, and seems somehow to include mother." How dear he is! He has seen Robert Lincoln[10] "once and much liked him, a very healthy, friendly, racy, masculine not uncivilized Westerner with wife and daughter to match. I think he will be very successful." Nurse's little brother came home from school and said that the Master made him *exasperate* his *h*'s, which seems to perfectly express the emotions of the poor *h* thro' its British vicissitudes.

June 4th

When I tell Somers[11] not to charge the cows with the chair, as I am sure they are afraid of me, he doesn't grasp the situation. I went out yesterday for the third time this year. They dragged the chair thro' a gate into a meadow and I lay in the sun whilst they picked me flowerets, with a cuckoo in the distance, circling swallows over head, broad sweeps of gentle wind slowly rustling thro' the trees near by; need I say I was happy?—Some one who wants these rooms[12] asked Miss Clarke if she had "got rid of the fidgetty old lady in the drawing-room." It is so comic to hear oneself called old, even at 90, I suppose! What one reads, or rather all that comes to us is surely only of interest and value in proportion as we find ourselves therein, form given to what was vague, what slumbered stirred to life.

---

[8] Her way of referring to her brother Henry (1843–1916), the novelist, throughout the diary.

[9] Alice James's maternal grandmother was Elizabeth Robertson, a daughter of Alexander Robertson of New York. She married James Walsh, eldest son of Hugh and Catherine Walsh, of Newburgh, New York.

[10] Robert Todd Lincoln (1843–1926), son of Abraham Lincoln, United States minister to England from 1889 to 1892.

[11] The bath-chair man.

[12] At 11 Hamilton Terrace, Leamington.

June 10th

I have just come across this in the *Imitation of Christ*[18] "No man doth safely appear abroad, but he who gladly can abide at home, out of sight." Considering how perfect practice has made me in the latter clause, what a pity it is I cannot profit by it abroad—but so are all our accomplishments wasted in this foolish world. From what Nurse tells me the Bachelers have sunk to the most abject and grocer-like respectability since the absurd clericule unearthed them from their slum and danced them up the aisle of the Parish Church to mumble his dead, dry-as-dust incantation over them, thereby desecrating the sacred fidelity in which they had lived for 20 years. They now shudder and go through all sorts of sophistications at the irregularities of their neighbors as shown in the too, too solid flesh manifestations which ornament the gutters so profusely. To be sure the possession of a wedding-ring after 20 years with a digit unadorned is eno[ugh] to turn the wisest head; and surely drawing the line at the "found out" is a weakness common to the most superior humanity. The illustrious *bourgeoise* with her *parfum* of tea and toast, who rules o'er them certainly sets them an example in her curious jugglings with the fragile ladies who are more or less closely related to the Divorce court. Some are arbitrarily shut out from the charmed circle whilst those more fragile bask in Royal smiles until they pass—shall I say?—to heavenly spheres, *tropical* would still be indulgent and more moral considering my Calvinistic descent.—Nurse has gone to the theatre and I have been trying to get her to take off an absurd hat in which she looks like a figure of fun, but in vain. She is as obstinate as a mule!

June 11th

Miss Minnie Wright came to see me yesterday P.M., the first creature I have seen in more than six weeks, save poor Miss

---

[18] *De Imitatione Christi* by Thomas à Kempis (1380–1471).

diminution

Palmer once, but she is so vague as to be hardly eno[ugh] of
an entity to dispel solitude. The Wrights I think I like as well
as any one I've seen in England. They are very sweet and
pure of nature, so honest as to be quite inadequate to the social
fib, with deliciously blundering consequences; they have the
intelligence by jerks, which seems to be that most *répandu*
and in the long run tells the more, the jerk always seems *such*
a luminous flash.

A dozen times a day, I find myself saying, "I'll write that
to A[unt] K."[14] I suppose I did so before; it only *seems*
oftener now, when I have to pull myself up. H. says he misses
Lizzie Duveneck[15] more and more, it is so with all, their loss
seems greater; I suppose it is the lessening number with none
to fill the ranks; besides Harry,[16] I have now only three friends
whom I have any right to call on from association and far-
backness, to say nothing of individual limberness.

As the wise tell us that everything has been said, how curious
it would be to know what will follow the present phase of
preoccupation with the *manner* of re-saying it.

June 12th

What a lightening it is of the burden to hear that the poor
wretches who have survived the floods in Pennsylvania are mentally paralysed! Everything seems to go to prove that blunted
sensibilities is the refuge of over-strained humanity and that the
appalling and terrible in the past has been neutralized in the
same way.—Mary Elliot and her Dr. John have just been
here; what a joy to see any one from home! Two such nice
creatures especially, Mary not quite so pretty, but then she

[14] Catherine Walsh, sister of Alice's mother, Mary Walsh James—the "Aunt
Kate" of the James family.
[15] Elizabeth (Lizzie) Boott Duveneck (1846–1888), daughter of the
amateur composer Francis Boott and wife of Frank Duveneck, the painter.
She was the "original" of Pansy Osmond in *The Portrait of a Lady*.
[16] Henry, the novelist, was often called Harry in the James family to
distinguish him from his father who was also Henry.

varies so from minute to minute and is much more mature and mentally firm but I liked *him* greatly, hardly having seen him before. He is frank and manly and ready to laugh, that most essential of all things; think of the multitudes who go through life on the cry! I have now read three vol[ume]s of Jules Lemaître *Etudes et Portraits*. Will he ever seem less to me? I suppose so. But how grateful shall I ever be for the intensity of that first impression, two months ago, my whole being vivified with the sense of the *Intelligent* revealed! One's mind stretching to the limits of his, absorbing him with every sense, such a subtle flattery emanating from his perfection in "putting it" as to make an absolutely ignorant creature like me vibrate, as with knowledge, in response to the truth of the myriad of his exquisitely subtle perceptions. Then his humour, his irony and his humanity!

June 12th

There is a very amusing distinction in the *Nation* about Mr. Parnell's "fib" in the House of Commons, the blackness of which seems to consist of his having *confessed* to it. Other statesmen lie but have always had the virtue to deny doing so; such bad ethics *must* be good politics! Think of a human being so devoid of humour as to be willing to descend in history in the phenomenally absurd position of the Attor[ney]-Gen-[eral,],[17] red-handed from Pigott cross-examining Mr. Parnell and making him responsible for the antecedents of the men he shook hands with in America! But the absolute want of humour in the Briton at large is the secret of the Irish question.

[17] Charles Stewart Parnell (1846–1891), Irish nationalist leader in parliament. The *Times* had printed two years earlier a series of letters, allegedly signed by Parnell, condoning the Phoenix Park murders in Ireland of May 1882. Alice is alluding to the hearings conducted during 1889 by a special commission investigating the charges. In February of 1890 Richard Pigott

I went out again today, and behaved like a lunatic, "sobbed," *à la* Kingsley,[18] over a farmhouse, a meadow, some trees and cawing rooks. Nurse says that there are some people downstairs who drive everywhere and admire nothing. How grateful I am that I actually do *see*, to my own consciousness, the quarter of an inch that my eyes fall upon; truly, the subject is all that counts!

Nurse asked me whether I should like to be an artist—imagine the joy and despair of it! the joy of seeing with the trained eye and the despair of *doing* it. Among the beings who are made up of chords which vibrate at every zephyr, of the two orders, which know the least misery, those who are always dumb and never loose the stifled sense, or the others who ever find expression impotent to express!—We met the man Brooks today with his grindstone, he looks canting eno[ugh]. What an absurd creature I am to have drawn such a rigid line now that No. 9 has arrived in the flesh. My heart was malleable during its period of incubation when Nurse was sure he was going to be twins and now that he is so virtuous as not to be, my heart is like granite. Eliza, who was a permanent appendage of Charlotte's person, whilst she did the house-keeping and errands, has become an excrescence upon the spindly body of white, pinched-faced Becky, aged ten years. Eliza is two and has never walked yet; she must be a bracing burden. Lavinia, who had a good place as slavey somewhere, returned home after the baby's birth for very joy at its advent, sacrificing her place.

---

acknowledges he had forged these letters. The Attorney-General was Sir Richard Webster. The *Nation* (May 16, 1889) had commented that "as Parnell is virtually on trial for promoting murder and outrage, the discovery that he was on one or more occasions simply untruthful, is irrelevant and unimportant."

[18] Charles Kingsley (1819–1875), author of *Westward Ho!* and other novels.

Labouchere[19] gives a list of clergymen and curates with an average of £130.0.0 income and between them *fifty* of what Fanny Morse[20] calls, "the deepening of the marriage tie." Nurse knows a family in Cheltenham, General Someone, who has 20. Sir W. Carrington whom the landlady knew had 22 by *two* wives. She nursed one of the daughters for many y[ea]rs, who lived with three sisters and they each had a separate jug for the daily milk and a separate loaf of bread and like the Jacksons ate alone! One of Mary Cross's brothers-in-law was one of 21 and Miss Chavasse[21] knew a family of 25 who used to be sent out in groups of eight, in different directions. They seem fond of 'em in the gross! The queer part is, that, as compared to our race and the French, they haven't philoprogenitiveness, but how feeble and diluted, of necessity must the parental instinct be, trickling down thro[ugh] 25. Just as the mind refuses to enjoy or to suffer save within limits, so does the heart refuse to love. Imagine being personally responsible for the cutting of 800 teeth! Thank Heaven, the Duke of Portland[22] is married. Five thousand presents to cover *his* nakedness!

Imagine hearing that some one here in Leamington whom I had never seen had said that I was "very charitable." I felt as if all my clothes had been suddenly torn off and that I was standing on the steps of the Town Hall, in the nude, for the delectation of the *British Matron*. This calumny arose, from my having given, I suppose, a sixpence to the Brookses *before* No. 9 was born.

Mr. Howells[23] letter made me so happy by saying that mine

[19] Henry Du Pré Labouchere (1831–1912), radical member of parliament from Northampton from 1880 to 1905, founder of the magazine *Truth* in 1876.

[20] Frances Rollins Morse (1850–1928), Boston social worker and art lover, a friend of the James family.

[21] Miss Chavasse had been Alice's nurse during her stay at Bournemouth in 1886 shortly after arriving in England.

[22] Contemporary reports of the marriage of the Duke of Portland to Miss Winifred Dallas-Yorke mention 500 (not 5,000) wedding gifts.

[23] William Dean Howells (1837–1920) had been a friend of the James family since the 1860's.

ad made father and mother seem living to him. No greater
appiness can come than finding that they survive, or can be
evived, in a few memories.

June 14th

Nurse met Becky Brooks and her *hangers-on* in front of the
Pump Room. She had Eliza, the excrescence, of course, on one
arm and was dragging by a red scarf *pinned* round his neck an
unfortunate dog with her other hand; four of the others were
of course tugging at the scarf so that Becky's slender person
often was upholding five others. When asked where the dog
came from she said, "The woman as wants to lose it, gave it us;
we's 'ad it all hafternoon." I think the dog must be sufficiently
lost by now!—What one never loses a sense of and never fails
to adore in England is the civility of all classes, not only to
their betters but to each other. Of course there are hideous
manners in *society* and in the Slums, but in the middle region
amidst the wise, the rational and the humble, among those
that count in short, civility I'm sure is the rule. Then these
creatures that come fresh from the hard, gritty, ragged interchange which passes for manners at home, actually don't perceive the difference, but Heaven forbid that I should begin
upon those that see not, it's too tragic! But one must be just,
the poor things have had nothing to perceive all their days when
suddenly brought face to face with all this complexity what
can they do but seek refuge in blindness. The landscape and
Somers taken alternately illustrate in a very instructive manner
how even the surface of our environment acc[oun]ts for us.
Yesterday I was lying in a meadow at Hawkes's farm, absorbing
like blotting-paper hay-ricks, hedges and trees composing themselves into a multitude of pictures with that felicity alone known
to this island, the foreground grey, with ghostly slants of
sunshine, vanishing to reappear in the distance, so succulent,

so smooth and so slow, so *from* all time and so *for* all tim
when Somers came suddenly within view and there he wa
the peasant of these fields! as robust, as unirritable, as "edg
less" as they are. I questioned him about some allotments tha
have been taken to build on just as the poor men have mad
their gardens after two years of work on the ground. He tol
the story slowly and easily, in his deep fat voice, ending wit
a comfortable laugh with no note of bitterness therein engen
dered by doubts as to the absolute nature of the landlor
making the sarcasm of the Yankee or the ferocity of the Frencl
man seem as impossible to him as a crop of dynamite to th
patient meadows.

The cuckoos imitate the clocks to perfection.

June 16t

What ghastly lives some people lead. The Bradleys, who mak
baskets, have a hen who in a polite manner lays *two!* eggs fo
my breakfast every morn. The daughter told Nurse the othe
day that her father had not been sober since Christmas. I
seems he has drunk all his life, that there are 15 children an
that [the] eldest son, a lad of nineteen who is a pattern of virtu
looks after everything and that his father maltreats him ho
ribly. This girl is so pretty, and what is better has grace, whicl
you see so rarely here. One of them is married and I suppos
the remaining 14 are ready at any moment to plunge int
matrimony. How overwhelming is the virtue of the poor! Thi
doesn't include their fondness for the conjugal state.

I have seen so little that my memory is packed with littl
bits which have not been wiped out by great ones, so that i
all seems like a reminiscence and as I go along the childisl
impressions of light and colour come crowding back into my
mind and with them the expectant, which then palpitatec
within me, lives for a ghostly moment.

H. writes that he has received an affectionate! ! ! letter fron

Wendell Holmes[24] a marvel explained by his near arrival in London. They say he has entirely broken loose and is flirting as desperately as ever. There is something so grim as to be out of nature in that poor woman's life and character. What is there but ugliness in any relation between two beings which doesn't work to soften their hearts and open their minds to their kind. Solitude is surely a flowery path to that!—Miss Percy from next door came in to see me, she is the most good-natured being and evidently looks upon me, funny as it seems, as a pitiable object. She asked me with the greatest conviction if I didn't get "awfully tired of reading!"—This pleased me greatly, it expressed so her round, bustling, cheery-in-the-morning personality. She strums for five minutes at a time on her rattle-trap of a piano and is in and out all over the place 20 times a day—has she ever dreamed "un songe merveilleuse-ment délicat, comme la solitude et le malheur en forment seuls dans les âmes qu'elles arrachent aux rudesses de la vie com-mune; l'idée d'une belle vie pleine d'ombre, vouée toute en-tière sans salaire ni retour, à la bonté et la résignation?"

June 17th

How absurd it is in any one to reply to Buchanan, as if he counted to any sane person for more than a jack-in-the-box, starting up to advertise himself.

Where do you suppose I went this morning!—into a hay-field amid the hay-makers; it was divine! Later among such silly sheep! The infinite gradations of light and shade simply in-toxicate one, how truly was it said that *weather* was unknown to us at home, here it is a complete absence of climate, altho' to prove how much richer results are to be obtained from a limited quantity, the native with a thermometer ranging from

---

[24] An allusion to Oliver Wendell Holmes (1841–1935), the son of Dr. Oliver Wendell Holmes, the "autocrat" of the breakfast table, later associate justice of the Supreme Court (1902–1932).

30° to 70° goes through more intensity of sensation in the
way of arctic cold and torrid heat than was ever dreamed of
among the philosophers of Prairie du Chien where Bob[25] said
that it went from 40° below to 105° in summer. They dress
so oddly, wrapping themselves in furs from head to foot they
go out and walk hard in the sun at 40°. They come home and
pass the evening in a huge vaultlike-room *sitting* in a low
bodice with the therm[ometer] at 50°. In summer a gossamer
gown, and a huge boa or fur cape over the upper part of 'em
truly are they not to be understanded of this Yankee!

June 18th

Alice Edwards told Nurse that—"Mother was awful bad last
night and this morning a lady brought a baby"—could there
be a more misguided lady?—This is No. 5, father twenty
eight mother twenty-three—one more tiny voice to swell the
vast human wail rising perpetually to the skies! I wonder if it
is indelicate in a flaccid virgin to be so preoccupied with the
multiplication of the species, but it fairly haunts me, something
irresistible and overwhelming like the tides of the sea or the
Connemaugh flood, a mighty horde to sweep over the face of
the earth.—It's rather strange that here, among this robust
and sanguine people, I feel not the least shame or degradation
at being ill, as I used at home among the anæmic and the fagged.
It comes of course in one way from the conditions being so easy,
from the sense of leisure, work reduced to a minimum and the
god *Holiday* worshipped so perpetually and effectually by all
classes. Then what need to justify one's existence when one is
simply one more amid a million of the superfluous?

I should be a valuable district visitor. Nurse was telling me of
her visit to the Bachelers and repeated something which Mrs.

[25] Robertson James (1846–1910), Alice's youngest brother, had been employed at Prairie du Chien, Wisconsin.

B. had said, using one of her expressions, when lo! I toppled
over in a faint! How little shall I ever know of life!

June 19th

Several people have been the last days to call, but I've seen 'em
not. Confronting the landscape in the A.M. leaves me without
further resistance and then an afternoon of prattle! after that
divine contemplation would be too much of an anticlimax. The
beauty tires me more than the chair, which only shakes the
muscles, while the former stirs unfathomable depths! Harry has
just sent me Sir Cha[rle]s Russell's speech,[26] how thrilling to
read it!

June 20th

I learn by a kind note this morn[ing] that Mr. Godkin[27] sent
me Sir Cha[rle]s' speech, which is very pleasing, he proposes
coming to see me but I have had to say nay. "How unspeakably
the lengthening of memories in common endears our old
friends!" In one's careless days, one little suspects how elderly
forlornities, out of sight, lap up crumbs of remembrance—not
but what my little world remembers me 1,000 times more than I
look for, I shall not sweetly say deserve. I went into the gardens
to day, the roses exquisite, the geraniums not got supreme com-
mand as yet. When will the race be emancipated from them?

June 21st

If I make this a receptacle for feeble ejaculations over the
scenery, what a terror it will be. I must, however, record the fact

---

[26] Sir Charles Russell, later Lord Russell of Killowen (1832–1900), was
a member of the Parnell Commission and revealed the Pigott forgeries. His
speech for the defense was regarded as a remarkable example of forensic
eloquence. He was later appointed Lord Chief Justice of England.

[27] Edwin L. Godkin (1831–1902), founder and editor of the *Nation.*

that to day I entered into Paradise; thro' the orchard an
gooseberry bushes to the garden in front of the Hawkes farm
house—a place to dream of! Let us dream then! Incredible as i
seems now, there was absolutely not one geranium *visible*. If th
orchard is a fair specimen, we do 'em better. That's one consola
tion. Nurse saw Charlotte Brooks with the baby appended c
course and inquired after its health. "He would be better i
Mother hadn't let him fall out of bed last night. She didn't fin
it out till 12 o'clock." She was going as usual for an hegg fo
Eliza, the Excrescence, who is the immediate jewell of their soul
altho' she has never walked and only says "la-la"; her fascina
tions for the general public are consequently not great.

We saw a one-eyed boy of twelve, very poor and rough, carry
ing in the tenderest manner a tiny baby! They have an amusin;
habit of using "swilling" for rinsing and washing. Nurse say
"I must go and swill my hands." I can't stop her.

Read *Révoltée*.[28] It is brilliant, but the people are al
rather too clever, as clever as he is—but it is full of beautiful an
deep emotion. But what a huge blunder, dramatically, artisticall
and morally not to have had André killed, life isn't as simple a
that and how stupid would it be if it were! What *is* living in thi
deadness called life is the struggle of the creature in the grip c
its inheritance and against the consequences of its acts; the
mother powerless by her tears to wipe out the wrong brough
about by her weakness and folly, the daughter to escape by revol
from the ignominy of her destiny—this is shadowed, but van
ishes in the smoke of a pistol-shot! Your terror of *insisting*, Jules
has made you of all beings fall into the *banal!!* How in eman
cipating ourselves we forge our chains.

I fancy that I have quite extinguished the Kingsleys. Imagine
her bringing Mrs. Harrison to call again. The Roseate one wil
find that a Yankee can be dropped with complete serenity, bu
that picking her up is quite another pair of shoes which she wil

[28] A comedy by Jules Lemaître.

ever make fit. How it lowers Ch[arle]s Kingsley to think that
e lived amidst such falsity and folly.

June 27th

There is one inestimable gain in the present moment however
desperate, it never can be yesterday and perpetually becomes
tomorrow.

> Whether at Naishápúr or Babylon,
> Whether the Cup with sweet or bitter run,
> The Wine of life keeps oozing drop by drop,
> The leaves of life keep dropping [falling] one by one.[29]

A gallant Briton has been bitten by a mosquito! at Henley.
In his extremity the dear soul naturally writes a letter and sends
it to the *Standard*, whereupon, from the Arctic zone of York-
shire to the tropics of Kent, endless victims start up, having also
had the dread experience, each with his theory and a description of his bite. One says that the survival of an egg of a mosquito thro' the terrors of an English winter is an unknown and
absolutely impossible thing, so that his mosquito must have been
imported for that one individual bite! So they flow on until a
creature inspired from Heaven makes "an authoritative statement" to the effect that mosquitoes have existed in England for
50 years! The others seem to have been struck dumb, as the
Standard has run dry by the *authoritative* one and the F. E. S.[30]
appended to his name! The adorable innocents!

Balfour[31] described as "Coercion tempered by facetiousness!"

---

[29] Alice is quoting Stanza VIII from Edward Fitzgerald's second (1868)
edition of the *Rubáiyát of Omar Khayyám*.

[30] Fellow of the Entomological Society.

[31] Politically, Arthur James Balfour (1848–1930) and William Ewart
Gladstone (1809–1898) were opponents. Balfour became chief secretary for
Ireland in 1886 during the second administration of Lord Salisbury (1830–
1903). This placed him for a time at the center of the Home Rule controversy.
Alice here alludes to Balfour's coercive administration of the Crimes Act,
when he was Chief Secretary, which reduced crime in Ireland to the vanishing

is good. His adoration of Mr. Gladstone seems to grow by the hour and is too delicious! The word that establishes beyond question, apparently to his own mind, the righteousness of any of his exploits, is that Mr. Gladstone did the same three years ago only more so. When will he have the courage of the more so! Truly a providential creature to hasten the solution and in his character of statesman what amusement and delectation will he afford for coming generations.

J. Lemaître says in a sentence of some one else what I blundered through a page in trying to say of him—"un livre qui me donne cette impression qu'il m'exprime tout entier, et me révèle à moi-même plus intelligent que je ne pensais."

June 28th

The *Standard* announces the marriage of the eldest daughter of the Prince of Wales to the Earl of Fife.[32] Think of their not having been able to catch a German princeling; surely the world is marching on! How pitiable the fate of the royalcules is! But why does the *Standard* feel it necessary to publish the divorced sisters? Some one said they were all four runaways. As the *Standard* admits of two *divorcées*, this may be true. How droll that with the Queen's lifelong horror of divorce that through her sons-in-law she should be so nearly related to so many unsavoury episodes, the common fate is hers, in being overtaken always by what is most offensive to us. What a beautiful moral to be drawn.

Read the third volume of George Eliot's Letters and Journals[33] at last. I'm glad I made myself do so for there is a

point; and to the fact that Balfour's various measures paralleled those taken some years earlier by Gladstone himself.

[32] Louise, Princess of Great Britain and Ireland (1867–1931) married Alexander, Duke of Fife (1849–1912). She was the third child and first daughter of Albert Edward, Prince of Wales (later Edward VII), and his wife Alexandra. Princess Louise was created Princess Royal in 1905.

[33] *George Eliot's Life*, as related in her letters and journals. Arranged and edited by her husband, J. W. Cross, (1840–1924) three volumes, 1884. Henry James had reviewed the work in the *Atlantic Monthly* in May 1885.

faint spark of life and an occasional, remotely humorous touch
in the last half. But what a monument of ponderous dreariness is
the book! What a lifeless, diseased, self-conscious being she must
have been! Not one burst of joy, not one ray of humour, not one
living breath in one of her letters or journals, the commonplace
and platitude of these last, giving her impressions of the Continent, pictures and people, is simply incredible! Whether it is
that her dank, moaning features haunt and pursue one thro' the
book, or not, but she makes upon me the impression, morally and
physically, of mildew, or some morbid growth—a fungus of a
pendulous shape, or as of something damp to the touch. I never
had a stronger impression. Then to think of those books compact
of wisdom, humour, and the richest humanity, and of her as the
creator of the immortal *Maggie*,[34] in short, what a horrible
disillusion! Johnnie seems to have done his level best to wash out
whatever little colour the letters may have had by the unfortunate form in which he has seen fit to print them. One hasn't at
the end the faintest idea of how she signed her name even, or
which of the three [names] she used, whether her letters were
long or short, all those details which are so characteristic. On the
subject of her marriage it is of course for an outsider criminal to
say anything, but what a shock for her to say she felt as if her
life were renewed and for her to express her sense of complacency in the vestry and church! What a betrayal of the much-
mentioned "perfect love" of the past! The letter in which she
announces her engagement to a friend and at the same time
assures her that Johnnie isn't going to grab her fortune is
deliciously English. What an abject coward she seems to have
been about physical pain, as if it weren't degrading eno[ugh] to
have head-aches, without jotting them down in a row to stare
at one for all time, thereby defeating the beneficent law which
provides that physical pain is forgotten. If she related her
diseases and her "depressions" and told for the good of others

---

[34] Heroine of *The Mill on the Floss* (1860) by George Eliot (Mary Ann
Cross born Evans, 1819–1880). The novelist had married John Cross in the
year of her death.

what armour she had forged against them, it would be conceiv
able, but they seem simply cherished as the vehicle for a moan
Where was the creature's vanity! And when you think of wha
she had in life to lift her out of futile whining! But the posses
sion of what genius and what knowledge could reconcile one to
the supreme boredom of having to take oneself with that super
lative solemnity! What a contrast to George Sand[35] who what
ever her failings never committed that unpardonable sin; it ever
makes her greasy men of the moment less repulsive.

July 4th

How can I better celebrate the Glorious Fourth than by announc
ing the glorious fact that I have been out already 15 times? I
wish my mind were not so cramped upon Somers, but his spine
does make the most blood-curdling oscillations from the perpen
dicular, and I can't but think of the horrors of that day with
Bowles![36] I work away upon his "higher nature" as hard as I can
and with success for I so leavened him with enthusiasm one day
that he *riz* to exclaiming when we reached home, "We've had
a lovely time! !" Catching my vernacular as well, which perhaps
isn't so desirable.

Canon Capel Cure[37] says that raffles are not "*direct* sin," a
thoughtful curve, I suppose, designed by Providence to circumvent the scoffer at Church Bazaars ! ! ! From the human being
point of view, how far superior Michael Davitt[38] is in the witness
box than Parnell, no wiggling, quibbling legal evasions and what
a light upon the "question" is Widow Walsh[39] ready to sacrifice

[35] George Sand, pseudonym of Armandine Lucille Aurore Dupin, Baronne
Dudevant (1804–1876), French novelist.

[36] Bowles, as well as Somers, was employed by Alice to wheel her chair.

[37] Edward Capel Cure was canon of Windsor, 1884, and author of *The
Words from the Cross* (1868).

[38] Michael Davitt (1846–1906), Irish revolutionary and labor leader, was
organizer with Parnell of the Land League.

[39] One of the widow's sons had been executed for killing a constable and
the mother had urged her second son, Michael, fifteen, also held for the crime,

two sons rather than treat with the enemy. Think of the fan-
tasticalities of the gosamer Balfour set to crush that indomitable
spirit. One can hear the derision of posterity.

July 5th

The troops of her *Christian* Majesty are now engaged in killing
3,000 Dervishes,[40] by depriving them of water. When the
desperate creatures make a rush to the river they are shot down!
Tommy Atkins is in the "best of health and spirits"—how rank
with *Humbug* is this Nation! It seems that Arabi refused on
some occasion to cut off water from the English saying it was
contrary to true religion to deprive even an enemy of water!

July 6th

How of all creatures to be envied is Father Damien.[41] To be
able to do something absolutely complete in itself, what more
could a human being ask for! That's where the Cath[olic]
Church has the pull—he must have known the joy of the
Martyrs. What a loss that men are entirely bereft of that soul-
satisfying resource in this knock-kneed generation of simply
relative right and wrong. They make too much of his heroism
for how simple to be *actively* heroic within absolute limits in Time

---

to meet his fate like his brother rather than be induced to turn informer. A
large sum was subscribed later in America to permit the widow and her remaining children to emigrate to the United States.
[40] Late in June 1889 an armed force of dervishes—Mohammedan nomad
friars—advanced toward Wady Halfa in Egypt with the reported intention of
raiding toward the north. In the early days of July, British artillery, cavalry,
and infantry killed several hundred including their leaders and hundreds died
of thirst in the desert when the British troops cut their water supply. The
action was criticized in some quarters as use of force on hungry nomad tribes
advancing it was said without aggressive intention upon the fertile plains
in search of food.
[41] Father Damien (1840–1889), Belgian missionary priest who labored
among the lepers in Hawaii.

and Paradise cock-sure for eternity! The active can't be much thrilled, of course, by the passive hero who is so little picturesque and reverberating as he lies hidden in reeking cellars and freezing attics, chained like a galley-slave to his oar of endurance for countless y[ea]rs.—Letter from Lady Clark[42] in much disgust over the Wales-Fife alliance. How can any man with the slightest parental instinct hand his pure, defenceless child over to a man whose life he knows to have been much on the same vile pattern as his own. Destitution and excessive luxury develop apparently the same ideals, the same marauding attitude towards mankind, and intensity of struggle for material goods, surely showing how perfect is the meeting of extremes. The stories which Nurse brings from Satchwell Street are no different in kind and little more shameless in degree than those they tell in London of the Prince's set. What difference is there in the spiritual essence of two viragoes fighting on their door-steps over a coal-ticket, left or not left by the district visitor and that of two great ladies at daggers drawn over their seat at some function or other?—all simply scrambling for something they haven't got.

July 7th

The great live apparently to a great extent upon the charity of their tradesmen, the poor upon that of the well-to-do, surely the nobler plan. The ladies of Satchwell Street hardly have been more childish or shown less dignity than the Royalties, in not going to the Duke of Portland's wedding because he wouldn't marry one of the three princesses, as they story goes. And they, too, have their arbitrary, virtuous rigidities for did they not stone out of the street the bride! whom the big Italian organ-grinder brought home the night of his wife's funeral. She was a little woman, they say, and he returned a fortnight later with another one as big and strapping as himself.

[42] Sir John Forbes Clark (1821–1910) and Lady Clark, the former Charlotte Coltman, of Tillypronie in Scotland, were friends of Henry James.

Miss Leppington came yesterday. She is as delicate and spiritual-minded as if she had bloomed upon our rock-bound puritan coast. She clings so to a "sense of sin," for it's not automatic simply, as is usual, but from conviction that *she* worships a God who made her thus!—she apparently likes it. How fatally the entire want of humour cripples the mind. What an awful loss it is that we can't see our own follies, they must be so much more exquisite than any one's else, but as vanity is what keeps the world agoing, after one or two convulsive laughs, the game would certainly be up!

Shall I ever have any convulsive laughs again! Ah, me! I fear me not. I had such a feast for 34 years that I can't complain. But a curious extreme to be meted out to a creature, to have grown up with Father and W[illia]m,[43] and then to be reduced to Nurse and Miss C[larke] for humourous daily fodder. Could you but hear the three-lettered chaff which I fabricate for 'em, for chaff of some sort I *must* have. In those ghastly days, when I was by myself in the little house in Mt. Vernon Street,[44] how I longed to flee in to the firemen next door and escape from the "Alone, Alone!" that echoed thro' the house, rustled down the stairs, whispered from the walls, and confronted me, like a material presence, as I sat waiting, counting the moments as they turned themselves from today into tomorrow; for "Time does not work until we have ceased to watch him."—There is a bit of brown wall that always brings up St. John's Wood,[45] so

[43] William James (1842–1910), Alice's elder brother, the psychologist and philosopher.

[44] After the death of Mrs. James, in 1882, Alice and her father moved from 20 Quincy Street, in Cambridge, to 131 Mt. Vernon Street in Boston. Here the father died at the end of 1882 and Alice lived alone in the house during 1883–1884, after which she went to live in England.

[45] During its residence abroad in 1855–1858, the James family had lived for a time at 10 Marlborough Place in St. John's Wood. Henry James's recollections of this period, including the theater-going, are recorded in Chapter XXIII of his *A Small Boy and Others*. (1913).

vividly, as I pass—that winter of 1854–55, all draped in Dec[ember] densities, with only three episodes standing out, as I remember: M[ademoise]lle C[usin]s[46] bonnet, *Henry VIII* and *Still Waters Run Deep*. Shall I ever forget Wolsey going to execution, or, "My sister is a most remarkable woman!" The joy of *Henry VIII* was somewhat obscured by the anguish of Aunt Kate's not being able to go. No greater misery ever befell a creature of woman born than that, thought I! I'm sure we went also to the pantomime at Christmas but I've completely forgotten it. M[ademois]elle Cusin's bonnet is equally vivid, but a more mixed delight. In the grey dusk of our P.M. walks we discovered an artist, but the pangs of parturition were most severe, for the millinery point of view of Neufchâtel and that of the Edgeware Road had not only to be revealed, but reconciled one to the other, by *me*, aged seven. It came forth green shirred silk and pink roses and I can remember how my infant soul shivered, even then, at the sad crudity of its tone; it doubtless soon gathered *depth* as the atmosphere of the season enveloped it, more and more.

July 11th

H. writes that he has been spending Sunday at Wilton House,[47] next best to having been there myself, for we saw the great Van Dyck together in '73, when Aunt Kate, he and I drove from the White Hart, humble pilgrims! Starting from the same level, the careless observer might think that my fall had been as great as his rise, living for 48 hours in the house with that glorious object—but who shall say—not I, surely, from my sofa whence I've learned such wondrous things. It is as if it were yesterday that I saw it—a breathless moment! Could it be there that the

[46] Mademoiselle Cusin was a Swiss governess, who served in the James family during 1855–1856 in London and Paris. *A Small Boy*, Chapter XX.
[47] The visit with Alice to Wilton House, residence of the Earls of Pembroke, was described by Henry James in *Transatlantic Sketches* (1875) and reprinted in *English Hours* (1905).

Moroni[48] is, that I've asked about so much. It isn't in Warwick
or Blenheim and those are the only houses I have seen. I remember just where it was in the room, simply a head. I needn't have
been in such a *funk* as I was before I left home that summer,
lest being such an entirely inartistic organization I should not
know what to *do* with the pictures, like poor Mrs. Ogle with a
joke, looking, as some one said, so helpless, as if she wanted to
hand it on as fast as possible—for I clung! Imagine the bliss of
finding that I too was a "sensitive," and that I was not only
"mute before a Botticelli," but that a Botticelli said an infinity of
things to me—and this in a flash of mutual recognition, after
the years of toil in trying to establish some sort of relation, either
of speech or silence, with the Botticelli of Boston. The first day
at the Nat[ional] Gallery, the portrait painter Porter[49] came in
—it was his first sight of an old master and he sauntered about
glancing casually here and there with no more ripple of emotion
than if he were at Doll and Richards'.[50] How the cheap quality
of his personality stood out!

I can never forgive these excellent folk for being such an
inartistic race. Amidst such opportunities for the picturesque,
born to a medium which transmutes all things thro' such infinite
degrees of the beautiful and the grim, to think of their having
had only one great Master! The landscape one can, of course,
readily understand even when most soaked in its beauty, may
by its arranged respectable expectedness exasperate to the last
degree the irritable spontaneous genius, holding within it, as it
does, the possibilities of the *bête*; but think of Rembrandtesque
London! ! One must acknowledge, however, that the one
Master took the atmosphere with sufficient solemnity and put it
thro' all its paces.

[48] Giovanni Battista Moroni (1525–1578), portrait painter of the Brescian
school, pupil of Il Moretto, exerted considerable influence on the art of
Van Dyke.
[49] Benjamin Curtis Porter (1845–1908), Boston portrait painter.
[50] The art dealers, Doll and Richards, were located at 145 Tremont Street
in Boston.

The *P[all] M[all] G[azette]* tonight points out the fact that Parnell, while under trial as accessory to murder, the deadly foe of the Queen, is made one of the Committee on Royal Grants! My dear, dear Cousins, of what substance are you made!

July 12th

H. says, with his usual felicity, of Bob that he is an "extraordinary instance of a man's *nature* constituting his profession, his whole stock in trade." *His* journey to Damascus casts a light upon the *naïfs* mysteries of the Bible.—It's amusing to see how, even on my microscopic field, minute events are perpetually taking place illustrative of the broadest facts of human nature. Yesterday Nurse and I had a good laugh but I must allow that decidedly she "had" me. I was thinking of something that interested me very much and my mind was suddenly flooded by one of those luminous waves that sweep out of consciousness all but the living sense and overpower one with joy in the rich, throbbing complexity of life, when suddenly I looked up at Nurse, who was dressing me, and saw her primitive, rudimentary expression (so common here) as of no inherited quarrel with her destiny of putting petticoats over my head; the poverty and deadness of it contrasted to the tide of speculation that was coursing thro' my brain made me exclaim, "Oh! Nurse, don't you wish you were inside of *me!*"—her look of dismay and vehement disclaimer—"Inside of you, Miss, when you have just had a sick head-ache for five days!"—gave a greater blow to my vanity, than that much battered article has ever received. The headache had gone off in the night and I had clean forgotten it—when the little wretch confronted me with it, at this sublime moment when I was feeling within me the potency of a Bismarck, and left me powerless before the immutable law that however great we may seem to our own consciousness no human being would exchange his for ours, and before the fact that *my* glorious rôle was to stand for *Sick headache* to mankind! What a grotesque I am to be sure! Lying in this room, with the resistance of a thistle-down, having illusory moments of throbbing with the pulse of the Race, the Mystery to be solved at the next breath and the fountain of all Happiness within me—the sense of vitality, in short, simply proportionate to the excess of weakness!—To sit by and watch these absurdities is amusing in its way and reminds me of how I used to *listen* to my "company manners" in the days when I had 'em, and how ridiculous they sounded.

Ah! Those strange people who have the courage to be unhappy! *Are* they unhappy, by-the-way?

July 16th

Owing to an unprecedented condition of affluence, Mrs. Bacheler has joined the "*Bew*rial Soc[iety];" hitherto only one could belong (two pence per week) and that one was naturally her lord and master. But she was not without her support for the dread moment, for she had an ancient night-gown of mine which she is cherishing for her shroud. It seems to be the climax of existence for 'em and one can't wonder for the thought of being buried higgledy-piggledy with odious creatures whom one has spent one's days in fighting with, must offend the æsthetic sense. This is another link with the great, it seems that the Prince has the same passion for deaths and burials as his mother. The whole family are devoted to them. All loss is gain; since I've become so nearsighted I see no dust or squalor and therefore conceive of myself as living in splendour.

Done the quarterly acc[oun]ts. My income a most interesting quantity, with the greatest capacity for diminishing itself and yet still existing. How thankful am I for my little. Conceive of being a millstone round the neck of one's brothers, as some poor wretches are, and not brothers like mine either!

Mrs. Sidgwick has sent me a paper upon *Madame de Sévigné*, the best thing I have read of hers. The dear lady is human, like the rest of us. I remember once talking to her about the awkward moments that come sometimes when the fruits of the family genius are lent to one, especially *verses* of deceased members, to

which she assented very warmly and said she always escape
from them, but her own products she has the greatest facility i
giving.—How base am I, but what should I do if I were not?
wish I didn't read so much rubbish. Nurse when she comes i
looks just like the buttony-boy in Leech staggering home wit
"Clarissa 'Arlowe for Missus," but it's well I can, for so man
hours slip away so and I can't read anything suggestive, tha
survives or links itself to experience for it sets my silly stomac
fluttering and my flimsy head skipping so that I have to stop
This is the great trouble with the substance-full Lemaître, som
of whose pages simply seem to intoxicate with their luminosity
It seems a waste not to have known him before, but then I thin
he fits now and yields me more in this present vacuity. What
curious psychological problem to solve, the spell cast over th
French race by the commonplace name of William. The follow
ing owing to the creature's intelligence is one of the most ex
quisite illustrations. In an article on an *adaptation* of one o
Shakespeare's plays, he (Jules Lemaître) says that the emenda
tions improve it very much, for "—le vrai Shakespeare, en effet
c'est celui que nous pouvons aimer, l'autre ne compte pas; l'autr
c'est William, si vous voulez, un accident, un rien." My dea
friend, you have reversed it, your nondescript play is decidedl
not Shakespeare, but the offspring of your mysterious and non
descript William—I should greatly like to know just what the
sound *William* stands for in your mind and that of your kind
One can't imagine an Anglo-Saxon being able ever to take the
Bible or Shakes[peare] seriously in French. One can only be
grateful to him, however, for dwelling so strongly upon the
tediousness of the great one's humour, which for the most is in
comprehensible and when not isn't humourous. To us, perhap
it's "William!"

August 4t

I must try and pull myself together and record the somewha
devastating episode of July 18th when Harry after a much
longer absence than usual presented himself, doubled by

William! !⁵¹ We had just finished luncheon and were talking of something or other when H. suddenly said, with a queer look upon his face, "I must tell you something!" "You're not going to be married!" shrieked I. "No, but William is here, he has been lunching upon Warwick Castle and is waiting now in the Holly Walk for the news to be broken to you and if you survive, I'm to tie my handkerch[ief] to the balcony." Enter Wm. *not* à la Romeo via the balcony; the prose of our century to say nothing of that of our consanguinity making it super[er]ogatory. The *beforehand* having been so cleverly suppressed by the devoted H. "it came out so much easier than could have been expected" as they say to infants in the dentist chair. (I always sympathized so with Ellen Gurney⁵² when she told of how she ran and slammed the drawingroom door when she heard, in the old war days, her brother Edward's voice suddenly in the hall downstairs, he having come home unexpectedly, as they always did in those days.) Poor Harry, over whom the moment had impended for two m[on]ths, looked as white as a ghost before they went and well he may in his anxiety as to which "going off" in my large repertory would "come on" but with the assistance of 200 grains of Bromides I think I behaved with extreme propriety. Wm. had only got to London the day before, having been for three weeks in Ireland and Scotland. He doesn't look [much] older for the five years, and all that there is to be said of him, of course, is that he is simply himself, a creature who speaks in another language as H. says from the rest of mankind and who would lend life and charm to a treadmill. What a strange experience it was, to have what had seemed so dead and gone all these years suddenly bloom before one, a flowing oasis in this alien desert, redolent with the exquisite *family* perfume of the days gone by, made of the allusions, the memories and the point of view in common, so that my floating-particle sense was

⁵¹ William James was in Europe during the summer of 1889. He had last seen his sister in 1884 when she sailed for England.

⁵² Ellen Hooper Gurney (1838–1886), sister of Mrs. Henry Adams, wife of Ephraim W. Gurney (1829–1886), professor of history at Harvard. Her brother was Edward William Hooper (1839–1901).

lost for an hour or so in the illusion that what is forever shattered
had sprung up anew, and existed outside of our memories—
where it is forever green!

August 5t

A note of farewell from Mr. Godkin with a tea-infuser. I'm glad
on Harry's acc[oun]t that he has gone, six weeks' visit is a long
strain. H. says he seemed to enjoy it greatly. I suppose I shall
never see him again, as he is getting on in years, and I'm *no*
getting on as to peregrinating. I'm sorry; he goes back so far.
One of the pleasantest summers I remember was the one we
passed together at Ripton in '74 or '75. He delighted so in
Father and how he roared over his jokes. We used to take such
long, beautiful rides thro' those roadless forests. What a charming country it would be if it were opened out and one could get
at it. They say that there is little doubt that Mr. Edmund
Gurney[53] committed suicide. What a pity to hide it, every educated person who kills himself does something towards lessening the superstition. It's bad that it is so untidy, there is no denying that, for one bespatters one's friends morally as well as
physically, taking them so much more into one's secret than
they want to be taken. But how heroic to be able to suppress
one's vanity to the extent of confessing that the game is too hard.
The most comic and apparently the chief argument used against
it, is that because you were born without being consulted, you
would be very sinfull should you cut short your blissfull career!
This has been said to me a dozen times, and they never can
see how they have turned things topsy-turvey.

August 9t

England is having one of its hysterical attacks over Mrs. Maybrick,[54] what a spectacle it is! Mrs. M. seems to be as debased

[53] Edmund Gurney (1847–1888), English psychologist and friend of
William James.

[54] Mrs. Florence Elizabeth Maybrick was convicted of murder, circumstantial
evidence showing that she had extracted arsenic from flypaper and administered

a villain as one could wish to find, and convicted herself out of
her own mouth. On the 6th the Ripleys came from London
and lunched. They told me a great deal of course that I wanted
to know about poor Aunt Kate.[55] Her illness seems to have been
less painful than we feared and she had every comfort and
care from them all. From some little things they said I am
thankful that as we could have done nothing for Aunt Kate,
H. and I were spared the contemplation of certain subsequent
developments. Poor human nature can stand but a slight strain
when it comes to tea-cups and salt-spoons. But it is all instructive,
and in that view,[56] "Altho' thou shouldest possess all created
good, yet couldest thou not be happy thereby nor blessed;
but in God, who created all things, consisteth thy whole blessedness and felicity; not such as is seen and commended by the
foolish lovers of the world, but such as the good and faithful
servants of Christ wait for, and of which the spiritual and pure
in heart, whose conversation is in heaven, sometimes have a
foretaste." (Imitation [of Christ,] chap. xvi.)

We have just, with "great valour and skill," annihilated 1,500
more Dervishes,[57] a "brilliant victory." After seven hours of
fighting the starved naked wretches were cut to pieces.

August 10th

I must record that on the 7th of August I was 41 years old! !
Glory, glory Hallelujah! Would oh, would it were 61! H.
says that the main desire in the British bosom, apparently, is
not to be left last with the host and hostess after an entertainment of any kind, so that there is at a given moment a regular

---

it to her husband, a Liverpool cotton merchant. She was sentenced to death
but this was later commuted to life imprisonment.

[55] Catherine Walsh had died earlier that year.

[56] The end of this sentence is blotted out in the diary.

[57] See note p. 43 above. The attacks of the dervishes had been continuing
during the past month.

stampede. The other night he was at some function at Lady
Knutsford's[58] and he was looking after Madame Taine,[59] helping M. Jusserand,[60] who had brought the Taines. They made
the circuit of the rooms and when they got back to where they
started they found the dense mass in retreat, a solid body of
backs presented to Lady Knutsford standing in one of the rooms
absolutely alone. When Madame Taine turned and saw her,
she stopped and exclaimed in horror and amazement, "Mais,
est-ce qu'on la laisse toute seule, comme cela?" and was for
rushing back to her, but M. Jusserand waved her on saying
"Cela ne fait rien, cela se fait toujours, etc."

August 12th

William was most amusing about Ireland—he seems sound eno'
on Home Rule, but how could a child of Father's be anything
else! ! He went to see the family of a little maid-servant they
have, and such a welcome as he had! The refrain, "The Lord
be praised that Kerry should have seen this day!" was repeated
every five min[ute]s during the two hours he was with 'em.
He says that they are an absolutely foreign people, much more
excessive than they are with us just like the stage Irishman.
He was very funny about evictions, and says the horror of them
entirely vanishes when you see the nature of the cabins, existence
without being so much preferable to existence within. He says
that it is the most extraordinary thing to see coming out from
the midst of all this filth, misery and squalor, this jovial, so-
ciable, witty, intelligent race, supported by, and living *entirely*
upon an ideal, etc., etc.

[58] Lady Knutsford was the former Lady Mary Ashburnham. She married
the Hon. Sydney Holland in 1883.

[59] Hippolite Taine (1828–1893), the French literary historian and essayist
and his wife had visited London during May of 1889.

[60] Jean Jules Jusserand (1855–1932), French diplomat and author, was attached to the French embassy in London at this time and had become a friend of
Henry James.

marrye X

Oh, the tragedy of it! when you think of the dauntless creatures flinging themselves and their ideal for seven centuries against the dense wall of British brutality, as incapable of an ideal inspiration or an imaginative movement as the beasts of the field.

Mrs. Bowyer told me yesterday that the presents of the Duchess of Fife were said to be worth £200,000. The Bachelers lie in bed till noon because they don't get so hungry in bed! Nurse has to make her Saturday visit late so that Mrs. B. may be dressed to receive. The dressing consists of pinning on, with a common pin, a bit of blue ribbon round her neck, said ribbon being an old bow off my pin-cushion which Nurse gave her some time ago. They have a new neighbour whom they feared drank, but it was only—"She was a bit boozey 'cause 'twas her wedding-day," number two, a perfectly legitimate moment and method of festivity, of course; "she has *beautiful* furniture and pictures!" her dower, doubtless. I saw, on Sunday in the River Walk, two workmen, about thirty, clean, intelligent, sober and serious and I did so long to stop and ask them what they thought of it all, but, ah! me, I'm hopelessly relegated among the smug and the comfortable.

August 13th

"Nous apprendrions de lui [un ange philosophe] qu'il faut savoir souffrir et que la science de la douleur est l'unique science de la vie. Ses leçons nous inspireraient la patience, qui est le plus difficile des héroïsmes, l'héroïsme constant. Elles nous enseigneraient la clémence et le pardon; elles nous enseigneraient la résignation, je veux dire la résignation dans l'effort, qui consiste à frapper toujours le mal, sans nous irriter jamais de son invulnérable immortalité. Sous cette inspiration les existences les plus humbles peuvent devenir des œuvres d'art bien supérieures aux plus belles symphonies et aux plus beaux poèmes. Est-ce que les œuvres d'art qu'on réalise en soi-même ne sont pas les meilleures? Les autres, qu'on jette en dehors sur

la toile ou le papier, ne sont rien que des images, des ombres
L'œuvre de la vie est une réalité d'homme simple, le pauvre
revendeur du Faubourg St. Germain qui fait de sa vie un poème
de charité, vaut mieux qu' Homère."—What a beautiful rhythm
this makes in my soul as I cradle myself for a moment in the
hope that those with *resignation in passivity* may, equally with
those with *resignation in effort*, not surpass Homer, but better
still, have some spiritual significance.

September 3rd

Life is simply a huge joke! The ghostly "Miss Peabody" *ma
terialized* into Katharine[61] on August 21. Let's have done with
it all!

November 16th

Kath. sailed on November 9th in the Umbria, and tomorrow
I hope for a cable telling of her arrival today. She seems de
cidedly to have "interrupted the Diary, Miss," as Nurse plain
tively predicted after her arrival (was ever a diary, by the
way, so honoured in its own country before?)—but that calam
ity perhaps isn't irretrievable. Notwithstanding the wear and
tear of Time and the burden of three invalids upon her soul and
body she seems as large a joke as ever, an embodiment of the
stretchable, a purely transatlantic and modern possibility. She
had, of course, an edition, up to date, of her pocket compendium
of use*less* information and she reassuringly and smilingly "in
formed" any of the population on any subject they might desire
I feel like a creature who, after a long draught of fresh air, has
crept back under an exhausted receiver closing down over her
again with a hopeless and all too familiar click. But it has hap
pened so often now since my scaffolding began to fall eight

[61] Katharine Peabody Loring (1849–1943), of Beverly, Massachusetts, has
accompanied Alice abroad and become her constant companion.

years ago, that after a few futile squirms I already breathe
and live and find my suffocation being therein the natural one,
for Heaven be praised! agonies do *not* repeat themselves, unless we wish it. We have each time something more to meet
them with and nothing is more true than that "à force de
s'élargir pour la souffrance, l'âme en arrive à des capacités
prodigieuses, ce qui la comblait naguère à la faire crever en
couvre à peine le fond maintenant"—but my soul will never
stretch itself to allowing that it is anything else than a cruel
and unnatural fate for a woman to live alone, to have no one
to care and "do for" daily is not only a sorrow, but a sterilizing
process. This is a scientific statement, not a lament, for I am
replete with the fertilization of the last three months.

November 18th

A cable this A.M. to say that she has arrived—so that episode has
vanished like a dream! I mustn't let the other episodes vanish
unrecorded, however, for the summer turned out a giddy whirl
for me! First William, instead of going to Switz[erland], came
suddenly back from Paris and went home, having as usual exhausted Europe in a few weeks and finding it stale, flat and
unprofitable. The only necessity being to get home, the first
letter after his arrival was, of course, full of plans for his
return plus wife and infants! he is just like a blob of mercury,
you can't put a mental finger upon him. H. and I were laughing
over him and recalling Father and William's resemblance in
these ways to him. Tho' the results were the same, it seems
to come from such a different nature in the two, in Wm., an
entire inability or indifference "to stick to a thing for the sake
of sticking," as some said of him once, whilst Father, the delicious infant! couldn't submit even to the thraldom of his
own whim, and then the dear being was such a prey to the
demon homesickness. H. says that certain places on the Continent bring up the old scenes so vividly, Father's sudden re-

turns at the end of 36 hours, having left to be gone a fortnight with Mother beside him holding his hand and we five children pressing close round him "as if he had just been saved from drowning," and he pouring out, as he alone could, the agonies of desolation thro' which he had come. But to return to our Mutton, William, he came with H. on August 14th on his way to Liverpool. He told all about his Paris experience where he was a delegate to the Psychological Cong[ress],[62] which was a most brilliant success. The French *most* polite and hospitable invited Wm. to open the Congress, and always had a foreigner in the Chair at the different meetings. I extracted with great difficulty from him that M[onsieur] Will-yam James was frequently referred to by the speakers. H. suggested that he might become another case of the great "Williams." He liked the Henry Sidgwicks and the Fred. Myers.[63] Mrs. S. tho' of such proud and ancient lineage, is the exact reproduction in her appearance of a Yankee woman who keeps a country store. Mrs. Myers paid him the following enigmatic compliment, "We are so glad that you are *as* you are!"

This reminds me of what Mrs. Kemble[64] said to H. about me after her first call, which was more enigmatic still. She arrived, poor lady, dreadfully out of breath from the stairs; I was greatly distressed, but my perturbation which had been prospectively great vanished, for Mrs. Kemble without her breath was a much less alarming quantity. H. told her, after, that I had been so troubled about the stairs, she said it was nothing more than what befell her always, and added, "Most fortunately your sister is an American lady, *a very different thing* from an English lady, I assure you." When I have seen her since I have always been in such an agony to be the *right* kind of a lady. In

[62] This was the International Congress of Physiological Psychology which was arranged to coincide with the International Exposition of 1889.

[63] Frederick W. H. Myers (1843–1901), poet and man of letters, was one of the founders of the Society for Psychical Research.

[64] Frances Anne Kemble (1809–1893), the celebrated actress of the early part of the century, was one of Henry James's closest friends.

the pursuit of knowledge I asked Nurse one day whether K[atharine] and I were different from English ladies in any way—"Entirely different, Miss!" "Why, how are we different?" "Not so 'aughty, Miss!" Truly discouraging! !

November 19th

What bottomless folly this Brazilian Revolution[65] is, confirmed in this morning's paper! and the dread Blaine[66] on our hands!

Just read this, Two Irishmen in Texas came across a snake and one chopped his head off and kept on pounding at the squirming body, whereupon his friend said, "Why don't you leave off, it's dead." "Sure and I know that, but I want to make the crature sinsible of his misfortune."

M. Delbœuf,[67] the Belgian psychol[ogist], told Wm. that he had a very rustic and untutored servant and one day some friends were dining and in pouring out the Wine she always lifted the glass up off the table and filled it behind their backs. Finally he said to her, "Versez-le sur la table," whereupon she poured it on to the table-cloth! This was a decidedly abortive brain-suggestion.

A young man took his young woman to a restaurant and asked her what she would have to drink with her dinner. "I guess I'll have a bottle of champagne." "Guess again!" quoth he.

Katharine has the most estimable habit of paying one compliments and delicately embroidering any outside reference to one's humble personality which may occur. I make it a rule always to believe the compliments implicitly for five minutes and to simmer gently for 20 more. That insures a solid gain

[65] Troops under Gen. Manuel Deodoro da Fonseca had deposed Pedro II and announced the formation of a republic.
[66] James G. Blaine (1830–1893) had become Secretary of State in March 1889 in the administration of President Harrison.
[67] Joseph Rémy Léopold Delbœuf (1831–1896), Belgian philosopher and psychologist, known for his work in logic and on hypnotism.

of 25 m[inute]s out of the 24 h[ou]rs, in which one is in peace and charity with all mankind.

[Several words blotted out] simply a creature who wants to turn her husband into a rather more extensive liar than she is herself. When will women begin to have the first glimmer that above all other loyalties is the loyalty to Truth, i.e., to yourself, that husband, children, friends and country are as nothing to that.

December 1st

What an indigestion of remarks *rentrés* I've had since Kath. left! I shall learn to cork myself up again before long and return to my state of "bottled lightning" as Wm. calls it, an expression which he culled from a story he read once in a Boston newspaper, where the heroine was thus described. I never can forget this either, which I read at the age of fifteen. A witness was asked to describe the appearance of the body of a man who was supposed to have been murdered. She said that "He looked pleasant-like and foaming at the mouth."

The whole Liberal-Unionist[68] party stinketh not more with *Virtue* than do I, when reproving Nurse. I shudder when I hear the inevitable peroration coming forth from my lips, "Nurse, it gives me great pain to have to speak to you thus, but I only do so for your *good! !*" Was there ever anything so dishonest?

Some one asked Kath. when she said she thought the *Temple Bar*[69] good, "Ah, do they take in the *Temple Bar* in America!" One has immediately the ludicrous vision of a number of the

[68] The Liberal Party had split on the Irish question and the "radical" Liberal-Unionists, under Joseph Chamberlain, disapproving Gladstone's first Home Rule bill, had joined the Conservatives in 1886 in forming a coalition government under Lord Salisbury.

[69] *Temple Bar Magazine* (1860–1906), originally edited by George Augustus Sala, was acquired by the publisher, Bentley, in 1866. It published essays and fiction.

T. B. being "taken in" by the two Great Continents. A curate on the same occasion said he thought "Boulanger[70] so very clever"—the one analytic remark possible to the British mind. "Clever! why, he has just been defeated and is nothing but a black horse."—"Ah! I never heard of his having a black horse, but I think it so very clever of him to go to Jersey!"

While I think of it I must note, lest unborn generations should think me a plagiarist, that a small joke I made about the cuckoo and the clocks, Kath. told me is in Dr. Holmes's *Hundred Days in Europe*.[71] I never saw the book and never read a notice of it. As great minds jump [together] this proves conclusively what I have always maintained against strenuous opposition, that my Mind *is Great!* Henry says that Wendell Holmes has had a most brilliant success in London and that he was as pleasant as possible, young-looking and handsomer than ever. Flirting as desperately too.—I suppose that his idea of "Heaven is still flirting with pretty girls," as he used to say. This that he said once still survives in my mind, that "Every man sees something of Mrs. Nickleby in his own mother," which reminds me of Alice repeating Prof. Farlow's[72] asking at their club table one night, "Why is every man's Aunt so entirely different from his Mother?" which is equally good, methinks. I remember the torpid A. G. Sedgwick[73] telling one day that he had gone to a telegraph office, written his tel[egram] and handed it to the clerk, and asked, "Is it plain?" "Plain, but peculiar!" O. W. H. said the absence of such possibilities is what makes one so homesick in Europe! to the disgust of the offended

[70] Gen. Georges Boulanger (1837–1891) had been elected Deputy for the Seine earlier that year but had fled France in April, taking refuge in England to avoid charges that he had mishandled public funds.

[71] Dr. Oliver Wendell Holmes's *Our Hundred Days in Europe* was written after his trip abroad in 1886.

[72] William G. Farlow was Professor of Cryptogamic Botany at Harvard and a Cambridge neighbor of the William Jameses for forty years.

[73] Arthur George Sedgwick (1844–1915), brother of Mrs. Charles Eliot Norton, was a friend of both Henry and William James during their youth in Cambridge.

Arthur. How funny it is to remember these trifling things but it is a joy to bring back the past in any way and I shall put down everything I can think of in this precious reservoir.—I shall have to stop reading French novels. A course of perpetual adulteries becomes more deadly wearisome and tedious than one can say, and makes one long to fly for excitement to one of Miss Yonge's[74] profligate groups of legitimate offspring, as far as *Morality* goes, and I don't think there is much to choose. It must be altogther consoling and exalting to feel that you have discovered and endowed y[ou]r race with one of the fundamental moralities as Dumas[75] must with his *Chastity*. He talks of it as if it were some Social Lotion (for outward application only, evidently) for the extermination of all evil, and stands awe-struck at his marvellous discovery, like a naïf infant.

In a fine speech by John Morley[76] at the Eighty Club, he says that to him—"A working-man who cannot get work is an infinitely more tragic figure than any Hamlet or any Ædipus." Beautifully and nobly said, *Honest John!* Think of the hideous despair of seeing y[our]self and children sinking into that black, seething, bottomless gulf which yawns before them from the cradle to the grave. John Morley must be rather disgusted at being vaunted to the skies for being commonly honest.

December 2nd

Nurse had one of her Sabbatical orgies yesterday; she starts forth at dawn and partakes of the "Spirit of our Lord" and her dissipations are only over at 8.30 P.M. How fortunate that in miracles, as in everything else, "ce n'est que le premier pas qui coûte" holds good. Given the first morsel, the feeding of uncountable millions follows after. When the parsonic worm who

[74] Charlotte M. Yonge (1823–1901) wrote 160 books, including many romances expounding the religious views of John Keble.

[75] Alexandre Dumas *fils* (1824–1895), French dramatist.

[76] John Morley, later Viscount Morley of Blackburn (1838–1923), had been chief Secretary for Ireland in 1886.

dwelt beneath me for so long came up to see me, I aired my
one bit of theological lore as I thought and asked him if they
didn't call their communion consubstantiation as distinct from
transubstantiation—'Oh! it sounds just like it only it isn't!'
When I asked *what* it was I received an equally lucid
reply. He proposed reading to me and I in all innocence declined and said that I got plenty of books from the libraries and
not until Kath. revealed it to me did it dawn upon my ingenuous
mind that he had spiritual food in his pocket. How I laughed
and thought of the old negro woman who, when remonstrated
with for stealing a goose and showing excessive piety, immediately after, at a revival meeting, exclaimed—"You don't
think I'd let a goose come betwixt me and de Lord?" My
goose wasn't stolen, but I hold the same sentiments. In the last
three days I've seen five people, a crush for me! There are
some half a dozen people who have come to see me once and
who have never come again, causing me to feel like a Barnum
Monstrosity which had missed fire. I wonder if it would pay
to have a long line of ancestry and come out at the end of centuries Miss Percy! She amuseth me more than a little and is
more *terre à terre* than any one I ever saw. She has a brother
with her who has been in Australia 17 years and is threatened
with complete blindness—she describes the situation as "dull"
for him. I asked her yesterday some questions about Australia,
especially about the money sent to the "Dockers' Strike" and
she replied, "You know there is an immense number of Irishmen in Australia." "But the Dockers weren't Irish." "No, but
they were on Strike and republicans and all that sort of thing!"
She doubtless considers the Irish question a Strike! Striking for
a republic.

Another of my inspired circle said, on her return from London, when I asked her what she had heard—"It was all on
public affairs and I never remember anything in which I am not
concerned myself." This one was not a scion of an effete race,
but is by way of having *Mind!*

The contact with life of the great mass seems to have the surface of a threepenny bit. The Wm. Sidgwicks came to luncheon one day whilst K. was here. It was the day after the French elections and I naturally referred to them with great interest and to the success of the exhibition, but they made the most languid responses. They *are* intelligent and usually widely interested, so it was the more disappointing.

December 11th

How sick one gets of being "good," how much I should repect myself if I could burst out and make every one wretched for 24 hours; embody selfishness, as they say [two words erased] does. If it were only voluntary and one made a conscious choice, it might enrich the soul a bit, but when it has become simply automatic thro' a sense of the expedient—of the grotesque futility of the perverse—it's degrading! And then the dolts praise one for being "amiable!" just as if one didn't avoid ruffling one's feathers as one avoids plum-pudding or any other indigestible compound!

December 12th

Harry spent Tuesday the 3rd with me. He is just back from Paris, as amusing as ever about his experiences, seeing things that no one else does. He seems to think that France is in an excellent condition. He saw a lot of men, and fell in love with Miss Eames,[77] the prima donna from Maine or wherever it is. He is very funny on the social subjugation of Europe by the Americans, which seems as widespread on the Continent as it is here. When it comes to Hurlburt[78] and James Gordon Bennett[79] it's rather hard of digestion. Mrs. Von Hoffmann[80]

---

[77] Emma Eames (1867–1952), American soprano, who sang at the Metropolitan Opera from 1891–1909.

[78] William Henry Hurlburt of the New York *World*. (See note on p. 193.)

[79] James Gordon Bennett (1841–1918), owner of the New York *Herald* and founder of the *Evening Telegram*.

[80] Baroness Von Hoffmann, the former Lydia Gray Ward, second daughter of Samuel Gray Ward.

old him that one night at her villa at Cannes the Comte de Paris had come to her and said that he heard that Mr. Bennett was there and he wanted her to introduce him as he was very anxious to know him. Mrs. V. H. went off reluctantly, not knowing *what* J. G. B. might do. She found him very reluctant and in short refused to budge, when she found to her horror the Count close at her heels. As soon as the ceremony was accomplished he asked James to allow him to present him to the Countess who wanted very much to know him and turned on his heel to go off and fetch her. Mrs. V. H. could stand it no longer so she planted her hands in Bennett's back and shoved him forward so that he could at least meet the lady halfway. The Archibald Groves[81] he saw in Paris; got rooms for them in his hotel where they stopped on their way to Tangiers. He said "how the drama of life rushes on and how out of it all poor chloroformed Edmund Gurney seemed." English women, he says, look entirely differently in Paris from what they do in London, not handsome but big and clumsy. The *New Review* has had a phenomenal success and in six months' time it is making a fortune. It's surely the flimsiest of the flimsy, and its success throws a light upon the intellectual demands of the moment, which isn't flattering. He told me a funny thing that happened last summer. He knows Mr. Geo[rge] Russell[82] but had never called upon him. One day he met him somewhere and he Mr. R. did something or other civil about H.'s umbrella, returned it to him or showed some other striking sign of morality on the subject so H. left his card at his door to thank him, when the servant saying he was at home H. walked in and paid him a call. A few days after he was at Waddesdon[83] and picked up the *New Review* when he found

---

[81] Archibald Grove was editor of the *New Review* (1889–1894), which published work by Henry James. Mrs. Grove was the widow of the late Edmund Gurney.

[82] George W. E. Russell (1853–1919), son of Lord Russell, Liberal member of the House of Commons for fifteen years, was also an active journalist.

[83] Waddesdon Manor, Buckinghamshire, the château-style mansion built in the 1880's by Baron Ferdinand de Rothschild.

himself to his dismay among the *Talkers* whom Mr. Geo. R. was then dissecting. H. unfortunately came directly after Lowell and was much more tenderly treated than that worthy which made it the more unpleasant for him. Mr. Russell of course supposed that H.'s call was a return of thanks for the paragraph! As no reference was made he must have thought H. superfluously modest. Mr. R. is extremely sensitive and he asked H. once how often he had been obliged to leave country-houses suddenly because he had been uncivilly treated therein and when H. said he had never done such a thing he seemed greatly surprised and said, "Why, sometimes I have gone off in the baker's cart."

One day when my shawls were falling off to the left my cushions falling out to the right and the duvet off my knees, one of those crises of misery in short which are all in the day's work for an invalid Kath. exclaimed, "What an awful pity it is that you can't say *damn*." I agreed with her from my heart. It is an immense loss to have all robust and sustaining expletives refined away from one! at such moments of trial refinement is a feeble reed to lean upon. I wonder, whether, if I had had any education I should have been more, or less, of a fool than I am. It would have deprived me surely of those exquisite moments of mental flatulence which every now and then inflate the cerebral vacuum with a delicious sense of latent possibilities—of stretching oneself to cosmic limits, and who would ever give up the reality of dreams for relative knowledge?

December 13th

The report of the Vigilance Association just come, most unpleasant in tone; the cant of the so-called Purity Party is more offensive than all the others, I think, but the professional philanthropist leaves his trail upon all he touches.

The German Emperor is quite mad, no sort of doubt. Vanity, Vanity, what a pitfall thou art! This from observation, *not* experience.

I was greatly touched a little while ago with Constance Maud's[84] talk about her music. She wants to devote herself to it seriously as a profession but as she is a daughter and not a son her tastes are set aside and she has to do parish work! and that pretty badly, I fear. Her compositions are very good, they say, and original, isn't it too bad? She says she doesn't know how she would live without her music. She is to be envied for such a passion. Ah! but she knoweth not that jewel beyond price, a moral passion, which can know no material obstruction, for which sorrow, loneliness and pain are food, which seeketh not for pleasure, but waiteth patiently till it flowers in happiness!

December 14th

A good letter yesterday from Alice[85] in which she says that she and Marg. go and hear Grace Norton[88] discuss or rather expound the erudite theme of the French ladies of the 18th century. Just conceive with Sainte-Beuve at hand and one's own chimney-corner, straining one's vision to make out the blurred outlines of those clearcut silhouettes through the fog of Grace's ineptitudes. Her clumsy and blundering handling of creatures whose whole *raison d'être* was the graceful, and the light and sure of touch, must be truly painful. Grace gave Mabel Quincy, as a wedding present, a copy of Montaigne with the "naughty" pages gummed together; could there be anything more deliciously droll!

Read the other day somewhere that the French women during the war had been *"sublimes et charmantes,"* a truly Gallic combination!

The negro lad who prayed, when leading a revival, "Lord, make Thy servant conspicuous," isn't bad! William expressed himself and his environment to perfection when he replied to

[84] Constance Elisabeth Maude, in addition to being a musician, published *Wagner's Heroes* and *Wagner's Heroines* in 1896, as well as writing novels and essays.

[85] Alice H. James (1849–1922), wife of William James.

[88] Grace Norton (1834–1926), sister of Charles Eliot Norton and a close friend of Henry James.

my question about his house at Chocorua, "Oh, it's the mos[t]
delightful house you ever saw; has 14 doors all opening out[-]
side." His brain isn't limited to 14, perhaps unfortunately[.]
The builder of his Cambridge house said that he had save[d]
$2,000 at least by going to Europe this summer. By listening
to every suggestion he heard and altering in accordance, th[e]
bills ran up. In talking with H. about the extraordinary adapt[-]
ability of the American to new circumstances he said, "He hasn'[t]
to cease being something else first; and then he is used all hi[s]
life to seeing people become anything in the course of fiv[e]
minutes."

Read Motley's Letters[87] with great interest. How the second
volume which relates of the Rebellion warms the heart by the
vivid memories it stirs. It all seems as of yesterday and ye[t]
so spiritually remote, for we seem to have passed beyond the
protesting and aggressive patriotism so natural and essential then
and the rejoicings over the victories, in view of the vanquished,
have almost a painful ring now. What a curious caprice of fate
that the poor man should have had to succumb to *Historicus*
as a son-in-law! He seems to have been honesty itself, and the
last creature for diplomacy, with his feminine tendency to
intensity. How tiresome all the lists of "people seen," which
seem to constitute such a large part of biographies, *Letters,*
etc., nowadays, nothing showing the slightest discrimination
said.

What a delightful, generous, and human sound Dr. Holmes'
Letters have, especially in contrast to the self-conscious Lowell.
It makes one understand Father's enthusiasm for the Doctor
who he used to say was worth all the men in the Club[88] put
together, and how indignant he used to be with Lowell's
manner of snubbing him, and admiring of the perfect way the

---

[87] John Lothrop Motley (1814–1877), American historian and diplomat.
His *Correspondence* (ed. Curtis), two volumes, was published in 1889.

[88] This was the Saturday Club which dined once a month at the Parker
House in Boston. The elder Henry James had been a member.

Doctor took it. In his *Memoir* of Motley, it's really touching how he dwells upon Motley's "beauty" and personal charm when one thinks of his own limitations. I remember Father coming home one Saturday from the dinner and telling, among other things, that Dr. Holmes had asked if he did not find that his sons despised him and seemed surprised when F[ather] said no, that he was not oppressed in that way—"But after all, it is only natural they should, for they stand upon our shoulders," exclaimed the Doctor, a truly dizzy height for the accomplished and elongated Wendell! The figure immediately presents itself of the two *à la* church-steeple.

Browning dead[89]—a pity he didn't die a little sooner before he made such an unpleasant spectacle of himself with Edw[ard] Fitzgerald last summer. How profoundly uninteresting to one are great men personally, as compared to the Bachelers, for instance. They seem so apart from their work.

I asked Harry if the French *listen* as the English do. He said they all talk at once, like American women. The English are irreproachable in that way, almost too good, for they don't encourage one by the way with inarticulate applause or dissent, and as the face is more often than not passive and expressionless, one is quite in doubt as to whether they are following one or not, so that embarrassing moments come. Nurse met Miss Blanche Leppington lately, and she said to her, "I was so glad to see Miss James looking better yesterday when I called, there is less going away of her face in weariness and pain!!"—Oh, my eye!!!

December 16th

Daudet's *La Lutte pour la Vie*[90] is wretched stuff. The climax,

[89] Robert Browning (1812–1889) had died in Venice on December 12. A few months before the end he had mistaken a reference made by Edward Fitzgerald to Mrs. Browning's poetry as a slight on her life and character. He had thereupon written his bitter "Lines to Edward Fitzgerald."

[90] Alphonse Daudet (1840–1897). His play *La Lutte pour la Vie* appeared in 1889.

a father killing the hero who has ruined and betrayed hi
daughter, forces upon one the futile and elusive nature of huma
means, for even the glow of triumph of an avenging murdere
must have but a momentary life, must fade and flicker ou
in the presence of his victim, stiff and stark, but yet complete
whilst he is still the same formless figure, vague and abortive

Halévy's *Notes et Souvenirs*,[91] combined with *L'Invasion*
are most interesting, psychologically, full of stories showing
French human nature *à nu*, tragic and comic, *pêle-mêle*. On
needs to read nothing else to understand the collapse. Th
mixture of *trahison*, *gloire*, wrongs, the invariable necessity
for a scape-goat and the awe with which they contemplat
themselves doing any common act of generosity or manlines
makes one feel as if they were hopeless babies for all time
Two Frenchmen in a horse-car in Washington when two ladie
got in and couldn't find seats said, one to the other—"Levons
nous, c'est noble!"

I wonder what part of me is fed by snubbing poor littl
Nurse. Every now and then I have to trample upon the desir
which rises within me. A survival of the savage, I suppose, a
sense that she is a dependent creature at my mercy for the
moment. Hideous! It's pleasant eno' to get out sometimes ir
the summer, but then one has to bother about the weather and
one's health every day, contemplate the clouds, and reflect
upon one's pains, whereas now it rains and blows without and
grinds away in the bones and I need never give 'em a thought.
Gadders will not believe me, but the days I go out are twice
as long in the passing as the shutup ones. I suppose that it
doesn't show the highest intelligence for a pathologic victim
to erect her standard as the normal, and label all variation:
therefrom as "queer and unnatural." I have, however, a faint
suspicion that the healthy, especially those called "healthy-
minded"—depressing quantities!—may see things equally out
of proportion. It pleaseth me to think so at any rate.

[91] Ludovic Halévy (1834–1908), French playwright and librettist.

I read in the *Nation* last night a notice of Miss Alcott's[92] *Life and Letters*, where mention is made of Harry's writing a review of *Moods* in the *North American Rev[iew]* which reminded [me] of Father's having met Mr. Alcott in the street one day and saying to him: "They are reading *Dumps* at home with great interest." " '*Dumps?*' " queried Mr. A. "Yes, *Dumps*, your daughter's novel!" said the pater. The suggestive *Moods* reduced to Dumps!

Lady Somebody in London was discoursing to me on the depravity of pick-me-ups and said she never took them but had beef-tea and milk—"For I find that God blesses *them*, but He never blesses the other!" She differs then from the little curate who, in discussing the Temperance fête, exclaimed, "It's sad that man should abuse God's good gifts!" Poor God must be busy stewing beef and distilling gin!

This touch of vanity of which I read yesterday maketh of an abbess of the 17th cent[ury] a woman and a sister! In the amusing memoirs of the Electress Sophia of Hanover,[93] she describes her sister Elizabeth, Abbess of Herford, as knowing, "every language and science under the sun and she corresponded regularly with Descartes"; she was also very handsome, but her nose was apt to grow red, and "all her philosophy could not save her from vexation," for when this misfortune overtook her, "she used to hide herself from the world." Dear friend, how I feel for you!—retrospectively, not to say introspectively, for which of us has not a red nose at the core of her being which defies all her philosophy, the courage of our features being the least attainable of all the heroisms.

[92] Louisa May Alcott (1832–1888). Henry James's review of *Moods*, written when he was twenty-two, appeared in the *North American Review* in July 1865.
[93] Sophia Dorothea (1666–1726) granddaughter of James I of England, married Duke Ernest Augustus, Elector of Hanover, bringing the throne of England to his son George Louis (George I) in 1714.

Tom Appleton[94] exclaimed on seeing Mrs. Browning's photo
with the long curls hanging down over her face—"The lap-dog
of the soul!"

To think of Browning's son disregarding his father's sacred
wish to be buried by his wife, in order, it must be, simply to
enhance himself.[95] But can the betraying creature so delight
in the praise of man as to think that the glories of the Abbey
reverberate in heaven! It seems so out of proportion to the
reality of things, because Browning by no possibility could
ever have had but a handful of following. What a com-
mentary that the only offspring of his and his wife's genius
and culture should grasp at the glory to be extracted from the
flimsy vulgar fashion of the moment! This applies to the
fashion, not the Abbey. Heaven forbid!

Christmas-day passed without disaster, and what more can
one ask! I had half a dozen giftlets, but the one that hit the
bull's-eye was a contribution from the Bachelers costing three
pence. I know the price because Nurse took a week to choose
it and I had to advance the money, this all unknown to the
B's. They were much distressed when they found it had not
cost more, as they had calculated upon spending nine-pence.
They have planned the investment for a year. They are admirable beings, always send their "love" to me instead of their
"duty." Bacheler couldn't wait until Wednesday to bring the
object (a little brass tray for pins), but left it on Monday,
thereby reminding me of the beloved pater—so the wise and
simple meet—who used to spoil our Christmases so faithfully
for us, by stealing in with us, when Mother was out, to the
forbidden closet and giving up a peep the week or so before.
I can't remember whether he used to confess to Mother after,
or not, the dear, dear creature! What an ungrateful wretch
I was, and how I used to wish he hadn't done it!!

[94] Thomas Gold Appleton (1812–1884), brother-in-law of Longfellow.
[95] Browning was buried in Westminster Abbey December 3, 1889.

A note just came in from H., in which he says that Browning *fils* had no choice, that the Florentine municipality behaved so atrociously about opening the cemetery, so the above indignation is rather uncalled for at this moment, but is, of course, highly valuable as showing how a super-exquisite soul like mine would be affected had the son acted just as he has not. H. says the ceremony [was] very impressive. But why will they insist on those tawdry wreaths! flimsy flowers with cards *attached*, "Miss Evelyn Smalley,"[96] etc., to enhance the solemnity of death and the Abbey!

I debated at dawn for a couple of hours or so as to whether I should stir up my palpitating heart and Jumping-Jack of a stomach by remonstrating with Clarkey and request her to transfer the thick layer of "matter in the wrong place," which ornaments the mantel-shelf, to some other portion of the cosmos, but my "amiability" had its way as usual—for what are the woes of dust as compared to an acrobatic stomach!

Capt. O'Shea[97] has laid a *nate* trap for Parnell, with his Divorce suit, just at this moment. From what one hears I suppose there is no escape for him. It will complicate matters a bit for the Liberals, doubtless, but Irish Home Rule like "Emancipation" is one of the immutable moralities and will triumph thro' whatever delays. But how base are politics! This putting things off until Death has won in the race and Mr. Gladstone is laid low! The hyper-refined Unionists have choice allies working for them. Pigott and this vile O'Shea who uses his wife's dishonour to destroy his foe, his own sensibilities having laid in wait for three years and more for a telling moment to raise their head.

December 30th

A young couple, bride 18, man 22, came here for their honeymoon. The day after the wedding he was found to have scarlet

---

[96] Evelyn Smalley was the daughter of G. W. Smalley, European correspondent of the New York *Tribune*.

[97] Parnell was named co-respondent in the divorce suit of Captain William O'Shea against Katherine, his wife.

fever and in ten days he was dead. How cruel it is when pain and sorrow come to young things,—they are so helpless; what can they do with it? What a rush of desire to go to them and wrap them about in one's long-accustomedness until the little bewildered soul has woven for itself some sort of casing.

January 11th, 1890

Harry came yesterday and I had as always a happy day with him. I should cry hard for two hours, after he goes, if I could allow myself such luxuries, but tears are undiluted poison! This is such a neat example of the abortive nature of human effort that I must give it. A few days after the first number of the *Speaker*[98] came out a friend who is very friendly and kind and often writes "to cheer me up," wrote me one of her good letters which she concluded thus: "don't embark on the Squeaker. There is such a miserably written article on Browning, but every one thinks they ought to be emotional and obscure on his topic. It is meant for imitation, I believe." As the said article is written by Harry she rather failed to cheer that time. After my sisterly susceptibility had recovered from the shock and I had towed my stomach and heart back into harbour, they having broken loose under the impression that they were to have a day to themselves, the comic of the situation overcame me; the disproportion and want of harmony between cause, intention and effect was so excessive. Harry's article so bad as to wreck the *Speaker* in the present and future, the good lady thro' benevolent intentions prostrating her pallid victim, she, doubtless, simply bringing up the subject to use the word "*Squeaker*," a Unionist *jeu d'esprit*, I suppose—carefully avoiding politics so as not to stir me up and seizing upon my one vulnerable point with such energy. It is rather complete. I *think* that I do not want her to find out her mistake, or

[98] Henry James's article, "Browning in Westminster Abbey," appeared in the *Speaker* January 4, 1890.

rather misdirection, but I *know* that there is a sprite within me that would be greatly gratified had she an inkling thereof; a sprite not only much entertained by the minute, illustrative complications which fall within its narrow range, but nimble to run in the follies of mankind, finding 'em so much more tonic than their virtues! How thankful I am that I never struggled to be of those "who are not as other ones are," but that I discovered at the earliest moment that my talents lay in being *more so*. Hold hard, my friend, the pride of abasement is a more insidious one than t'other!

January 12th

How the Brazilian affair, death of the Empress and that poor old man, disgust one with the hideous brutalities of democracies. Were it not for the barrier of the ludicrous, one would fain lapse. What a curious nature though, that of the reactionary, deliberately turning his back upon opportunity, refusing to handle the tools of his moment and stamping himself failure. Being to the mind as some diseased vegetable growth which nips efflorescence, and burrowing all his days in a *cul-de-sac* instead of floating with the current of expansion and getting all the fun he can grasp at in the passing.

The crank Stead[99] has given himself away in the most lovely manner in his *Review of Reviews*, in which I believe he aspires to address the Universe. He gives the heads of his belief 1st God, 2nd England, 3rd Humanity!! poor little appendage! How men are fated to prick with their own hand the bubble of their pretensions.

Miss Bond who is struggling to keep a little shop, with an old mother of 84 on her hands, bad health and all sorts of horrors, said to Nurse the other day something which made Nurse say, "Miss James isn't a Leamington lady, she is Ameri-

[99] William Thomas Stead (1849–1912) founded the *Review of Reviews* in 1890.

can," whereupon Miss Bond exclaimed "That's why she is so different." In what do you suppose the difference consisted!— the poor woman was in great distress because she was moving out of this parish into another and she feared that I would refuse to help her any more! I have heard of charity regulated by religions, subdivided into sects, but it was a revelation to find it had parochial limits! like the man Stead's Humanity, altho' I suppose he would humbug himself with the word Imperial.

You would be amused if you saw the paces thro' which I put poor little Nurse; in the winter she has to applaud me Mind in summer me beauty! In my moments of modesty, don't scoff, I have 'em, I consult her about my letters and you may be sure she knows too well which side her bread is buttered to do aught but admire. In the summer when we pass an old frump more sour than the last I throw myself upon her mercy and ask her if I am as dreadful to look upon as that. When she comes up to time with a reassuring negative, and I sink back on my cushions, in my black-goggled, greenery-yallery loveliness, pacified—for the moment! Ah, but such heart-rending objects as one sees with no acrid strain to stiffen the sinews, creatures dropped out in the race and left all limp by the way side, decorating with pathetic tags of lace and pitiful ruffles their squalor. Creatures born with no chance, as if made of the scraps left over in the great human factory, and thrust forth weaponless to fight in the hideous battle. Canon Leigh says they all drink, but this is a figment of his temperance brain, I fear, for they don't look as if they had ever known even the momentary satisfaction of that passion gratified.

January 13th

Poor little Portugal has succumbed before the Big Bully[100] and the *Standard* and P[all] M[all] G[azette] are glorious

---

[100] An allusion to a British ultimatum to Portugal forbidding its plans to expand the empire in Mozambique and Angola.

over the "resolute attitude"—the mastiff confronting the toy-terrier! Compare the slump before Bismarck on the Samoa question. Katharine said when she came back from London that she had lunched one day at Mrs. Ashburner's with Mrs. May Boreham, born Dabney, and Annie Richards[101] and that they all agreed that they liked English people, individually, extremely, but that taken *en masse* their bullying brutality made them simply odious. This was rather interesting, as Mrs. Ashburner and May Boreham have both English husbands. I wonder if the latter didn't tell her husband after she got home, one would feel so disloyal in discussing his people behind his back, but doubtless he wouldn't have the faintest idea of what she felt; they are mostly such pachyderms. This is the sort of thing that well people are always saying to the weak and they have no conception of their cruelty—A poor old maid here was at some parish meeting and the Vicar's wife said to her, "you know we don't ask you to help us in this work, because *you faint!*" branding the poor thing with incompetency because last year, after a hard day's work, she had grown faint on one occasion. But it is impossible that the two ever should understand one another, for when most sympathetic, the well let fly their wildest shots. A while back I was greatly enjoying a friend from home who went far back and in whose presence the past revived for a bit, when suddenly she removed herself to the planet Mars by asking me whether I was in pain anywhere at that moment. She stood at the foot of the sofa, but she had no gift to divine that pain was as the essence of the Universe to my consciousness and that ghastly fatigue was a palpable substance between us. How could she?—We were emotionally blended, but what common ground had we physically and especially as I had bluffed off all her investigations!

The gentlemen of the Round Table must be amused at the contemplation of how seriously they are taken in the 19th

[101] The Ashburners, originally from England, had been neighbors of the Jameses in Cambridge, and one of them, Annie, had married an Englishman named Richards.

cent[ury] by their compatriots. I read a bit of M. Twain's book[102] and found it tedious eno', but this isn't the point, 'tis horror that these holy and moral quantities should be made fun of! To let the wit play lightly about what has long been taken with solemnity is a somersault for which the muscles of their minds are not limber eno'. These developments are most amusing to contemplate, they are so naïfs in giving themselves away to the scoffer.

January 29th

I have had a dev'lish head-ache and no mistake! I sought for *Roosian*[103] symptoms, but all in vain, 'twas too, too familiar Yankee! There is no hope of my sowing a microbe, Providence, with its improvident wasteful ways, will forget to send any to my address simply because 'twould sweep away so clearly my little rubbish-heap. An infant bacillus would make one bite of me!

My being, however, has been stirred to its depths by what I might call ghost microbes imported in my Davenport which came from home ten days ago. In it were my old letters. I fell upon Father and Mother's and could not tear myself away from them for two days. One of the most intense, exquisite and profoundly interesting experiences I ever had. I think if I try a little and give it form its vague intensity will take limits to itself, and the 'divine anguish' of the myriad memories stirred grow less. Altho' they were as the breath of life to me as the years have passed they have always been as present as they were at first and [will be for] the rest of my numbered days, with their little definite portion of friction and serenity, so short a span, until we three were blended together again, if such should be our spiritual necessity. But as I read it seemed as if I had opened up a post-script of the past and that I

---

[102] *A Connecticut Yankee at King Arthur's Court,* 1889.
[103] The influenza epidemic of 1890 was called at first "Russian influenza."

had had, in order to find them *truly*, really to lose them. It
seems now incredible to me that I should have drunk, as a
matter of course, at that ever springing fountain of responsive
love and bathed all unconscious in that flood of human tenderness. The letters are made of the daily events of their pure
simple lives, with souls unruffled by the ways of men, like
special creatures, spiritualized and remote from coarser clay.
Father ringing the changes upon the Mother's perfections, he
not being of the order of "charming man who hangs up his fiddle
outside his own front door," for his fireside inspired his sweetest
music. And Mother's words breathing her extraordinary self-
less devotion as if she simply embodied the unconscious essence
of wife and motherhood. What a beautiful picture do they
make for the thoughts of their children to dwell upon! How
the emotions of those two dreadful years, when I was wrench-
ing myself away from them, surge thro' me!—The first haunted
by the terror that I should fail him as I watched the poor old
man fade day by day—"his fine fibre," William said, "wearing and burning itself out at things too heavy for it"—until
the longing cry of his soul was answered and the dear old
shrunken body was "lying beside Mary on the hilltop in Cambridge."—Mother died Sunday evening, January 29th, 1882,
Father on Monday midday, December 19th, 1882, and now I
am shedding the tears I didn't shed then!

February 1st

Listen to the twin souls, Georgie Coss and the Countess of
Shrewsbury,—dowager, I believe. Georgie is fourteen; her
mother died a year ago of a horrible cancer, her father, an
unknown agglomeration of molecules, brothers and sisters fluctuating in number, sometimes six of 'em at other moments,
nine. This in quantity only, quality never fluctuating, always
bad. Georgie has been snatched from their midst—a brand
from the burning—and placed in frigid glory and respectability

with a "Lydy" in the Holly Walk, in charge of six children at
one shilling per week!!! Altho' she has had several spiritual
guides, having been to Bible classes and Sunday schools, etc., etc.,
she has apparently assimilated very imperfectly the parsonic
pap to the effect that she should be content in that position
in life in which God has placed her, at any rate as regards
clothes, for she came a short time since and told me that her
young soul aspires to "a change" of those garments, which we
all find, no matter in what "position" God may have placed
us at the moment, are greatly benefited by an occasional visit
to the wash-tub. I, not wishing to excite what in speaking of
the White-Chapelites the *Standard* called "their cupidity," told
her "that her case must be thoroughly investigated before she
had a stitch from *me!*" Nurse went forthwith to interview an
Authority upon Georgie's lingerie, who was horrified at hearing of her "graspingness," but allowed that she had only *one*
of each of those garments the nature of which has been delicately
suggested above. *Now*, methinks, 'twould have been the moment for the parson to step in and show Georgie, while the
iron was hot, the iniquity, when not born to "a change," of
"grasping" at one, point out all she has to be thankful for,
having six children for a shilling a week when she might so
easily have had twelve for sixpence, etc., etc. But the parsons
are a flaccid set, and so it has been decided without the interven-
tion of the Established Church that she is to have "a change"
lent to her for a 12 month and that if, meanwhile, she "grasps"
at nothing, at the end of the year, when in rags and tatters,
they shall be her own. Altho' we *have* Georgie so neatly, I am
afraid we shall find it harder to circumvent Lady Shrewsbury's
cupidity, not having caught her young. She has been doing, in
more ways than one, the U.S. last summer and not only tells,
without a blush, but boasts that she didn't pay a dollar in an
hotel or rail-way train all the time she was gone, but bled the
native! Her transactions seem to be on a larger scale than
Georgie's, but her "position" doubtless ensures uninterrupted

relations with the wash-tub and the mangle, so she naturally turns to a wider field whereupon to exercise her genius as a bird of prey.

February 10th

I'll not use that word recommended by Kath. but which is denied with her other rights to *Woman*, but I shall proclaim that any one who spends her life as an appendage to five cushions and three shawls is justified in committing the sloppiest kind of suicide at a moment's notice.

Mary Cross, the excellent, came from London to see me and spent two days at the Regent. How good she is!

Since I last wrote the fierce dog next door thought one day that he would partake of Miss Percy's pug puppy for lunch. The results were pleasing for the neighbourhood. I collapsed and had to send for my Primrose Knight—Dr. Wilmot. Altho' a devoted fox-hunter he shuddered most successfully over the laceration of the pug, illustrating quite triumphantly the theory of the infinitesimal for had he been among a group of English *Gentlemen* gazing at some poor object hunted to its death by 20 hounds, he ne'er would have winked. To be sure this homeopathic operation in a garden didn't gloriously display the passion for "manly sport" inherent in the "brave Briton," nor was it arranged for the amusement of the Gentleman——and I beg its pardon—the Fox!

The Ripleys write that Great-Grandfather Hugh Walsh[104] left Ireland, in a broken-hearted condition, in his youth because he was not allowed to marry a young lady, with whom he was in love. What his social position was they know not but he must have had some money, for he settled at Newburgh, on the Hudson and consoled himself by starting a Soap!! factory. He later took to building sloops. He married and named one of his daughters after his first flame. He must have come like

[104] Hugh Walsh, grandfather of Alice's mother.

Grandfather James[105] from that debased Ulster, what a humiliation for *Me*. I suppose they didn't suspect what was to spring from them or they would have managed better. Katie and Henrietta Rodgers were very funny about Great Grandfather Robertson,[106] who came from Rannoch in Perthshire, they say. After he had made his fortune in linen in New York he returned to Perthshire and collected the bones of his forefathers and put a monument over them. He then took to his bosom his third wife and sailed away. After they had been at home a little while, he found that the bride had pinched Aunt Wyckoff[107] (Cousin Helen Perkins's Mother) who was his youngest and favorite daughter, so he rose in his wrath and shipped her back to Scotland and she was heard of no more! They say that the old blue Robertson Canton china, which came from cousin Helen, thro' Mother to me and is now at Harry's in De Vere Gardens,[108] must be 200 years old quite. Katie Rodgers with perfect solemnity assured me that the Robertson descent could be traced back to Robert Bruce, King of Scotland! I asked how—"Oh, why, Robert*son*, son of Robert—er—er—Bruce!" She showed me the coat-of-arms but whether it was of the house of Robertson, Bruce or "Er—er," I couldn't clearly make out. Henrietta who seemed a scoffer said, "Well if you *have* got a coat-of-arms it's dreadfully out-at-elbows." Methinks that the collection of the ancestral bones by the old gentleman sounds more like pauper, than royal antecedent. But I must relate the consul's visit—the sixth who has visited *me* couch since I've been in England![109]

[105] William James (1771–1832), Alice's grandfather of Bailieborough County Cavan, Ireland, established himself in the United States shortly after the American Revolution.

[106] Alexander Robertson, grandfather of Alice's mother, came to the United States shortly before the Revolution and attained civic prominence in Manhattan. The Rodgers were maternal relatives.

[107] The Wyckoff-Perkins relatives of the Jameses are described in the sixth chapter of Henry James's *A Small Boy and Others*.

[108] Henry James's address in London was 34 de Vere Gardens, W.

[109] The diary does not relate the visit.

Here is a beautiful, touching tale. An old couple near London somewhere, who had lived together for half a cent[ury], were beyond all work and had had to sell all their things and had nothing before them but the dreaded Union, where they would have meat and drink, to be sure, but where they would be divided; they could meet all but that, so one day they went out together and never came back, and their old bodies were found tied together in the river. How perfect a death!

The men of the House of Savoy seem alone to have that sense of the picturesque which lifts them out of the vulgar and flimsy platitude of contemporary monarchs. As the Duke of Aosta lay dying, he told the priest who was standing by his bedside to go and rest. The old man turned away and a man who was standing among the others stepped forward and took his hands and said "Thanks"—the priest then expressed some sorrow and affection for the duke—when "Thanks" was repeated with much emotion—as the room was dark the confessor said "I don't know who you are?"—"I am his brother."

In all the five y[ea]rs I have been in England I have never heard or read of a word said by "our family" which would give one reason for supposing that they had the faintest conception of what they represented, save on its flimsiest side. Andrew Lang's[110] "unusually usual grocer" is infinitely more capable of a lyric burst than they. When you think, too, that with teeth drawn and trimmed claws they are caged within the ignominies of a Constitutional Monarchy and that flowers of rhetoric alone are left to give them, for a moment, the illusion that they share the birthright of their humblest subject and are not slaves but men, they seem paltry eno'.

What expresses more perfectly the folly of the philanthropic mush of this age than this contempt of the sympathetic man felt 2,000 y[ea]rs ago by the adorable Chuang Tsiu?—"the

[110]Andrew Lang (1844–1912), folklorist, poet, journalist.

sympathetic man being simply a man who is trying to be some
one else all the time and so misses the only possible excuse
for his own existence." At least, so *Oscar* reports him.

February 13th

In a rash moment, panting to rise out of the trivial and draw
a breath of *life*, I read one of Father's letters to a [word blotted]
friend. It fell perfectly flat—Ah, what a wilted moment was
that! I felt as if I had committed a desecration. Dear old
Geo[rge] Bradford is dead, aged 83—*the* flower of New Eng
land maidenly bachelorhood, the very last, I fancy, of his very
special kind. May all tender, benignant thoughts go with him!

Mary Cross said that she had read in Herbert Spencer's
Autobiography, which had been lent to her, the following
H[erbert] S[pencer] one day in talking to Huxley, said that
the only thing to hope for was to make a little mark before one
died, to which Huxley—"Oh, no matter about the mark, if
one only gives a shove." At first it makes Huxley seem the
bigger animal of the two, which he is, no doubt, but surely
H[erbert] restores the balance by repeating it to his own harm
if he doesn't make it tip a little thro' the superior weight of
voluntary virtue over spontaneous. Shade of my Father, visit
me not if that heresy fall upon thine ear!

No collector has greater joy over his specimens than have
I with my human bric-a-brac, the Bachelers. They are so un
like our accidental, mush-room poor, so many generations of
poverty have gone to the making of 'em. They are so decent
penned in their rudimentary sensations as compared to us
the sport of fugitive, fantastic emotions—they are truly *precious!*
—In this world *pour rire* this methinks takes the cake. Two
thousand years of Christianity, as interpreted by the pious of
all nations, necessitates that when a poor girl goes wrong she
should be ejected from all Societies to which she belongs, *in-
stituted* for the purpose of keeping her in the straight path!

In this way "we" endear ourselves to our neighbours. This summer it was proposed that a society should be formed for the "protection" of the London barmaids, who went in large numbers to Paris to the Exposition.

I am in a Porcupine fit with little Nurse—she is no more bewildered than I am and we both have simply to undergo it as one of the endless forms of moral dyspepsia. There is one comfort—she doesn't suffer 100th of what I do. It's her genius for prevarication that I can't bear up against. Instead of remembering that it is the only defence she has against my caprice. I preach to her and tell her that I would rather have her tell 20 honest lies than act one, which must be as clear as mud to her befogged little brain. Think of being dependent upon the whims of another for bread! And how can we, the *haves*, ever hope to enter remotely into the inspiring motives of the *have-nots*? She truly is also *taught* in the rules of a Guild to which she belongs to conceal certain things if the revealing of them endanger her livelihood—pious conversation is one. If it is not relished by the patient, relinquish the topic and confine yourself to intercessory prayer which may do good and at any rate wont endanger your place! I often wonder if she is interceding with the Most High for this reckless sinner. I rather imagine she considers the case too hopeless. The head of the *Guild* is a certain Rev. Something, who writes these guides for conduct. One thing I am glad to have learned that we are quite wrong in thinking that our servants lie because they are Catholics—Since I have been in England I have had half a dozen attendants, "lady nurses" among them and they have all been robust fibbers. They have all been pious, too, but those who have had the most ardent thirst for the "Spirit," etc., are stronger in prevarication than in direct lies, as if their genuflexions had developed the dramatic element and their minds become attuned to the evasive clerical circumlocution. I once tried an *Intelligent* Companion. She began by a "literary" remark in order to meet the requirements of the situation. It

was to the effect that "Longfellow was such a *deep* poet," and
the climax of her being seemed to have been reached on some
occasion when James T. Fields[111] took her in to dinner. Altho
she showed such tact in choosing my native geniuses we parted
shortly most amiably and expensively, to continue on so high
a key was too great a strain. I believe she was a Cousin of
Wilkie Collins[112] who had always been very kind in helping
her. I fell back again upon the pious fibbers. I had sounded their
depths and they could have no more surprises for me. I suppose, however, that in a self-righteous manner I shall continue
to chastise the prevaricator. I must hasten to add that I am
intelligent eno' in the stress of circumstance to be a great adept
in "the thumping lie"—but it is very complicated to use it
often as it involves so many more, like the passion of love
which, according to Massimo d'Azeglio,[113] should be shunned
of youth because "it involves a course of perpetual lying"!!
Vide his charming *Memoirs*. The ennobling and superlative
Passion!! Will mankind ever be *Brothers?*—Julia Marcou
whose father was French, told me that one of her friends in
Paris who was just married told her of her excitement in going
out alone for the first time and how frightened she was in
finding that a gentleman was following her. As she approached
her house, her terror increased *lest she should meet her husband!! for he would think that she had encouraged the man!*
She suddenly took out her purse, and handed the creature a
penny whereupon he turned upon his heel and she was saved
from seeing her husband degrade himself. Julia told all this
as quite natural. Surely there is an unbridgeable gulf betwixt
the Northern man and he of the Latin races!

---

[111] James T. Fields (1817–1881), Boston publisher, editor of the *Atlantic
Monthy* from 1861 to 1871.

[112] Wilkie Collins (1824–1889), popular Victorian novelist, author of *The
Moonstone*.

[113] Massimo d'Azeglio (1798–1866), Italian statesman and author. His
memoirs throw much light on the Risorgimento.

February 15th

'Tis wonderful how easy 'tis to be profound, in all innocence too, thereby losing unfortunately a moment of inflation, a thing always to be cherished. Some one was describing a Mrs. B. and said that she was very ambitious of success for her husband, conventional success, of course, she meant, politics was the line, whereupon I said, "She is a simple organization, then?" which created much confusion and had to be justified by pointing out that the pursuit of any "success" to be seen of man is simply a survival of the finite ambition of the savage. He scalped his victim, she must transmute his tomahawk into an imperceptive soul and a thick skin, turn all her energies to the grosser elements of life, circumventing envy, malice and all uncharitableness—But what of the success made up of all delicate shades and subtle tones, that makes no sign, but is known alone to the bosom that attains it?—that floods the mind with infinite delight when least expected—that has never mistaken pleasure for that shy bird happiness whose song is only to be heard of the ears of the soul.—Surely it has not sunk deeply into the mind of Man that—*The Kingdom of God cometh not with observation: neither shall they say, Lo, here! or Lo, there! for behold, the Kingdom of God is within you.*

February 17th

I find myself as the months pass more and more stifled by the all pervasive sense of pharasaism in the British constitution of things. You don't feel it at first and you can't put your finger upon it in your friends, but as the days go by you unfold it with your *Standard*, in the morn. It rises dense from the *P. M. G.* in the evening, it creeps thro' the cracks in the window frames like the fog and envelopes you thro' the day. I asked H. once how it struck him from his wider and varied field not wanting my view to become cramped upon conclusions drawn from my centimetre of observation, he said that he didn't think it could be exaggerated. It's woven of a multiplicity of minute details and incidents which elude you in the telling but which seem to exist in the texture of things and leave a dent in the mind as they file past. A monarchy to which they bow down in its tinsel capacity only, denying to it a manly movement of any sort; a boneless Church broadening itself out, up to date; the hysterical legislation over a dog with a broken leg whilst Society is engaged making bags of 4,000 pheasants, etc. etc., or gloating over foxes torn to pieces by a pack of hounds; the docility with which the classes enslave themselves to respectability or non-respectability as the "good-form" of the moment may be; the "sense of their betters" in the masses; the passivity with which the working man allows himself to be patted and legislated out of all independence; thus the profound ineradicables in the bone and sinew conviction that outlying regions are their preserves, that they alone of human races massacre savages out of pure virtue. It would ill-become an American to reflect upon the treatment of aboriginal races; but I never heard it suggested that our hideous dealings with the Indians was brotherly love masquerading under the disguise of pure cussedness.

It would have been highly immoral, when Kath. was here, not to get as much work out of her as possible, so the second week she began upon Woking. I had got discouraged about cremation, having been told that it was very fussy and expensive, so she wrote for the circular to be sent by the Cremation people, when, lo! it's as simple and inexpensive as possible, only six guineas and one extra for a parson. Me ashes are to be put in an urn, and sent home, not as a parlour ornament for William's new house, but to be buried beside Father and Mother in the cemetery at Cam[bridge],—so that we shall not be myths as Harry suggests we might otherwise become. 'Tis a great waste that I didn't die whilst K. was here; she could have carried home the urn in her top berth and as she

lay convulsed with seasickness it would have greatly assuaged
her grief to have such a palpable assurance that that portion of
me hitherto so susceptible to the dread thing was reduced to
ashes. It seems delightfully clean to elude in this way that early
riser, the unpleasant wurrum, and I am greatly in hopes that

> "The worms crawled in
> And the worms crawled out,"

will not be true of my return to dust.

Then we began upon my Will, which I wanted to make
over again, leaving out, of course, those who had offended me
since my last, as a cousin of Lilla Walsh's used to do, who
re-made hers every few weeks. K. told me that as long as I
indulged in no amateur legal terminology but confined myself
strictly to my vernacular it would be all right, so she wouldn't
allow me even one decorative bequeath. She wrote to the
Consul at Birmingham to ask him if it had to be signed in his
presence and he said yes, so hearing that Lizzie Putnam was at
Banbury and was coming to spend a certain afternoon, K.
telegraphed to the Consul, as it was so good to get a Boston
witness. The arrival of this august personage the Consul
naturally caused me to "go off" and I had to be put to bed—
when the most amusing scene followed. I lay in a semi-faint,
draped in as many frills as could be found for the occasion, with
Nurse at my head with the thickest layer of her anxious-devoted-
nurse expression on, as K. told me after, when thro' a mist
I vaguely saw five black figures file into my little bower, headed
by the most extraordinary little man, all gesticulation and
grimace, who planted himself at the foot of the bed and strok-
ing my knees began a long harangue to the effect that he and
his wife had both "laid upon a bed of sickness" which seemed
to constitute uncontrovertible reason for my immediate recovery.
K. with difficulty restrained him from reading the Will aloud
there and then—he has doubtless not forgiven this dam thrown
across to arrest the flood of his eloquence—It was so curious

for me, just like a nightmare effect and I felt as if I were assisting at the reading of my own Will, surrounded by the greedy relatives, as in novels. After they had filed in and out several times and become tangled in as much resounding red-tape as the creature could reel off for the occasion they went off downstairs to an "elegant" tea where the Consul entertained them with his whole history and the digestive processes of his domestic circle, which seem to be in a sadly disorganized condition. He asked K. whether she was related to "Our great Minister to Portugal Geo. B. Loring"—imagine the condition of a Peabody-Loring having such an insult hurled at her! And he also wanted to know whether Postmaster James and I were consanguineous. I, not having been *born* (ahem!) was able to take things more easily, besides Mr. James, I believe, was a man to be related to whom would have been an honour. Miss Blanche Leppington, who had been asked to be a witness, told K. after that she hadn't looked at my face but that she felt as if she "ought to keep her eye fixed upon Miss James's *hand!*"—she also said the scene—"Will remain in my thoughts as the most pathetic I ever saw and in my imagination as the most picturesque and American!"—I can't complain of not being taken seriously and I think it is the first time that *picturesque* and *American,* which are usually supposed to neutralize one another so completely, were ever conjoined. In recounting the story to H. he said, "You can't say you've done nothing for your Race since you've brought that about in your own person."

February 20th

Beatrice Bowyer came in yesterday in all her beautiful young radiance to see me on her engagement. She seemed like a creature transformed, having lost all her shyness and her face beaming with happiness; she has always been handsome but now she is beautiful; may her present sunshine know no cloud-

marriage ✓

ing! A lovely vision to keep by one to illuminate the memory! How an engagement always warms and stirs the spinsterial heart. Here, however, is the opposite view: our super-excellent slavey, Louisa, said to Nurse last night that you must be as happy as you can be while you are young because after, you "*never* can be." When Nurse asked why, "because you'll be married and how can you be happy with a man at your back all the time!" She then went on to say that she never would marry as long as she could possibly help it. She seemed entirely persuaded that marriage was a fate which could not be eluded, but simply postponed, and a husband an absolute evil without even momentary, illusory seductions. Her mother on Valentine's day gave birth to olive branch number seven which explains doubtless the intensity of her convictions. The baby is to be called "Valen*times*' Jacob," according to Louisa. She went home once for the day and when asked how she enjoyed herself she beamed and said that she had enjoyed herself greatly, for "Father had me on all day!"

This is how justice is meted out A.D. 1890:

"Mr. Benzon may esteem himself fortunate in having got off with a sentence of three months' imprisonment, although the Marquis of Ailesbury was good enough to bear testimony to his previous good character. The charge of forgery was not proved, and he was found guilty of having obtained various sums of money on false pretences. Contemptible to the last, the wretched creature shed tears frequently during the hearing of the case. Why any sort of sympathy should have been felt for him, surprises me. It seems to have been based upon the notion that if a man "nob" spends £250,000 during two years in racing, he ought to be allowed to fare sumptuously at Monte Carlo, and to gamble at the tables there by means of forged cheques and cheques upon banks where he had no assets." (*Truth.*)

"Two instructive instances of police-court justice are cited in a letter written to a Cheshire paper by Mr. Devine, of the Gordon Memorial Home, Manchester. In one of them an unfortunate and friendless London boy, well educated and brought up, but desperate with poverty and starvation, determined to try and get into prison, but without stealing or doing anything to be ashamed of. He accordingly walked to Euston Station, got into the first train he saw, and was, in due course, arrested at Stockport and charged with traveling without a ticket. This boy was sentenced to one month's imprisonment, one of the magistrates stigmatizing him as a 'blackguard and a scamp.'" (*Truth*.)

Here is our dear friend the "one sympathetic man" who makes things smooth for us.

"Yet another case from the same school. A lad of thirteen had been embezzling the school money and truanting for eight weeks. The father, on discovering his son's delinquency, soundly thrashes him, is summoned, at the instigation of soft-hearted neighbours, for assault, and condemned by a discriminating magistrate to a month's hard labour. The man's family is thus, for the time being, deprived of its bread-winner; whilst the boy, since then, has disappeared from school and home, to qualify no doubt in the school of life for a higher standard.[114]

Little Harry[115] said once to his mother: "Oh Mamma, I've such a broad stomach-ache!"

But to return to the Consul; from what Kath. told me of his talk he was a typical being, a Western politician—Only "accepted the Birmingham place as a personal favour to President Harrison," etc., etc. The sort of creature whom one has never seen but who swarm in the West and South Western— I suppose, dread thought! What a blessed arrangement 'tis that our own vulgar ones are mitigated for us by the power to divine more or less the circumstances responsible for 'em and are consequently simply relative in their offensiveness—

[114] Letter from a school manager to the *Standard*, February 19, 1890.
[115] This was Henry (Harry) James (1879-1947), nephew of the novelist, oldest son of William James.

but how can they be anything but *absolute* to the foreigner? I had such a curious impression of a type in seeing Mrs. R. L. Stevenson in London. From her appearance Providence or Nature, which ever is responsible for her, designed her as an appendage to a hand organ, but I believe she is possessed of great wifely virtues and I have heard some excellent letters written by her to H.,—but such egotism and so naked! ! giving one the strangest feeling of being in the presence of an unclothed being. It is the most supremely absurd thing to hear Americans denying any grotesque possibility which is said by a traveller to have taken place on our fluid continent. One day in London I heard Mary Porter in my room informing two English ladies of the manners and customs at home, her standard being the artificial and sophisticated Newport. I couldn't stand it and immediately to Mary's disgust told some Western anecdotes. K. told me these two tales when she was here. One day last spring at Asheville, N. C., on their way North she overheard at the table a father and mother and two daughters talking. *Father*—"It's delightful to be in a hotel where you can eat dinner without gloves on." *Daughter*—"Why, Father, I think it's quite rulable to do so when the family is alone." *Father*—"Your mother doesn't think so. I always have to eat my dinner and play whist with my gloves on." This she actually heard, so there must exist a gloved and "rulable" race somewhere in the broad land. Kath. also told me that she was once on one of the big Mississippi steam-boats. In the evenings they used to have a hop in the saloon off which the state-rooms opened. At the doors of their rooms the Mammas sat matronizing their daughters; as they grew tired, they gradually "re-tired," put themselves in their berths, re-opened their doors and continued their duties from that vantage ground!

February 21st

From the "Standard"

"The following extraordinary letter, addressed to the Chairman, caused great amusement at a meeting of the Richmond Board of Guardians yesterday morning:—

THE HERMITAGE, BARNES, FEB. 19.

DEAR SIR,—The small number of inmates attending the Sunday services at the Richmond Union Workhouse Chapel is a deplorable fact, and the Guardians have acted wisely in discussing the subject, and suggesting means for an improvement of the present condition of things. I have no desire to interfere in any way with your chaplain, though I would be glad to help him in making his congregation more numerous. With that view I beg to make application for the post of assistant chaplain, which I am willing to fill without any fixed salary. I have had considerable experience in reforming the worldly, and I believe I could solve the great problem which is now troubling the Guardians. I only ask for payment by results. If there are three hundred inmates, I think in the course of a few months I could get two hundred and fifty of these at the Sunday services. I would only stipulate that the Guardians should pay me four pence per head for every addition to the present number regularly attending the chapel, with an extra penny per head for each case in which I bring a Roman Catholic to the Established Faith. I would also undertake to make the musical services attractive, if the Guardians would allow me to put the best singing inmates in surplices, which the lady visitors might make for them. I would, with your permission, introduce full choral service, with an occasional orchestral accompaniment. This I could make easy, as one of my sons plays the oboe, and the other the fife, while my daughters are proficient in the 'cello, the cornet, and the double bass. I can also do a little on the trombone, and I would willingly undertake the conductorship. I do not doubt that in a very little time, with bright and cheerful services, I could bring the whole of the inmates to chapel regularly. As a minister of the Establishment I am very anxious to commence my duty forthwith, and shall be glad if you will lay my letter before the Guardians at their next meeting, feeling assured that my inexpensive offer will be gladly accepted. Believe me,

Yours very truly,

PETER THOMAS M'CULLUM.

The Guardians declined the offer with thanks."

'Tis surely a moment of Religious pallor when the rescue of a soul from Rome has the modest value of five pence! There is one gain certainly, the ancient superstition as to spring and youth being the joyous periods is pretty well exploded, as the one is the most depressing moment of the year, so is the other the most difficult of life. Spring not only depresses us physically, but in proportion to the revelation of natural beauty "la souffrance innée . . . de n'être que nous, le désir vague d'en sortir et de nous mêler à l'être universel"—overwhelms us and fills us with despair. And what joys of youth equal this blessed moment of middle life, when serene and sure of our direction all the simple incidents of daily life and human complication explain and enrich themselves as they are linked and fitted to the wealth of past experience. Whilst the blank youthful mind, ignorant of catastrophe, stands crushed and bewildered before the perpetual postponement of its hopes, things promised in the dawn that the sunset ne'er fulfils. Owing to muscular circumstances my youth was not of the most ardent, but I had to peg away pretty hard between 12 and 24, "killing myself," as some one calls it—absorbing into the bone that the better part is to clothe oneself in neutral tints, walk by still waters, and possess one's soul in silence. How I recall the low grey Newport sky in that winter of 62-3 as I used to wander about over the cliffs, my young soul struggling out of its swaddling-clothes as the knowledge crystallized within me of what Life meant for me, one simple, single and before which all mystery vanished. A spark then kindled which every experience great and small has fed into a steady flame which has illuminated my little journey and which, altho' it may have burned low as the waters rose, has never flickered out—"une pensée, unique éternelle, toujours mêlée à l'heure présente." How profoundly grateful I am for the temperament which saves from the wretched fate of those poor creatures who never find their bearings, but are tossed like dryed leaves hither, thither and yon at the mercy of every event which o'ertakes them. Who feel no shame at being vanquished, or at crying out at the common lot of pain and sorrow, who never dimly suspect that the only thing which survives is the resistance we bring to life and not the strain life brings to us.

March 3rd

I am continually amused by my naïve irritation before the *Church.* To have reached middle age and to be able to contemplate as an absolutely new discovery what is traditional and automatic in the daily life of most of one's kind is a gain in so restricted a career, for it is *El Dorado* of impressions, moral amazes, mental tortuosities and spiritual repulsions—as if I had opened up at the end of the 19th cent[ury] a virgin mine of ecclesiastical iniquities! Nurse I think has had a mild attack of influenza; at any rate she looked and felt very poorly for a few days, but she kept up bravely. I collapsed too for a few days and cultivated as much "prostration" as possible, but all in vain; the little beasties are too wise to think that they can make a feast off the pale fluid that stagnates in my veins, so I shall drag on a bit longer. But what does it matter!—a few head-aches more or less and 'twill be o'er. 'Tis rather droll tho' that my having a few more head-aches *should* be essential to the development of the race. But droller than my head-aches is the ardent out-pouring of one, "The Hon. Reginald Brett," whose young (?) soul has been vexed to the length of a column in the *P. M. G.* over the Arthurian blasphemies of Mark Twain. Calm thyself, Reginald! take Mark as a refined humourist or a vulgar buffoon as may be the bent of your taste, but do not make thyself the butt, dear Brett! for the merriment

f your unscrupulous cousins beyond sea, by taking him with
olemnity—few things are worth it, perhaps neither you nor
, how much less, then, M.T.! The muddle in thy ingenuous
nind shown in the following methinks is curious eno' to pre-
erve.

"If cruelty has obtained in European struggles for causes which
ppear to us, judging with fuller light, inadequate or vain, it must
ot be forgotten that in America the most savage war of modern
imes—in which thousands of helpless prisoners were starved to
leath on one side, and wounded men crawling from the field of
attle were shot in cold blood on the other—was relentlessly waged
etween men of one race and one speech!"

Dost think that the war was waged with no object save as a
vent for savagery? or is the freeing of millions of human beings
rom bondage a cause unworthy to lift up the hearts of wives
o send forth their husbands and mothers their sons to battle?

The intelligent and most sympathetic Massimo d'Azeglio
nakes a reflection showing how almost impossible it is to grasp
he "foreign" situation. In making some very true remarks
pon Democracy differing from Autocracy in being a many
eaded tyrant, a despotism from below instead of from on high,
e adds, comparing Russia and the United States (time, the
Rebellion) "I am constrained in justice, to ask pardon of the
Russian despotism for placing it in the same balance with Amer-
can despotism, for whilst Alexander Romanoff breaks the
hains of his slaves Abraham Lincoln only breaks the chains
f his enemies' slaves." The impression given by this, of that
mbodied benignancy, poor old tragic Lincoln freeing slaves
nly, *quâ enemy's* slaves with a preserve, perhaps, of his own
n the background at the White House shows the marvellous
ossibilities of non-apprehension. "Voisenon[116] raconte qu'il se
rouvait un jour chez Voltaire, à une lecture d'Alzire, avec

[116] Claude-Henri, Abbé de Voisenon (1708–1775), author of light verses
nd tales and a friend of Voltaire. *Alzire ou les Américains* was a tragedy by
Voltaire produced in 1736. The son of Jean Racine was Louis Racine (1692–
763).

Racine fils. Ce dernier crut y reconnaître un de ses vers, e
répétait constamment entre ses dents: 'Ce vers-là est à moi.
Impatienté de ce gémissement incessant, l'abbé s'approche d
Voltaire et lui dit à l'oreille: 'Rendez-lui son vers, et qu'il s'en
aille.' " Good! The pest who is perpetually crying plagiary is
I suppose, the paltriest of all animalcules.

March 7th

H. writes this morning that Messrs. Geo. Curzon[117] and Augus
tine Birrell,[118] of opposite views, bot[h] told him that Labou
chere was entirely squashed by the Attorney-Gen[eral] in hi
attack on Lord Salisbury,[119] and that the evidence he brough
to support his case was of the flimsiest. For one who pride
himself so upon his calm superiority to the weak beings who
are led into pitfalls thro' convictions, 'tis rather a grotesque
episode. Our favourite and most cherished, and believed in
quality seems always to betray us at some triumphant momen
in our puppet career. Be careful Labbie! Creatures like you are
only possible as long as they are successful; your moral flimsi
ness and the strain you put upon the aesthetic sense are such
that if you fail in worldly shrewdness and are led away like the
hysterical, you fall like a house of cards. Nothing more need
be said on the subject after this bit from Sir Charles Russell's
speech on the amendment to the Parnell Report motion.[120]

"The most painful incident in the debate has been the silence
with which expressions of congratulation to the Irish members
have been received on the opposite benches; but when charges have

[117] George Curzon (1859–1925), later 1st Marquess Curzon of Kedleston
[118] Augustine Birrell (1850–1933), essayist, author of *Obiter Dicta*, 1884
and 1887.
[119] Robert Arthur Talbot Gascoyne-Cecil, 3rd Marquess of Salisbury
(1830–1903), was Prime Minister 1886–1892 (the second of his three terms
of office).
[120] The special Parnell Commission brought in its report on February 13,
1890, ruling that the attempt to link Parnell to the Phoenix Park murders
was false, since Pigott confessed he had forged the incriminating letters.

een flung at their heads, and the worst construction has been put
on the facts against them, hon. members opposite have thought it
becoming to cheer (hear, hear). I think you are pursuing a very
blind course. You are seeking to drive from public life and from
the leadership of an important party a man who can point to great
achievements done, not for Ireland alone, but for the empire,—
for the weakness of Ireland is the weakness of the empire (hear,
hear), and the improvement has added strength to the empire
(cheers). He can point to solid achievements accomplished in ten
years equalling what has been accomplished for Ireland in the
preceding eighty years. He has been helped in that by a growing
spirit of intelligence and sympathy in the minds of the English
people, inspired and fostered by the man of genius who leads this
party (loud cheers). But, if you are only wise enough to see it, he
has done more than that. He has shifted the political fulcrum of
Irish politics to the floor of this house (hear, hear). He has drawn
away from secret associations great popular forces into Constitutional action, that may or may not have had its attendant evils
and blots. No one will deny it has had this effect—unless, indeed,
your policy prevents it; it has made Fenianism and secret societies
cease to be a political factor in Ireland today (hear, hear). Above
all, he has taught the Irish people to have faith in Parliament and
in its sense of justice. He has taught them to look to Parliamentary
methods for redress. You are not pursuing a statesmanlike course.
Had Mr. Parnell stood by his class, and been actuated by the
selfish interests of his class; had he forgotten that he was an Irishman; had he forgotten that as an Irish representative the cares of
his country were his first concern; had he stood, as Grattan
phrased it, 'offering himself in the market of St. Stephen's'; had
he refused to listen to the cry of calamity from his country,—a cry
too often misinterpreted as a cry of sedition and treason,—had he
done these things, you would have regarded him as a decorous
member of Parliament (cheers). Today the man who has done all
those things that I have shown, and who has acted as I have said,
you seek to dishonour (cheers). Are there no men amongst you
magnanimous enough, statesmen enough, to try and lift up this
question beyond its personal character? (Loud cheers.) Do you
not see that behind Mr. Parnell stand a nation and a nation's hope?

(Cheers.) Do you not see that if you wound him you wound and insult them? (Cheers.) Do you not see that by that course you are not healing, but embittering an international quarrel that all good men who have the interest of the State at heart would wish to see ended forever? You will, by your party vote, carry this motion. If you achieve that victory it will be at best a Pyrrhic victory, and in achieving it you will have displayed neither the qualities of statesmen nor of patriots (prolonged Opposition cheers)."

From Standard, March 7th

The behaviour of the Unionist and Tory is simply the *bête* carried to its supreme expression. It is truly a great misfortune for a people to be so destitute of inspiration, and so completely without humour, as to be left absolutely naked to itself. If you could read, too, the chorus going up to heaven on all sides over the love of *Manliness* and *fair play* in the Briton's bosom! those qualities of which they are always assuring the rest of the world they hold the monopoly. The Englishman, however should not be held accountable for being mentally so abject before the Irishman—he is helpless for there is absolutely nothing in his organization wherewith he can conceive of him, and his self-respect naturally has no other refuge save in loathing and despising him. He has no wings to his mind to bear him whither his leaden feet are inapt for carrying him, so that it is only now at the end of seven centuries that he is beginning faintly [to] divine that in Ireland, above all other lands, there are impalpable spiritualities which rise triumphant and imperishable before brutality.

March 9th

Often in the stillness of the night the voice of a woman, hardly human in its sound, saying without pause, in a raucous monotone, "You're a loi-er. You're a loi-er" mingled with the drunken notes of a man and with a feeble gin-suckled wail for chorus reverberates within me. One night as I was going to bed in De Vere Gardens (not al fresco, but under H.'s roof) these hor rible sounds rose from a passage at the side of the house. Nurse discovered that it was a man and woman fighting over a baby! —A bundle of rags containing a spark of human life sending up its piteous protest—it was like a descent into Hell. I asked Mary Porter one day, who was then living at the East End in the midst of it all, whether she ever escaped from it, if it didn't dwell within her and haunt her thro' all the hours. She didn't seem to know what I meant—Ah! she has no stomach, happy mortal! It would be curious to know what liar means to them, it seems such a very sophisticated form of reproach. Mrs. Lathbury told me that she found the East Enders had an infinitely finer perception of right and wrong than she had! What satisfaction can there be in humbugging oneself in that fashion?

Imagine my "going-off" on hearing the result of the St. Pancras election![121] Naturally the imminent prospect of 700 more elections in the pit of me stomach isn't seductive. How strange 'twould be not to be under the dominion of that mighty organ, save digestively. No fiat of the fateful three was ever more irresistible than the decrees sent forth by that pivot of my being! Mentally no fate appalls me, but morally no crawling worm was ever so abject as I am before the convolutions of that nest of snakes coiling and uncoiling themselves. What pain remotely approaches the horror of those hours, which may swamp one at any moment, passed, second by second, hanging as it were by a cobweb to Sanity!

How revolting Sarah Bernhardt[122] acting in a Passion Play! She is a moral abscess, festering with vanity.

[121] The St. Pancras by-election was contested by the Conservative-Unionist Harry G. Graham and the Liberal Thomas H. Bolton. An independent, John Leighton, also ran and created the fear that he would split Bolton's vote. Bolton had come out flatly for Irish Home Rule and received strong support from Gladstone. He won by a majority of 108 votes. The independent received only 29 votes.

[122] This must have been theatrical gossip, for Bernhardt never acted in a Passion Play. She did produce a drama based on the life of Joan of Arc later this year. It was described by one of her biographers (Baring) as "a commonplace and cheaply patriotic play."

"If they desired company," said Mr. Balfour last night of the fellow-members whom he puts in prison, "let them exercise, as they had a right to do, with the other prisoners." "Pickpockets!" cried out an hon. member. "Yes," retorted Mr. Balfour, "he drew no distinction." Mr. Balfour knows perfectly well that he does draw a distinction, and that this bit of bravado was no less mendacious than it was insolent. Otherwise why do not he and his colleagues take logical measures against the "Condemned Criminals" of the Commission Reports?" (*P. M. G.*, March 20th)

This is a characteristic example of Mr. B. in his rôle of Great Statesman, la fine fleur of the Aristocracy and the idol of the Gentlemanly Party. One is as an American still so under illusions as to *Noblesse Oblige* and all the other fine hereditities that you can't fail to be horribly shocked in finding these men with roots far back in the past as devoid of gentlemanly instincts as the most discredited mushroom Western politician. But Balfour seems of all of them most bent upon discrediting hereditary responsibilities and ne'er to have suckled a generous, manly or noble tradition with *his* mother's milk. But why let oneself get hot over such an ephemeral creature—"Their brazen insolence," as Wm. says, "will be judged by history," to which we can well afford to leave them.

The women seem to do here constantly what so rarely happens at home, marry again. 'Tis always a surprise, not that I have any foolish young inflexibility about it, for I am only too glad to see creatures grasp at anything, outside murder, theft or intoxication, from which they fancy they may extract happiness, but it reveals such a simple organization to be perpetually ready to renew experience in so confiding a manner —playing the old tune with variations, simply. As they do it within a year or two the moral flesh must be as healthy as that pink substance of which they are physically compact, the torn fibres healing themselves by first intention, evidently. The subjective experience being what survives from any relation, you would suppose that the wife part of you had been sufficiently developed in one experiment, at any rate that you would like to contemplate the situation a bit from the bereft point of view —but, no, they are ready to plunge *into love again* at a moment's notice—as if 'twere quantity, not quality, of emotion that counted.

One had expected to see Bismarck[123] disappear in the course of nature and his hideous anachronisms gradually follow, but to have him "crushed," *more suo*, by his Nursling, too, is as rejoiceful as it is droll. 'Tis rather alarming, however, for altho' as H. says his internal policy seemed worthy of Boulanger, he *did* make for peace, while this whipped syllabub young man rushing it makes one feel as secure as if he were a child playing with matches in a powder magazine.

"It is not in my power to reward your services according to their full value. I must, therefore, be satisfied at assuring you of my never-ending thanks and of those of the Fatherland. I bestow on you the dignity of a Duke of Lauenburg as a sign of these thanks, and I shall send you my life-size portrait." WILHELM, I. R.

Console thyself, Bismarck! the portrait might have been colossal. I should like to be Wilhelm for half an hour; he is such a perfect specimen; more completely under the illusion of his own individuality and absolutely remote from the possibility of taking his relative measure than any known contemporary quantity.

Nurse's father is a National School Master in Prestbury near Cheltenham, which she told me when she first came, with immense pride, was "the hot-bed of Ritualism!" This is how the Spirit ferments within the pedagogic bosom. In talking about

---

[123] Otto von Bismarck (1815–1898) resigned as Chancellor of Germany March 18, 1890, as a consequence of continuing differences with Wilhelm II. He was created Duke of Lauenburg.

the Christmas tree I said, Why, what a big one it must take
for 300 children, to which Nurse replied that only about half
of the children were asked as there was not room enough. "How
does he choose them, the best scholars, I suppose?" "Oh! no
he asks only the children that come to Sunday school, so that
the Chapel children won't get in!" This the great Christian
festival symbolizing the Brotherhood of Man! too, too lovely!

March 25th

Henry came on the 10th, and spent the day, Henry the patient
I should call him. Five years ago in November, I crossed the
water and suspended myself like an old woman of the sea
round his neck where to all appearances I shall remain for all
time. I have given him endless care and anxiety but notwithstanding this and the fantastic nature of my troubles I have
never seen an impatient look upon his face or heard an unsympa-
thetic or misunderstanding sound cross his lips. He comes at
my slightest sign and hangs on to whatever organ may be in
eruption and gives me calm and solace by assuring me that my
nerves are his nerves and my stomach his stomach—this last a
pitch of brotherly devotion never before approached by the
race. He has never remotely hinted that he expected me to be
well at any given moment, that burden which fond friend and
relative so inevitably impose upon the cherished invalid. But
he has always been the same since I can remember and has
almost as strongly as Father that personal susceptibilty—what
can one call it, it seems as if it were a matter of the scarfskin,
as if they perceived thro' that your mood and were saved thereby
from rubbing you raw with their theory of it, or blindness to it.

I was so pleased to come a little while ago across the following in a letter of William's to Wilkie in February, '66, after his
return from Brazil:[124] "Harry, I think much improved, he is

[124] William James had been a member of the Agassiz expedition to Brazil,
1865–1866. Garth Wilkinson (Wilkie) (1845–1883) was the third son in
the James family.

a noble fellow—so true, delicate and honorable." All of which is as true in 1890 as then. I was of course much gratified to find this further on, "—and Alice has got to be quite a nice girl"— hasn't it the true fraternal condescension in its ring! I am afraid that I have fallen from such altitudes since at various moments. To give a specimen of Harry's absolute unworldliness and inability to conceive of the base, notwithstanding his living so much in the world, he writes à propos of Cousin Henry Wyck- off's will and the fear that Albert, or rather the depraved Mrs. Albert Wyckoff, should contest it—"I suppose William will get, at any rate, his $5,000; there would be a baseness in Mrs. W. grudging that and her having to do that sort of thing if she does contest that may shame her from it." The beautiful and babe-like innocence of this view of Mrs. W., who spends all her time betting at horse-races, being so overcome by the superiorities of the adored William as to be shamed into virtue is truly touching. H. seems cheerful about his play[125] and to be unable to grasp my flutterations about it. What a "state" I was in when he told me six months ago as a great secret that he had embarked. I had to tell some one about it, or have exploded, so of course there was nothing to turn to but little Nurse. I could cry, if it were not so much better an investment to laugh, over my poverty in the way of receptacles for my overflow— such a contrast to the vast and responsive reservoirs of the past. Nurse undergoes it all passively, finding it a pleasant change from the iniquities of the parson and Mr. Balfour which she has in such monotonous alternation.

March 30th

I have an exquisite 30 seconds every day: after luncheon I come in from my rest and before the window is closed I put my head out and drink in a long draft of the spring—made

---

[125] This was Henry James's dramatization of his novel, *The American*, originally published in 1877.

of the yellow glory of the daffodils on the balcony, the swelling twiggery of the old trees in front, the breathless house-cleaning of the rooks, the gradation of the light in transition, and the mystery of birth in the air. What hours of roaming could give me a more intense absorption of the ever-recurring Miracle than those few moments which sink into my substance!

The "home" feeling which you can with good will and if such be the need of your being—after the home full-grown and seemingly indestructible! into which you were born has melted away under your eyes—fabricate between any four walls, is to my great delight possessing me more and more here in these two rooms. The illusion is greatly fostered by the succession of the seasons which has taught me just what to expect, so that I recognize the seen before in their chiaroscuro effects and know with what tint of spectacles to heighten the depths and soften the crudities. To the perverse it must seem contemptible that a day should be made worth living by a ray of light shed athwart it, suggestive of past rays and pregnant with those to come. But the wilful love their miseries, and have no desire to save wear and tear by being friends not only with themselves, but with the wall-paper and the sofa-cushions, to say nothing of the "shiffoneer," that nucleus of the lodging house scheme of adornment. I must allow, however, that I haven't been strong before the anti-maccassars and the Nottingham lace curtains, I simply won't assimilate 'em! There were 17 when I first came and I have gradually eliminated them and at the end of three years there is no sign left. I had to go slowly on account of Clarkey's feelings, but they were too depressing and neutralized all higher suggestion!

In a letter from H. this morning he tells of the engagement of the "charming Sylvia Du Maurier[126] to Arthur Davis [Davies] a remarkably fine and handsome young fellow, altho' as yet a penniless barrister—he has 'taken' everything takeable in the

[126] Sylvia du Maurier, second daughter of the artist and novelist George du Maurier, married Arthur Lewellyn Davies.

way of scholarships and prizes and he and his five brothers have
cost their father never a penny for their University Education
—a homeruler and athletic and handsome." It is that sort of
creature so beautifully adjusted morally, mentally and physically, cropping up here so often, that makes you feel that they
are the exceptional people, the race that counts after all—so
that with your heart-strings vibrating you forget and forgive,
almost love, perhaps, the vast and solid mass from which they
have bloomed, standing placid and complacent, knee deep in the
National slough. There is such a charming face one sees here
among the youngish men, altho' it often descends unlessened,
a look of such beautiful purity, innocence and simplicity, a
serenity unimpaired by the complications of experience, a look
of being as incapable of a theory as if they had emerged the
hour before from the Womb of Nature.

Mrs. Bowyer brought her son to see me one day this winter,
a nice typical youth, so clean and inarticulate! I see that the
pious pile erected by the Duke of Newcastle for his private
devotions at Clumber has cost £50,000, perhaps that's why he
can't afford a tooth-brush. Louisa Loring's[127] dentist in London
told her that he had three kinds of tooth-powder, that he would
give her what he gave to Americans and people who brushed
their teeth properly, the second was for those who sometimes
brushed them and the third—pure pumice—for those, who, like
the Duke of Newcastle, had *never* brushed them. Since his investment in American candy I think he will be forced into the
outlay, for to digest so sweet a Duchess will be toothachy.

March 30th

"How the poor live." Here is an instance taken from some evidence recently given in the Hebburn police-court:

"Inspector Snowdon said that he went to Simpson's house No.
8 Williams-lane, Hebburn Quay, on the 15th ult. He had gone for

[127] Louisa Loring was a younger sister of Katharine P. Loring.

two school-board fines which had not been paid. Simpson was getting some tea. All the children were present. Mrs. Simpson came out from the front room. She had a few rags on, hanging about her, but not sufficient to cover her nakedness. All the furniture in the house was two chairs, one without a back, and two iron beds, one of them in ruins, while there was a mattress black and glazed with filth. The children were in a filthy condition, hanging in rags and swarming with vermin. The house smelt dreadfully. There was no food in the house except a few potatoes. He afterwards went again to the house, but the door was fastened. He forced the door, and was led to believe that some person had been in the house, but looked all over the house without finding any one. On striking a match and looking up the chimney he found George there resting with his feet on one side and his back against the other side. There was no fire on. The boy said he often went there when any one was coming into the house. The girls told him that they slept in the bottom of a cupboard, and the mother on one of the shelves."

Yet the father of this miserable family was a carpenter in Armstrong's, and his wages since the beginning of the year had averaged 25s. 7d. a week. Thanks to the "Children's Charter," he and his wife (who is stepmother to all the children except the youngest) are now undergoing two months' hard labour.

(*P. M. G.*, April 5th.)

In measuring such as the above Mrs. Lodge's story of the baby which was rescued from some den of misery is of inestimable value. The child was taken to a Home of some sort, laid in a spotless crib and all the comfortable layer of soil removed, when it began and roared all night and kept all the other children roaring for three days. The matron in despair sent off for the mother, who, on seeing it, immediately said: "Why, lay it on the floor"; which being done, the child went sound asleep all night. But what could wring the hearts of pious old maids more than a baby lying on the floor of squalor?— baby meanwhile in bliss.

April 6th

The Emperor William seems to be a young man "with whom it is always fourth of July,"—as some one said of old Coggswell, the postmaster in Newport. Mr. Tom Hazard, at the expiration of the second Mrs. C., asked him if he wouldn't like to come to a *see-ance* at his house, when he could hear his wife and touch her hand, to which C. promptly replied "Oh, no, Mr. Hazard, thank you. I think it best to let bygones be bygones always!" A few months after, the third Mrs. C. was being led to the altar.

Aunt Mary Tweedy[128] asked Miss Mary Hazard whether they had heard yet from their sister Anna, who had just died; to which she replied, yes that she was better—she had been a great invalid—but did not come down to breakfast yet!

Read the "Madonna of the Future"[129] yesterday, it was long since I read it and it came with a new sense of beauty. His old things are always good to go back to.

April 7th

I remind myself all the time of a coral insect building up my various reefs of theory by microscopic additions drawn from observation, or my inner consciousness, mostly. The one that resists the best and is most constantly re-enforced, and against which fewer of those wretched little demolishing trifles arise, to which one has always, in conscience, to close one's eyes,—is that this most excellent people can't harm anything that they don't know; they don't learn things in the air, and by absorbing one of your surfaces they cannot construct you and divine the

[128] Mary Tweedy (Mrs. Edmund Tweedy), while not actually an aunt of the James children, was so called by them because she was the half-sister of their Temple cousins, whom she had adopted after the death of their parents. The Tweedys were neighbors of the Jameses at Newport.
[129] "The Madonna of the Future" first appeared in the *Atlantic Monthly* in March 1873.

nature of the others.—Whether this crystallized within me whilst I was being carried off the tug at Liverpool, my arms round the necks of two soapless children of the sea, the only occasion when I may have been said to have been in the "world," or not, I was strongly impressed from earliest days that they have not "intuitive natures," as the man, who kept the house we were in at Princeton one summer, said of his wife—how Father laughed in telling it—Her intuitions, by the way, consisted of cooing rubbish to the flowers under our windows at dawn with long, perfectly straight, straw-colored hair hanging round her. The Briton can easily be forgiven his incapacity for such subtleties! Here is an illustration or two: After Mrs. Lathbury[130] had been coming for a year or two in the friendliest and kindest manner to see me, she asked me about the ways of living at home and I said I should have to have a house of my own or live in a boarding house; that it was like the Continent, there not being this excellent lodging-house arrangement. She asked me to explain the nature of a boarding-house, which I did to the best of my ability—when she said, "Would you have a room to yourself?" Now she had never seen me actually going to bed so she felt no security as to my knowledge or preference for the common laws of decency when her eye wasn't upon me and she had received no impression during our very frequent and agreeable interviews which would have made the question superfluous and that my habits in the main made for refinement.

I remember Mary Peabody telling me of having met a young man, one of the Macaulays, when she was traveling with her mother in Switzerland. He must have found them attractive as he joined them and travelled with them for a week and made himself very pleasant. After they had been home for a year, a long letter suddenly arrived from him saying that he thought they might like to know what had been happening in Europe since they had left, so he went on to narrate in minutest detail all the various events of which they had read every morning

[130] Probably the wife of the journalist and editor, D. C. Lathbury.

at their breakfast-table. The amiable young man pictured them as buried in the heart of the forest, I suppose—but, as Mary P. said "What a blow to our vanity to find what he must have thought of us and our opportunities when we were together, that we should need such a letter." Mary P. who is unusually intelligent and au fait, too! but the dear soul had never been to Boston and actually seen that there were books and newspapers there, and Mary P.'s being intelligent for a week, for he must have seen that, whilst under the propagating rays of his orbs, was very insufficient ground for the wild generalization that she was permanently so. Mr. Nettleship, the oculist, came to see me in De Vere Gardens, and at the end, when he was extracting golden drops from Kath., he asked her if this was a "flat" and seemed very much surprised by it and said "You have them in America and do people in your rank of life live in them?" Whether debased or exalted he didn't say. Now houses of flats are in every quarter of London, but it had never penetrated his consciousness because the end of his nose had never been abraided by contact with the walls thereof—and I think he had a vague impression that we had imported this one from the U. S. Mrs. Gladstone told Harry, à propos of the G. O. M.'s exquisite Italian, that two or three days after her wedding she was standing in the drawing-room and heard some one coming downstairs singing in the most beautiful tenor voice an Italian song, "Fancy, my surprise and delight on going out into the hall to find it was Mr. Gladstone! I had no idea that he could either sing, or that he could speak Italian." Think of being engaged and married to a man and not having learnt thro' your pores that he had a tenor voice! But what a phenomenal being is Mr. Gladstone, his wealth of resource, even as a lover, so vast that he could afford to leave dormant a tenor voice and Italian song!

Mrs. Charles Buxton[181] told me one day that Mrs. Mat[thew]

[181] Charles Buxton (1823–1871), son of the philanthropist Sir Thomas F. Buxton, married Emily Mary, eldest daughter of Sir Henry Holland in 1850.

Arnold[132] had heard of her brother-in-law's (Mr. Forster) death in the English papers when she got to New York, he having died whilst she was on the ocean,—I said, "You mean she heard the telegraphic news in the American papers." "Oh, no, you know she would read it in the English papers when she arrived in New York." It seemed one of those dark places of the human mind into which light never enters so I struggled no more. Mrs. Arnold came very kindly to see me one day before she went the second time and spoke very cordially of her visit and we were discussing the domestic difficulty when she told of having staid in some house in the West where they had quite too few servants, only a man and a housemaid. I asked if there was no cook. "That I cannot say, I didn't see her if there was one." "But you had food to eat?" "Oh, yes!" "Did the lady cook, do you think?" "Oh I think not!" The dear lady had so lost her bearings, from the fact of there being so many fewer visible housemaids than there "ought" to have been that she could not draw upon her imagination for a cook, her eyes not having actually beheld her. One could run on with the like trivialities, *ad infinitum*.

Mrs. Buxton was by the way very much surprised to hear that Matt[hew] Arnold's lectures had been such a failure and said that she knew it for a fact that he himself thought they were brilliantly successful and that he fully expected to give a second course that summer on his second visit. He wrote his much discussed article instead, in which he found balm, let us hope.[133]

---

[132] Arnold married Frances Lucy, daughter of Sir William Wightman, a judge, June 10, 1851.

[133] Arnold had lectured in America during 1883–1884 on "Numbers; or, The Majority and the Remnant," "Literature and Science," and on Emerson, The press was largely critical and hostile. In 1888 his various essays about his trip were published in Boston under the title *Civilization in the United States: First and Last Impressions of America.*

f I can get on to my sofa and occupy myself for four hours, t intervals, thro' the day, scribbling my notes and able to read ne books that belong to me, in that they clarify the density and nape the formless mass within, Life seems inconceivably rich –full of "l'allégresse de la certitude acquise. La raison a aussi es émotions et c'est par frissons que se propage la lumière."

The *Standard* this morning devotes the first paragraph of its ummary of news to the thrilling fact that the infant daughter f the Duke of Portland was christened in Windsor Chapel in resence of the Queen! Toward the end of the column comes nention of the "impressive" gathering in Hyde Park of the vorking-man on the eight-hours question—the first shall be last nd the last shall be first! How I wish I could have seen a ew of the faces of these Masters of the world in whose hands ur material future lies, who can say how immediately. Should he governments of Europe show the cowering abject attitude vhich they took on the first of May, what an impetus it will ;ive, it will almost seem as if one might live to see the remodel-ing. I shall always be a bloated capitalist, I suppose, an igno-niny which, considering all things, I may as well submit to, racefully, for I shouldn't bring much *body* to the proletariat, ut I can't help having an illogical feminine satisfaction that ll my seven per cents and six per cents with which I left home iave melted into fours. I don't feel as if four per cent were quite so base!

Could anything exhibit more beautifully the solidarity of the ace than that by simply combining to walk thro' the streets on he same day, these starvelings should make Emperors, Kings, 'residents and millionaires tremble the world over! Those vho have every opportunity for acquiring wisdom, inheriting ioble, humane and generous instincts have found no more in-pired means of allaying their mutual rapacities than shooting lown vast hordes of innocent men, as helpless as sheep—Whilst

these creatures, the disinherited with savage instincts all un-
subdued, have divined that brotherly help is the path to Victory!
What one of us, with his sentimental, emotional sympathy, ever
stood by his fellow, starving, and watching his dwindling wife
and children for weeks? And yet at every strike thousands of
the unfed, the unclothed, and the unread, stand or fall together
and make no boast.

May 13th, 1890

Harry came on Thursday 8th. He had been to Chester to see
the Comptons[134] to make arrangements about *The American*.
It is to be brought out in the Provinces and acted there thro' the
winter and taken to London in the spring. This is thought best
as it will give Compton plenty of practice in the part. H. says
he will have to work over them immensely. The Comptons
think very well of the play and feel sure it will be a success,
and they are much better judges of that than any one else
with their immense experience of audiences. H. was very much
struck with their British decency and respectability which was
much revealed to him as he penetrated into their interior. Such
a contrast to that of second-rate or first-rate for the matter of
that, French actors with whom prolonged personal intercourse
would be simply impossible. Compton having asked him about
Newman's clothes in these early days reminded him of the
following—Some ladies in London were being coached for a
play by a Frenchwoman, an ex-actress, I believe, Lady Archie
Campbell,[135] who was one of the ladies, arrived the first day
dressed as a Pierrot, the part she was to act. On beholding her
the Frenchwoman exclaimed—"Voilà bien une Anglaise, qui

[134] Edward Compton (1854–1918), the actor, and his wife, the former
Virginia Bateman (1853–1940). He produced Henry James's dramatization of
The American in 1890 in the provinces and in London, where the play ran for
seventy nights.
[135] Janey Sevilla Callander (d. 1923) married in 1869 Lord Archibald
Campbell, younger son of the 8th Duke of Argyll.

se fait faire son costume avant d'avoir pensé à son rôle!" H.
was also here April 15th—it is so reposeful to see him, he is
so unsuggestive as to the conduct of life—the angle of one's
cushions or the number of one's shawls.

"L'inertie de la bête devant *l'irrévocable* a presque toujours
l'aspect du courage." This is not flattering but which of us has
not given within a faint paralytic smile over her "Courage,"
however careful her vanity may have been not to dispel the
superficial illusion.

May 17th

The Queen's call at Waddesdon[186] sounds as if it were a
reward of virtue, the good Rothschilds having had their curtains drawn in their house in Piccadilly (vide "Speaker") as
the naughty working men filed past to Hyde Park for their
demonstration on May 4th. Just conceive of the Prince of Wales
not having gone to the Park! to think of losing all one's opportunities after that fashion. The king of Italy seems alone among
them all, to have any imagination and to get some fun out of his
limitations. But the poor things are such slaves! The Queen
stopped on her drive the other day and watched a performing
bear, she also laughed; whereupon the next morning there was
a Standardesque leader upon "this strange and not altogether
wise fancy" (perhaps "act"!) "of the Queen!" The Princess
Mary (Duchesse of Teck)[187] was to open something or other
at the East End. She was so late, that a noble Lord began the
proceedings without her. She came in the middle, and the next
thing on the programme to be done immediately after was the
singing by children of a song beginning "Mary, wake up!" The
noble Lord had of course no higher inspiration than to pass
this and hurry on to the next, thereby depriving the poor

[186] Queen Victoria had visited Waddesdon, country home of Ferdinand
Anselm de Rothschild, earlier that month.
[187] Princess Mary, Duchess of Teck (1833–1897), mother of Princess Mary,
later Queen Mary (1867–1953).

Duchesse of even that tiny ripple of human life whereby to refresh the arid desert of the arranged where she is fated to browse.

"The comments which appeared in our columns on Monday last on the case of the man Mark Henry Vaille, who fell dead suddenly through starvation, has created considerable interest,—so much so that a question was asked in the House of Commons concerning it. A representative who has been making inquiries about the case found that Vaille lived at 231, High-street, Shadwell.

"Our representative was directed to a dark, narrow, dreary-looking passage, and was told that the house lay at the bottom of this. The passage opened upon a small yard, covered with refuse, which sent forth a most objectionable stench. No. 231 is 18 feet high, with one room down and one upstairs. A lad of fourteen opened the door, and upon being asked said that he and his brothers lived in that room now their father was dead. The room—or den—was not more than ten feet long, eight feet wide, and seven feet high. There was no fire in the grate, and, judging by the damp, clammy walls and putrid atmosphere, there had evidently not been any for some days past. The window consisted of three broken panes, and some rags stuffed in where panes should have been. The only furniture was portions of two chairs, a broken table, an apology for a chest of drawers, an old wooden frame covered with a lot of dirty rags answering for bedstead and bedding, together with an ancient Dutch clock and two or three cracked platters.

"The lad who had opened the door said his mother was in the Banstead Lunatic Asylum, suffering from melancholia brought on through starvation. He had three sisters: Matilda, aged twenty-four and married, and Annie, aged twenty-two, in service; Martha, eighteen, in a school; and three brothers, all at home, younger than himself. He called them to him,—a set of wan, dirty little fellows, though intelligent. Their names were William, aged nine; Harry, six; George, four. His own name was Edward John, and he was fourteen years old, he said. Asked how his father had lived, he replied, by dock-work, but, being only a casual, he did not get much, except when the wool sales were on. All the money that his father earned he brought home, and 'he was a good, kind father,' added the lad, pathetically. 'For the last few weeks Matilda, who lives in Wapping, has given us food, but she cannot give us much, as her husband does not get much work. He works at the docks.

" 'The landlady lives upstairs,' continued the boy, with a half-frightened look; and at that moment she arrived on the scene,—a little wizened-face old dame of sixty. She said her name was Mrs. Mallison; but when this was overheard by some neighbours they all shouted out, 'No, it wasn't; it was Mrs. Brennan.' Whatever her name, however, she at once commenced about the Vailles owing her several weeks' rent at 2s. a week. At the present time the children have nothing to rely upon except the charity of a few poor neighbours and the sister Matilda. On Wednesday afternoon a parish officer called for the first time, and desired to take all the children to the workhouse. This Matilda and John flatly declined to allow. The father was buried at the expense of the Dockers' Union. John is a lad who is anxious to get into a situation, he says, where he might go to school a bit as well as work for himself and brothers. He is intelligent, and seems full of ambition, with an intense fondness for his little brothers." (*P. M. G.*)

The father was a very good man, who got a job to do, and as the money for it was being handed to him he fell dead at the master's feet! He had eaten nothing that the children should have more—and I gave £6.0.0 the other day for a trumpery wedding present! You can't, however, go out and give them what you have, simply.

I almost pauperized Miss Bond by helping her to float a little shop—have had to stop off short, yet she does not seem to think me a fiend incarnate! The most abject case of destitution of which I have heard of lately is that of the Dowager Duchess of Manchester,[188] whose jointure is only £2,000 a year! When you think of the rapacious hordes thro' which a box of matches, or an egg for her breakfast has to work its way before it reaches her, she is truly a pitiable object!

---

[188] The Dowager Duchess of Manchester, the former Countess Louise Fredericke Auguste, daughter of the Comte d'Alten of Hanover, had lost her husband in March 1890. In 1892 she remarried and became the Duchess of Devonshire.

This is valuable as showing the relative value of women and herring:

"For those men to whom the pastime of jumping on their mothers or their wives is a pleasant relaxation from the monotony of every-day life, Hampstead will, for the future, possess exceptional attractions, if the sentence recently passed upon a certain Henry Willet is to be accepted as a precedent. This worthy individual had for years past subjected his wretched wife to a systematic course of cruelty. He had continually threatened to kill her, either by jumping on her, dashing out her brains, or by inserting a pin or needle behind her ear in order to penetrate her brain. The culminating point, however, was reached when he brutally assaulted her in bed by pressing his knees into the lower part of her back and attempting to strangle her, a piece of playful pleasantry which led to his arrest. The Solons on the Hampstead Bench expressed their horror at his unnatural behaviour, and, by way of making an exemplary example of this monster, fined him—ten shillings!

"And now look on this picture. The Bury magistrates on Saturday sentenced a woman named Mary Blomley to one month's imprisonment, without option of a fine, for stealing three red-herrings, valued at three pence, from a greengrocer's cart. Notwithstanding that Mary had been previously convicted, such a sentence for such an offence is a disgrace to the Bury bench. Sir Henry James[139] the member for the borough, is one of the advocates of lighter sentences. I hope that upon the first favourable opportunity he will give a little advice on this subject to the Bury J. P.s."
(*Truth.*)

May 20th

Where do you suppose they have discovered Self-Sacrifice now? In the heroic bosom of Stanley![140] who on his own showing

---

[139] Sir Henry James (1828–1911), later Lord James of Hereford, was Attorney-General in 1873–1874 and from 1880 to 1885.

[140] Sir Henry M. Stanley (1841–1904), African explorer and journalist. Dorothy Tennant, a sister of Margot, later Lady Asquith, became Lady Stanley.

laps up the *agréments* of African travel as I do my afternoon tea. Henry told me on one of his late visits that he had asked Miss Dorothy Tennant, who he says is a most charming creature, something about Stanley and she had said: "Oh, dear old Stan. that will never come to anything." How can a refined woman marry a man of such coarse, crude and rudimentary fibre? "The Bullet and the Bible" expresses him to perfection.

I had an almost Gallic sense of the injustice of Fate the other day, unusual with me, for I am not rebellious by temperament and trampled down as much as possible all boresome insurrections, having fortunately early perceived that the figure of abortive rebel lent itself much more to the comic than the heroic in the eye of the cold-blooded observer, and that for practical purposes surrender, smiling, if possible, is the only attainable surface which gives no hold to the scurvy tricks of Fortune. I was awfully tired one afternoon and was going to bed when Constance Maud's name was brought up, asking if I would not see her for a moment as she was going to America the next day. I scrambled into bed, and she, tall, straight and handsome, with shining eyes and glowing cheeks told me that she was going to my land, whilst my highest privilege, shriveled and rickety, was to go to bed in hers! What a tide of homesickness swept me under for a moment! What a longing to see a shaft of sunshine shimmering thro' the pines, breathe in the resinous air and throw my withered body down upon my mother earth, bury my face in the coarse grass, worshipping all that the ugly, raw emptiness of the blessed land stands for—the embodiment of a Huge Chance for hemmed in Humanity! Its flexible conditions stretching and lending themselves to all sizes of man; pallid and naked of necessity; undraped by the illusions and mystery of a moss-grown, cobwebby past, but overflowing with a divine good-humour and benignancy—a helping hand for the faltering, an indulgent thought for the discredited, a heart of hope for every outcast of tradition!

I went out for the first time May 18th a very early start for me. Bourget[141] said to Harry: "Je n'ai jamais osé avoir de l'esprit devant Dumas." How extraordinary it is to see that wittiest and most infinitely perceptive of races, individually surrendering itself to a Colossal Vanity, that quality from which springs all the grotesque in life! The impish passion displayed by that "Unknowable Reality behind Phenomena," for making the creature self-destructive, the very quantities which make him strong before his fellows insidiously eating into his own vitals, is delightsome to watch from a sofa for an unsentimental spinster. Can it be, perhaps, that the *Unknowable Reality* simply jokes with Phenomena? as they say that the American Public does with all the serious things of life—or is it only that mankind is so dense that it cannot perceive all the cowardices, follies and self-love unless they are carried to the limits of the grotesque?

Miss Ireland told me that Mrs. Kemble said, on her first visit to the United States that "the women seemed just like white mice screaming!"

Two friends borrowed Father's *Literary Remains*,[142] which William curiously names "of the *late* Henry James" like those "widows of the late So-and-So," who die in the newspapers—the first regretted that he (Father) "had never known anything of the Broad Catholic Church"—*i.e.*, the centimetre of washed-out Anglican Evasions. The second, thought "it such a pity that Darwin was not known to him." The dear old gentleman doesn't seem to have had an opportunity to acquire the elements of general "Culture"—does he? À propos of Darwin, I was reading an article of Emile Montégut's[143] the other day, in

[141] Paul Bourget (1852–1935), French novelist, was a friend of Henry James.

[142] *The Literary Remains of the Late Henry James*, edited by William James (Boston, 1884), contains a series of miscellaneous papers and excerpts from the works of Henry James, Sr. (1811–1883).

[143] Émile Montégut (1825–1895), French critic.

which he points out to the *strieg-for-lifeurs*, who are of course all fierce radicals, that the representative of a long line is a perfect illustration of their gospel and should be cherished by them as an exquisite *specimen* of the survival of the fittest. This self-evident proposition is of course not new but I had never seen it so neatly expressed, especially, and it caused me pleasure.

June 9th

I have this morn[ing] a beautiful letter from Harry[144] of 25 pages in answer to a few lines I wrote to him, after reading the *Great Play!*[145] I was greatly thrilled and touched by the implication which his letter gave that he cared for my opinion as an opinion,—the smallest flatteries of one's kin outweighing the acclamations of a multitude—these last so familiar to me! When I look back upon the unrippled stream of fostering and indulgent domestic receptivity down which I have floated all my days—I wonder that I am not a more objectionable and impossible wretch than I am. H. is staying in Venice with the Curtises,[146] in the Palazzo Barbaro; Miss Wormeley—how the name recalls old days!—there too.

June 10th

The Sapient *Standard* has given me endless delectation since I have read it, the last six years, but *à propos* of the Channel Tunnel it surpasses itself. Sir Edward Watkin,[147] has brought

---

[144] The greater part of this letter, dated June 6, 1890, is reproduced in the first volume of *The Letters of Henry James* (ed. Lubbock) (New York and London, 1920).

[145] His dramatization of *The American*.

[146] Daniel S. and Mrs. Curtis, the former Ariana Wormeley, were for many years friends of Henry James. Mrs. Curtis's sister, Katherine Prescott Wormeley, was translator and editor of the works of Balzac in the United States.

[147] Sir Edward William Watkin (1819–1901), member of the House of Commons for many years.

it up again in the House; here is a bit of his speech, and a leader in the *Standard* upon it:

"It was urged that the tunnel would create a frontier. Why France already had fourteen railways running into Belgium, eight into Germany, seven into Switzerland, two into Italy, two into Spain, and a third was now in course of construction. They were told that the tunnel was dangerous, and that, instead of leading to peace, it would lead to war. It was absurd to say that an aperture about twice the size of the door of the House would cost some 30 millions to defend (cheers). Why should they not be allowed to continue their experiments, and why were they to be suffered to fall into decay? He appealed to the right honourable gentleman to give them fair play, and to allow the experiments to continue. Proposals had been made for bridging the channel, and laying a tube in it, and there were the discoveries of coal. All these altered circumstances afforded a justification for a renewal of the proposals. If the Government continued to crush out the scheme with the weight of its majority, it would have to justify its action in the face of the constituencies, and say why they would have no one go to the Continent except on the stormy surface of the sea."

"The main arguments against the proposal are so cogent as to be absolutely conclusive in the estimation of people who prefer the safety of England to the escape of seasickness, and Military Estimates of reasonable proportions to big dividends for private speculators. The advocates of the scheme have laboured, but laboured in vain, to persuade people that a means can be devised for rendering it absolutely impossible for the English end of the tunnel to fall into the hands of a foreign force landed on our shores. It is easy to make it appear—on paper—that such a circumstance would be to the last degree improbable; though, even on paper, no stronger argument can be adduced. But improbability, in a matter of this moment, will not be regarded as sufficient, or anything like sufficient, by an Englishman who loves his country. We cannot play with chances in a question of this kind. No doubt it is easy—on paper, as we say—to put the English end of the tunnel under military control. It is equally easy to provide a means by which the soldiers in charge of the tunnel should either flood it or cut off rough communication in some other way. But everybody with a grain of sense and a scruple of caution, must perceive that either the means relied on might fail to operate, or might be put in motion too late, or that the English guardians of the tunnel might be surprised and mastered. The persons who project, and would fain construct, Channel tunnels know nothing of the art of war, its surprises, stratagems, disappointments and catastrophes. There is an old proverb that all is fair in love and war, and we should like to see the Foreign General, or the Foreign Statesman, who would regard anything as unfair that, in the event of a conflict with this country, put him in possession of a means of rapidly pouring troops into it. The philosophic historian might condemn the act of treachery; but that would not undo what the act of treachery had effected. When the possibility of unscrupulousness on one side, and of hesitation or bungling on the other are considered together, the man seems to us almost insane, always supposing he cares for England, that would urge or sanction the project. Even if the risk could be made what is called infinitesimally small, we should be a community of lunatics to run it. There are some things of such supreme importance that they impose absolute certainty as their only sufficient and adequate safeguard. Nature has provided us with that certainty by placing a barrier of waves between the ambition of Continental conquerors and the liberties of England. That they and their countrymen should wish to evade the obstacle, to turn our flank, or to take us *en revers,* is perfectly intelligible, and in a philosophical spirit we can admire their ingenuity, in much the same manner as we admire the authors of the 'Trojan Horse.' But in regard to Sir Edwin Watkin and these *dona ferentes,* our feeling for them is one that could not be adequately expressed by any classical quotation. Doubtless, they mean well. It is their want of foresight and want of statesmanship that we complain of and lament."

Conceive of the Bold Briton announcing *without a blush* that he is only saved from annihilation by the silver streak! When you consider that it has been established from all time that it takes three Frenchmen to equal one J[ohnny] B[ull] the spectacle of the swarming Island cowering before this small aperture is more delicious still; and the wicked naughty "Foreign Gen[eral]" too who surely would not *scruple* according to the *Standard*, to use the time-honoured stratagems of war against the dear innocents, completes it all. This is the cry of the Military party in especial—think of Switzerland!—too delectable.

June 15th

How exquisite it is when it all sings within,—but what a price to pay! The ways of the pious bewilder one so!

"Mr. Farrell, the foreman of the jury, sent a telegram to the Queen at Aix-les-Bains yesterday, urging upon her Majesty favourable consideration of Mrs. Davies's telegraphic message. The Rev. E. Hancox, Primitive Methodist Minister at Crewe, in the afternoon sent a telegram to the Queen, stating that all the churches in Crewe were praying for Richard's respite. . . ."

They were trying to get the two Davies boys who had killed their father respited, and the papers were full of this sort of thing. Did the Rev. Hancox, doubting the efficacy of prayer, want the Queen to nudge Jehovah a bit, or was it an intimation that as they were all praying away so hard in Crewe Jehovah might get ahead of her? Practically it seems unwise to pit the spiritual and temporal powers against each other, in such impious and sceptical fashion; for it must surely be destructive of faith in Deity or Monarch; at any rate it's too much of a strain upon mine!

It is very curious to watch them abjectly prostrating themselves before their God, singing praises to His Glory, proclaiming that all His works are for good and yet when the least of the multifold miseries which oppress humanity falls to their lot, how they cry out against His decrees, entreat Him to avert their calamities as if propitiating some power of evil whose deeds are of darkness. Constance Maud told me of her sorrow at some moment when it was thought that her Mother was dying and how she prayed to God to spare her life—the sincerity and strength of the feeling which she showed increased the shocked sense which filled me as I listened. One cries out, bowed down in supplication, for strength, but how can any creature measure her judgment with that of the Doer of all Good, how can she propose to make her paltry necessities an element for the modification of another's destiny, how can she thrust her miserable plaints into the presence of Majestic Death? I remember how horrified I was to the core of my being when some said to me in that month when Father lay dying, refusing to eat, that I must urge him and tell him that he must eat for *my sake!!* Imagine my wanting to stay the will of God and add a second to the old man's hours!

June 16th

What a sense of superiority it gives one to escape reading some book which every one else is reading. I never would read Amiel,[148] and so far I have not succumbed to Marie [Bashkirtseff's] *Journal*.[149] I imagine her the perverse of the perverse and what so dreary to read of, or what part so easy to act as we walk across our little stage lighted up by our little self-conscious foot-lights? Every hour I live I become an intenser devotee to *common-sense!* À propos, how does it advance matters for the race to have Mr. Augustine Birrell tell an audience of the people that a man who cares more for poetry than the poor-laws is an "intellectual fop"? Surely the people, even with a big P, are worth something better than such pure silliness. Since I have read him in the *Speaker*, I have got used

[148] Henri-Frédéric Amiel (1821–1881), Swiss diarist and critic of French Protestant ancestry.
[149] Marie Bashkirtseff, (1860–1884), a Russian diarist, who kept one of the most intimate journals of the nineteenth century. It was begun in Nice in 1873 and breaks off eleven days before her death.

to A. B., and I am not so irritated away from his substance by his manner as I was. Intellectual foppishness by the way applies to it excellently in its strain for the quaint and desire to be precious and odd, with always the self-conscious echo in its train of "Isn't that good?" I asked Harry one day if he felt it and he said, yes, and that the curious part of it was that it existed in his features in the same way; that after he said anything there was a movement of his nostrils and a smack of his lips immediately suggestive of self-applause. He is probably "shy," as they say in Boston, as was Michel Angelo, too!

"It could not fail to be a disagreeable moment for Mr. Balfour when Honest John Roche, the leader of the Clanricarde tenantry, —the man who has five times suffered imprisonment of the cruelest kind under his administration,—filed past him on his way to receive the welcome of the Speaker, amid the enthusiastic cheers of the Opposition last night." *P. M. G.*

If it were not for Mr. Balfour and the Parson to heat my blood I should be at the enviable age when:—"Il n'y a rien qui soit mauvais, il n'y a que des choses tristes ou drôles."

> Forget not, Earth, thy disappointed Dead!
> Forget not, Earth, thy disinherited!
> Forget not the Forgotten! Keep a strain
>   Of divine Sorrow in sweet undertone
> For all the dead who lived and died in vain.
> Imperial Future! when in countless train
>   The generations lead thee to thy throne,
>   Forget not the Forgotten and Unknown!"

"They are by Mr. James Williams,[150] Fellow of Lincoln College, Oxford, and are contained in the volume of verse called *A Story of Three Years*, published in 1883. The lines are as follows":—

[150] James Williams D.C.L. (1851–1911), Fellow of Lincoln College and All Souls, reader in Roman Law at Oxford. Author of many legal studies, he also published volumes of verse, some tales, and a study of "Dante as a Jurist" (1906).

A MEMORY.

Brave soul, so true and noble, thou hast spread
  White pinions for thy flight upon the deep,
The sorrows of the olden time are dead.
          Why should we weep?

Thou didst not grieve at others' happier fate,
  And thou didst mark the gallant ships go by,
Hull after hull with store of precious freight,
          Without a sigh.

Failure was thine, as men account success;
  'Twas better so, perchance, else Heaven might
Have granted us one honest soul the less
          To teach us right.

No crime was it that thou couldst not prevail
  To set thy beacon on the shore of time;
They who strive not, not they who strive and fail,
          Commit the crime.

Earth hath no reverence for fruitless toil;
  Eternal Justice looks with keener gaze,
And on the stricken head will pour the oil
          Of well-won praise.

June 18th

It is very curious how for the last year or two I perpetually come across in my reading just what I have been thinking about, curious I mean, of course, because my reading is so haphazard. It reminds me of Wm. in old days when his eyes were bad and I used to begin and tell him something which I thought of interest from whatever book I might be reading, when he would invariably say, "I glanced into the book yesterday and read that." I wonder what determines the *selection* of memory, why does one childish experience or impression stand out so luminous and solid against the, for the most part, vague and

misty background? The things we remember have a *first-
timeness* about them which suggests that that may be the reason
of their survival. I must ask Wm. some day if there is any
theory on the subject, or better, whether 'tis wórth a theory.
I remember so distinctly the first time I was conscious of a
purely intellectual process. 'Twas the summer of '56 which we
spent in Boulogne and the parents of Mlle. Marie Boningue[151]
our governess had a *campagne* on the outskirts and invited us
to spend the day, perhaps Marie's fête-day. A large and shabby
calèche came for us into which we were packed, save Wm.; all
I can remember of the drive was a never-ending ribbon of dust
stretching in front and the anguish greater even than usual of
Wilky's and Bob's heels grinding into my shins. Marie told
us that her father had a scar upon his face caused by a bad
scald in his youth and we must be sure and not look at him
as he was very sensitive. How I remember the painful conflict
between sympathy and the desire to look and the fear that my
baseness should be discovered by the good man as he sat at the
head of the table in charge of a big frosted-cake sprinkled o'er
with those pink and white worms in which lurk the caraway
seed. How easy 'twould be to picture one's youth as a perpetual
escape from that abhorred object!—I wonder if it is a blight
upon children still?—But to arrive at the first flowering of me
Intellect! We were turned into the garden to play, a sandy
or rather dusty expanse with nothing in it, as I remember, but
two or three scrubby apple-trees, from one of which hung a
swing. As time went on Wilky and Bob disappeared, not to my
grief, and the Boningues. Harry was sitting in the swing and I
came up and stood near by as the sun began to slant over the
desolate expanse, as the dréady h[ou]rs, with that endlessness
which they have for infancy, passed, when Harry suddenly
exclaimed: "This might certainly be called pleasure under
difficulties!" The stir of my whole being in response to the

[151] Mlle. Boningue is also remembered by Henry James in Chapter XXII of
A Small Boy and Others.

substance and exquisite, *original* form of this remark almost makes my heart beat now with the sisterly pride which was then awakened and it came to me in a flash, the higher nature of his appeal to the mind, as compared to the rudimentary solicitations which usually produced my childish explosions of laughter; and I can also feel distinctly the sense of self-satisfaction in that I could not only perceive, but appreciate this subtlety, as if I had acquired a new sense, a sense whereby to measure intellectual things, wit as distinguished from giggling, for example.

July 18th

How well one has to be, to be ill! These confidences reveal to you, dear Inconnu, so much mental debility that I don't want to rehearse herein my physical collapses in detail as well, altho' I am unable to escape a general tone of lamentation. But this last prostration was rather excessive and comic in its combination, consisting of one of my usual attacks of rheumatic gout in that dissipated organ known in the family as "Alice's tum," in conjunction with an ulcerated tooth, and a very bad crick in my neck. By taking a very small dose of morphia, the first in three years, I was able to steady my nerves and *experience* the pain without distraction, for there is something very exhilarating in shivering whacks of crude pain which seem to lift you out of the present and its sophistications (great Men unable to have a tooth out without gas!) and ally you to long gone generations rent and torn with tooth-ache such as we can't dream of. I didn't succumb and send for my Primrose Knight, having no faith in anything but that time-honoured nostrum Patience, with its simple ingredients of refraining from muscular contractions and vocal exclamations lest you find yourself in a worse fix than you are already in!

July 28t

I lay in a meadow until the unwrinkled serenity entered int
my bones and made me one with the browsing kine, the stil
greenery, the drifting clouds, and the swooping birds.

July 29t

I have had a blow! I have been counting day by day that th
blessed Henry would be back by Aug. 1st, when Lo! he has pu
it off to the 13th. He does not suspect that I have been badl
ill, so 'tis all right. I have taken to being sentimental and home
sick for him, I generally rather enjoy a romantic pose when h
is off,—"an orphan," as Gen. Butler (wasn't it?) used to say
a friendless wisp of femininity tossed upon the breeze of hazar
in the land of the stranger, etc., etc.

When a French book is bad 'tis bad indeed, nothing coul
be poorer than *Toute une Jeunesse* of Coppée,[152] milk and wate
is strong drink to it. There is a review of Anatole France's[1]
La Vie Littéraire in the *Speaker*, of such an incredible crudit
that it's inconceivable that any reputable sheet which desired a
intellectual standing could have printed it. The book, Vol. II., i
full of subtlety, beauty, grace and humanity, oh! the coars
possibilities of the British fibre. Dear old Mr. Boott came one da
before I was ill, stopping over one [train].[154]

August 13t

As they drop off, how we bury ourselves, bit by bit, along th
dusty highway to the end! The especial facets of our being
which turned towards each one will nevermore be played upor

---

[152] François Coppée (1842–1908), French novelist and short-story writer.
[153] Anatole France (1844–1924), French novelist, critic, and man of letters
[154] Francis Boott (1813–1904), father of Elizabeth Boott Duveneck and a
friend of Henry James for forty years.

by the rays which he gave forth. How darksome then the last stages if we have not made our own his individual and inextinguishable radiance, to warm the memory and illuminate the mind.

August 17th

Anatole France says somewhere: "Tout vaut mieux que de s'écouter vivre,"—which is not to be denied surely, but if destiny, Anatole, offers you no other opportunity you will find that if you lend an indulgent and imaginative ear you may strike, even from that small shrill key-board, all the notes of melody, comedy and tragedy.

August 18th

There has come such a change in me. A congenital faith flows thro' me like a limpid stream, making the arid places green, a spontaneous irrigator of which the snags of doubt have never interrupted [n]or made turbid the easily flowing current. A faith which is my mental and moral respiration which needs no revelation but experience and whose only ritual is daily conduct. Thro' my childhood and youth and until within the last few years, the thought of the end as an entrance into spiritual existence, where aspirations are a fulfilment, was a perpetual and necessary inspiration, but now, altho' intellectually non-existence is more ungraspable and inconceivable than ever, all longing for fulfilment, all passion to achieve has died down within me and whether the great Mystery resolves itself into eternal Death or glorious Life, I contemplate either with equal serenity. It is that the long ceaseless strain and tension have worn out all aspiration save the one for Rest! And also that the shaping period is passed and one is fitted to every limitation through the long custom of surrender.

LE RÊVE.

Vous me demandez qui je vois en rêve?
Et gai, c'est vraiment la fille du roi;
Elle ne veut pas d'autre ami que moi.
Partons, joli cœur, la lune se lève.

Sa robe, qui traîne, est en satin blanc,
Son peigne est d'argent et de pierreries;
La lune se lève au ras des prairies.
Partons, joli cœur, je suis ton galant.

Un grand manteau d'or couvre ses épaules,
Et moi dont la veste est de vieux coutil!
Partons, joli cœur, pour le Bois-Gentil.
La lune se lève au-dessous des saules.

Comme un enfant joue avec un oiseau,
Elle tient ma vie entre ses mains blanches.
La lune se lève au milieu des branches,
Partons, joli cœur, et prends ton fuseau.

Dieu merci, la chose est assez prouvée,
Rien ne vaut l'amour pour être content.
Ma mie est si belle, et je l'aime tant!
Partons, joli cœur, la lune est levée.

GABRIEL VICAIRE[155]

[155] Gabriel Vicaire (1848–1900), French writer of satirical light verse.

South Kensington

1890-1891

September 12th

TWAS NO GO! I went under on Saturday, August 2nd and administered an electric shock to Harry which brought him from the Paradisino at Vallombrosa to immure himself, without a murmur, in my squalid indigestions. He avenged himself upon Katharine, who received his telegram on August 6th, and by September 2nd had dug me out and transplanted [me] to these comfortable quarters, hoping for a French cook, the only cure for dyspepsia and I feel already much less like a mildewed toad-stool. There seems a faint hope that I may fizzle out, but the Monster *Rebound*, which holds me in its remorseless clutch, I am sure will gather itself up for many another spurt. Dr. Baldwin[1] from Florence has been staying with Harry—I didn't see him but H. and K. both extracted the consoling answer to "Can she die?" that "They sometimes do." This is most cheering to all parties—the only drawback being that it will probably be in my sleep so that I shall not be one of the audience, dreadful fraud! a creature who has been denied all dramatic episodes might be allowed, I think, to assist at her extinction. I know I shall slump at the 11th hour, and it would complete it all so to watch the rags and tatters of one's Vanity in its insolent struggle with the Absolute, as the curtain rolls down on this jocose humbuggery called Life!

[1] Dr. W. W. Baldwin, friend of Henry James, was an American expatriate physician who had a flourishing practice in Florence for many years.

K. brought some sweet potatoes to Miss Blanche Leppington —she writes: "The yams are queer but good. I told the good-man of our house to try them, he and his wife. I think he expressed the general sentiments. "Yes, he liked them very well, not but what he felt you wouldn't like to be tied up to them, the same as you were to a potato." This expresses the national attitude so perfectly to the "boiled potato," which haunts and pursues at every turn; when mashed they call it "very rich."

Katharine calls my Philippics *Jacqueries*, I think that "Jim crackeries," as Howells says, is better. Two friends said, one to the other—"So Miss Tennant has caught a lion."—"A tiger, rather."—"No, surely Stanley is the King of beasts."

Dr. Baldwin says that as soon as an Italian has a pain that he not only sobs, but the whole household surround him in chorus. Lately he was called to a gallant colonel and found a large, handsome man lying on a bed all gorgeous with pink silk and lace draperies, crying his eyes out because his throat was sore. Dr. B. went to stay at the Spencer Walpoles[2] who govern, I believe, the Isle of Man; in the house was a Lord Bateman, who was very pompous and fussy and à propos of something he did Dr. B. said to him—"Lord Bateman,[3] you remind me of Lord So-and-So in Texas—A man came up to him and said—'If you'll only hump yourself the boys won't mind it if you are a Lord.'" This gave joy to the gubernatorial circle and produced a shower of cigars from Lord B. Clarence King[4] told Harry that a man in Wisconsin, where, it seems, it's very hard to keep grass green—took a friend to see the

---

[2] Sir Spencer Walpole, K.C.B. (1839–1907), was Lieutenant-Governor of the Isle of Man from 1882 to 1893.

[3] William Bareman Bateman Hanbury, 2nd Baron Bateman, (1826–1901) was Lord-Lieutenant of Hereford from 1852 to 1901.

[4] Clarence King (1842–1901), celebrated geologist and first head of the U.S. Geological Survey. An intimate friend of John Hay and Henry Adams, King was a brilliant conversationalist and wit.

grave of his son—"You have got this beautifully green" said the friend—"Yes, I promised my son on his death-bed to keep his grave green and I'll be damned if I don't, if I have to *paint* it." *There* is the alternative for you, which, as Mrs. Mary Parkman said, always existed in the Yankee mind.

September 15th

I had a tooth out the other day, curious and interesting like a little lifetime—first, the long drawn drag, then the twist of the hand and the crack of doom! The dentist seized my face in his two hands and exclaimed, "Bravo, Miss James!" and Katharine and Nurse shaking of knee and pale of cheek went on about my "heroism" whilst I, serenely wadded in that sensational paralysis which attends all the simple, rudimentary sensations and experiences common to man, whether tearing of the flesh or of the affections, laughed and laughed at 'em. As long as one doesn't break in two in the middle, I never have been able to see where the "heroism" comes in. Harry had a most eccentric accident in Florence. The evening he arrived he was seized after dinner with a very severe pain in his throat; having had a bad tooth-ache he supposed it had to do with that. The next day he spent with the dentist, and went in the afternoon from the hotel to stay with Dr. Baldwin, his throat becoming more and more sore so that he immediately said to the Doctor, "You must look at my throat"—"Why, you have got something sticking in it and it's green!" He tugged and tugged and brought out a long haricot vert which had wound itself about the root of his tongue, which was already beginning to ulcerate. Think of the dentist, gazing into his mouth all the morning, not having seen a green object.

Emotional expression is infinitely rich and varied of form— the moonlight causes a Yankee butcher to say to his wife— "It's such a beautiful night I can't lie still another minute for I must go out and do some slaughtering."

September 18th

Mrs. Cuyler, who lives in Morristown, New Jersey, was at the Lakes gazing upon some exquisite view and she turned to a chance American and said, "What a lovely spot!" "Yes, I should say so too if I didn't come from the most beautiful place in the world." "What place is that?" "Morristown, New Jersey." This reminds me of the Briton who said to Harry on the Continent that he longed for London because it was so brilliantly lighted at night, compared to all other cities. I asked H. what protest he had made. "Silence!"

In the *Paris Illustré* there is an announcement of Bourget's marriage,[5] in which it says that the stories that the young woman is rich are not true, that her only dower is her beauty and youth, and that any one who knows the "noble heart" of the great analyst knows that he is capable of making a love marriage. I have no doubt that any Frenchman is capable of thinking himself "noble" in doing so. I read somewhere of some Frenchman who prayed every day that physical suffering should be spared him as he was entirely unable to endure it, whereas moral suffering he snapped his fingers at. I wonder if they know what moral suffering is? In the letters and memoirs that one reads they seem to howl alone over the betrayal of fate, their dearest friends, or such-like flimsinesses.

September 24th

This is what H. calls the "Swan-Song." Imagine my entertainment in getting from Mary Cross the *Daily News* extract, a

[5] Bourget married Minnie David on August 21, 1890, and she became a friend also of Henry James.

[6] Pasted in at the bottom of the page under this date is the following clipping:

CHURCH CHARITY

To the Editor *of the* Pall Mall Gazette.

Sir,—The offertories in the Bournemouth churches on Sunday last show the following results:—

Church Expenses and Building Funds	106	12	1
The Poor	2	7	6
Education	0	3	0

European Reputation at the first go off! How fortunate for the male babes that I am physically so debile!

To the Editor of the Nation:

SIR,—For several years past I have lived in provincial England. Although so far from home, every now and then a transatlantic blast, pure and undefiled, fans to a white heat the fervour of my patriotism.

This morning, most appropriately to the day, a lady from one of our Eastern cities applied to my landlady for apartments. In the process of telling her that she had no rooms to let, the landlady said that there was an invalid in the house; whereupon the lady exclaimed: "In that case perhaps it is just as well that you cannot take us in; for my little girl, who is thirteen, likes to have plenty of liberty and to *scream* through the house."

> Yours very truly, INVALID.

ENGLAND, July 4, 1890.

"An invalid American lady, who has for some years past lived 'in provincial England,' has written to a New York paper to tell how now and then 'a transatlantic blast, pure and undefiled, fans the fervour of her patriotism.' On the last occasion it came in the form of 'a lady from one of our Eastern cities,' who happened to apply to the writer's landlady for apartments. It was in the process of informing the visitor that she had not at that moment any apartments to let, that the landlady happened to observe that she had an invalid lodger. 'In that case,' promptly replied the 'lady from one of our Eastern cities,' 'it is perhaps just as well that you cannot take us in; for my little girl, who is thirteen, likes to have plenty of liberty, and to scream through the house.' "[7]

Miss Clarke told me the story at a desperate moment so I sought a desperate remedy. In comparing notes with H. I find that had I brought forth *The Tragic Muse*, I could not have gone through with more *author-processes*. As so often happens in works of genius I had to leave out the chief points, fearing

---

These are monstrous figures!—Yours obediently,

> H. Ashworth Taylor

24, Hereford-square, S.W., March 14.

[7] *Daily News*, July 29 1890.

length and the editorial veto: which was that Miss C.'s passive manner of relating the tale illustrated very well the absence of reaction in the British masses against the accidents of life, making an instructive contrast of type to that of the aggressive infant from beyond sea and the inability of the American Mother to imagine a momentary suppression of the screams in favour of the Invalid; but Shakespeare may have felt Othello commonplace! We were much surprised in coming to this expensive spot to find not only many but vociferous children rushing thro' the corridors, shouting as if they were at Saratoga—the explanation is that they are *Australian*, the atmospheric effect of the new land—'tis all in the environment.

"Another of the good stories told in 'London Street Arabs' is that of a little boy of six, who declared that he loved Christmas-day because on Christmas-eve he hung up his stocking, and next morning he found a present inside. 'What did you find last Christmas?' was Mrs. Stanley's question. 'A ha'penny,' he replied, smiling with pleasure at the recollection; but he added, truthfully, 'I put it in myself overnight.' "

How blessed it is that our ha'pence never run short, we give them to ourselves complacently to the end. It is so amusing watching Katharine and even little Nurse managing me, and the feeling of acquiescence and sense of their wisdom and [my] desire to play into their hands and meet them half-way, is very curious and diverting.

> When I am dead, my dearest,
>   Sing no sad songs for me.
> Plant thou no roses at my head
>   Nor shady cypress tree.
> Be the green grass above me
>   With showers and dewdrops wet;
> And if thou wilt, remember,
>   And if thou wilt, forget.
>
> CHRISTINA ROSSETTI

"An inquest was held on Thursday at Hull, touching the death of Miss Amy Cullen, aged thirty-three. Miss Cullen, who resided by herself, was found dead in bed on Wednesday morning, having poisoned herself with 'vermin killer.' It appeared that deceased has been engaged to be married to a clerk named John Aston. Mr. Aston stated that he had known the deceased for many years. He was engaged to be married to her, and that engagement took place within the last fortnight. On Monday night he had requested her by letter to break off the engagement. On Tuesday morning he received a letter from her. It was dated August 19th, and was as follows:—

DEAR JACK,—You have done right in letting me know the truth in time, instead of leaving me to find it out when it was too late. I think I can give you a motive. You could not marry one woman while loving another; but no woman will ever love you as I did. Perhaps you hardly realized how dear you were to me. You cannot gauge the depth or intensity of that love which you thus carelessly fling away as a thing not worth keeping. Pride would forbid me saying this to you if I had not made up my mind not to live; but what I could not say living I can say dying, for, oh, my darling, I cannot live without you. After the one glimpse of heaven that you have shown me I dare not face life with the prospect of never seeing you again. By the time you have received this I shall be no more; but don't reproach yourself, dear. It was to be, and you could not have acted otherwise than you did. Good-by, Jack. If there is a God, may He bless and keep you, my darling, and make you happy.
AMY.

I should like to think that you have my piano. I have told Willie that I wished you to have it, but perhaps you will only shrink from it and hate it because it belonged to me.

"The jury returned a verdict to the effect that death was caused by poison, self-administered by deceased while labouring under mental depression caused by the abrupt manner in which the engagement between deceased and Mr. Aston had been broken."

What a beautiful sincerity and dignity! How happy and wise to go in the illusion of her sorrow and never learn that "Jack" is a figment of her fancy, born simply of her rich and generous possibilities.

Katharine had a delectable moment last night as audience to the following—little Nurse came in having been to tea with her aunt; "Well, you've got back, did you have a pleasant time?" "Yes, Miss, very, and my Cousin Tom walked home with me and talked about all sorts of things and asked me what I thought of the effect of commerce upon things now." "He meant, I suppose, whether it elevated the Race." "Yes, that was just it and you know I don't know anything about those things." "Oh, Nurse, how cruel! when I have done nothing but talk to you the last five years about the lamentable condition of the race!" "But you never have said anything about Commerce, Miss." "But I have told you of the debasing influence of Balfour and the parson upon men." "Oh, if he had only said politics, Miss, then I should have known." Such a revelation of my nullity before the jeering K. was a humiliation indeed.

Ah, woe, woe is me! I have not only stopped thinning but I am taking unto myself gross fat, all hopes of peace and rest are vanishing, nothing but the dreary snail-like climb up a little way so as to be able to run down again! And then these doctors tell you that you will die, or *recover!* But you *don't* recover. I have been at these alternations since I was nineteen and I am neither dead nor recovered—as I am now forty-two there has surely been time for either process. I suppose one has a greater sense of intellectual degradation after an interview with a doctor than from any human experience. There is an account of a wedding in the *Standard,* of some New Yorkers—three presents are mentioned, a golden dinner-service from an uncle, a golden dessert-service from a brother and "a book from Lady Something Thynne"—how thin it *do* sound. Can you imagine anything so vulgar as the *gold?* The bride instead of a bouquet had a silver prayer book in her hand, I told H. with disgust, to which he said, "Surely a lady who can eat off gold ought to be able to pray out of silver!" Kath. showed me with great satisfaction her seal with a thistle upon it for device. I asked if she had not thought upon the possible reflections of the impious. This let in a new light, to her amusement, and she said it was chosen by her grandfather—"prophetically" I whispered. 'Tis funny how the most elastic accept without question what came to them before the development of the reactionary moment.

October 4th

A man has committed suicide in St. Paul's which I allow is inexcusably sloppy of him but it has caused a delicious fuss and fluster among the shovel hats. The Cathedral will have to be re-consecrated, they fear, but perhaps they may be able with their highly developed muscles of evasion to wash out the stain of blood by an "Act of Reconciliation!" I can never accustom myself to the word "Celebration" as a religious function; it is so inevitably confounded in the American consciousness with the reverberations of the Glorious Fourth. The Australians also have ice-water for breakfast and the husband lets his wife come into the room first and seat herself at the table first like Americans. Since I have heard of these resemblances the screams of the children are much less terrible. Imagine my amusement in Leamington to find that little Nurse had brought a history of the early Christians from the library in order to confront me with the moment when the tender off shoot of Rome had separated from its Anglican parent! The finding seemed to evade her so she concluded as I became more ill to abandon my conversion then, but yesterday she brought Renan's *Saint Paul*[8] from Cousin Tom hoping to find therein, mayhap, the historic episode. She *is* a good little thing in her faithfulness to her friends whose number is not to be counted and includes all

[8] Renan's *La Vie de Saint Paul* was published in 1869.

classes, but she is much more thrilled by the Porters, a chimney-sweep's family at Hampstead, than by the maid of the Countess of Buckinghamshire whose acquaintance she re-made the other day. She knew the sweeps in '85 when we were at the Toynbee Hall Barnet Cottage thro' July and August. On Sunday she went to see them and says that they have got on so and have such linguistic and grammatical embellishments and ambitions for themselves and lack-a-day! piano-ones for the infant Willy, all this in the face of the Influenza and its devastating consequences in the shape of rheumatic fever, etc. Isn't it touching? No drink, you see! The Bachelers, whose income is 3/6 per week, a pension which he gets from the Militia band in which he played the "Coronet" for 25 years, and abandoned owing to cataracts on both his eyes, gave Nurse three handkerchiefs costing three pence apiece and Mrs. Charlton, our super-excellent charwoman used to bring a cauliflower and vegetable marrow now and then, out of their allotment garden. They seem neither [of them] to feel the pressure of poverty to the painful extent of the Duchess of Westminster[9] who from a letter which I read somewhere had to inflict the following humiliation upon herself; she writes to the committee of some association for the furtherance of Art Education, I think among young women, that when she had promised to subscribe £20 for five years, she hadn't realized how irksome it would become and that she must consequently retract it—such ignominies must be a large price to pay for being a Duchess! Harry told such a touching episode of his late travels. After the Passion Play they stayed for a week at Garmisch, a most lovely Tyrolean Valley, where gentle sunny Nature was complemented by smiling benignant peasant[s] outvying each other to seduce by gracious greeting the barbarian invader, Mrs.—[10]

[9] The widowed Duke of Westminster, Hugh-Lupus Grosvenor (1825–1899), had married Catherine Cavendish, daughter of the 2nd Baron Chesham in 1882. He owned about 30,000 acres in Cheshire and Flintshire and 600 acres in London, also Grosvenor House Gallery and many race horses.

[10] Henry James had traveled to the Passion Play with his American friends, the Daniel Curtises, whom he had visited in the Palazzo Barbaro in Venice.

Truth points out the fortuitous conjunction of Archdeacon Farrar[11] with a stipend of £2,000 a year, saying at the Church Congress that the Church would be out of touch with the masses until a Mendicant Brotherhood was established! Some years ago the Bishop of Exeter, I think, justified himself for having confirmed some imbeciles by relating that one of 'em "silly Billy," had on his death-bed given expression to the following glorious reflection—"What does silly Billy see, three in one, and one in three!"

William has for several years past read the Bible to his boys and expounded! as he went. The other day little Billy exclaimed—"But Father, who is Jehovah *anyhow?*" This must have been a blow after three years of complacently supposed lucidity. Some years ago, when Harry was five or thereabouts, Wm. undertook to explain to him the nature of God and hearing that he was everywhere asked whether he was the chair or the table. "Oh no, God isn't a thing He is a spirit, He is everywhere about us, He pervades"—"Oh, then he is a skunk!" How could the word "pervades" suggest anything else to an American child! Her Yankee Grace of Marlboro,[12] who it seems isn't smiled upon by London, surely a sign of Grace, enriches her references to herself by the constant introduction of her Grace-ship into her anecdotes. She was telling of a visit she had made to some Rothschild and how he had given her every object she admired. Her receptivity had finally drawn its line before something and she left saying "Oh, no *not* that!" But when she reached her own house a footman came to her with a parcel saying "Here is a parcel, your Grace, which his Grace's valet gave me to give your Grace!"

[11] The Very Rev. Frederic William Farrar (1831–1903) had been appointed Archdeacon of Westminster in 1883.

[12] The Duchess of Marlborough was an American, the former Lilian Warren, daughter of Cicero Price, a commander in the U.S. Navy, and of the widow of Louis Hammersley of New York. She became the second wife of George Charles, 8th Duke of Marlborough, on June 29, 1888.

What is absorbingly interesting is the extraordinary ingenuit
of Providence in utilizing the paltriest instruments for th
greatest "shoves." If the irreconcilables only knew it the
would find it more cleanly and amusing to wait serenely fo
the doomed moment when the extinct survival dances gayl
to his own destruction and by some grotesque inevitable ac
of folly strips himself for even the animal intelligence. Thin
in the last decade of the undermining of the monarchical trad
tion by the Prince of Wales and his "Semitic bankers and Amer
ican Adventuresses," the Orleanists with their Boulanger, no
even a bag of wind, and the colossal William and his ful
length portraits! How it fills one with wonder to see peopl
old eno' to have stored experience never apparently suspectin
that of all the arts the art of living is the most exquisite an
rewarding and that it is not brought to perfection by wallow
ing in disabilities, ceaseless plaints of the machinery of life an
the especial tasks fallen to their lot. The paralytic on his couc
can have if he wants them wider experiences than Stanle
slaughtering savages, the two roomed cottage may enclose a
infinitely richer, sweeter domestic harmony than the palace; an
the peaceful cotton-spinner win victories beside which thos
of the reverberating general are dust and ashes—let us no
waste then the sacred fire and wear away the tissues in th
vulgar pursuit of what others have and we have not; admittin
defeat isn't the way to conquer and from every failure imperish
able experience survives.

October 12t.

Surely, this poor lady's situation is pathetic. Katharine knew
at Hyères an English lady who had married a Spanish or Frenc
cavalry officer. He died leaving her with a daughter. She late
married a curate, by name Hobson or Hodgson by whom sh
had nine children. One day K. was calling upon her and th
eldest daughter who was a fantastic miss suddenly jumped u

and seized two photos standing on the table and presented them to her, saying, "Look at this, then at that, and imagine how Mamma after having been the wife of the one can ever have married the other."

There, indeed, were the fierce mustachios of the dashing defunct, and the pasty stodgy Hobson in melancholy contrast. On the other side of the room was the sister of the lady, the wife of an M. P. reproaching her with the superfluity of the pledges given to Hobson, "How can we talk to the people at the East-End if you in the clerical line persist in having such families!" Between this upper and nether mill-stone the poor lady sat unremonstrant and unmurmuring!

Answer to a Cambridge Exam paper. "Very little is known of the early life of Christ. The little that is known we get from Archdeacon Farrar."

October 20th

Mr. Boott said last summer that he never got used to the immutable Englishry of it. The day after he landed it always came again as a surprise; "as if he had waked up in Parent's Assistant." William, writing after a snow-storm at home, says— "The light is shrieking away outside." Howells says of New York—"Such an uproar to the eye." A curious conjunction of books, Kath. reading me *Don Quixote;* Nurse *David Copperfield;* and I to myself Maupassant's *Fort Comme La Mort*— between these two robust ones *David Copperfield* is feeble eno', Micawber the only substance. Maupassant's story "The Coward," a man shooting himself because he is sure he won't have the right attitude in a duel which he is to fight the next day, is most admirable, how it is the paraphernalia only that masters us! The prizes pursued and the man who attains fill one with joy at never having had the ghost of a chance in the race.

October 25t.

K. says this is a shocking hotel; she is always coming, at the turn of the stairs, upon a waiter and chambermaid, rebounding at sound of her, from osculatory relaxations. How different their life from ours! We toil not to be sure, but do we ever attain the Ideal as they must in the surreptitious kiss?

K. went the other day to a beautiful old house at Mortlake Temple Grove. It has been for many years a private school to prepare infants for Eton, etc. and was originally built by Sir William Temple. She described all the luxuries and beauty provided for the pampered young ones and Nurse, a few day after, went to the Wandsworth infirmary where she has a friend nursing and brought back as *pendant* the following—a little girl of twelve dying of consumption so thin and shriveled that she seemed only five or six. Her mother was in a mad-house from drink and her father had died the week before in a drunken fit, and there she lay trying to smile over some biscuits just given to her; a little boy with a crooked spine dying of cancer and so on! Nurse went to old Mrs. Bond's funeral in Leamington; the family, daughter and grandchildren, stood by the grave and, after a long wait, a parson came, pulled a book out of his pocket, read over the service, turned on his heel and walked away—not only never spoke to the family but did not even look at them!

October 26th

William uses an excellent expression when he says in his paper on the "Hidden Self"[13] that the nervous victim "abandons" certain portions of his consciousness. It may be the word commonly used by his kind. It is just the right one at any rate

[13] William James's paper "The Hidden Self" had appeared in *Scribner's* in March 1890. Alice is referring to her brother's discussion of Binet's "contractions of the field of consciousness" in hysterical persons.

altho' I have never unfortunately been able to abandon my consciousness and get five minutes' rest. I have passed thro' an infinite succession of conscious abandonments and in looking back now I see how it began in my childhood, altho' I wasn't conscious of the necessity until '67 or '68 when I broke down first, acutely, and had violent turns of hysteria. As I lay prostrate after the storm with my mind luminous and active and susceptible of the clearest, strongest impressions, I saw so distinctly that it was a fight simply between my body and my will, a battle in which the former was to be triumphant to the end. Owing to some physical weakness, excess of nervous susceptibility, the moral power *pauses*, as it were for a moment, and refuses to maintain muscular sanity, worn out with the strain of its constabulary functions. As I used to sit immovable reading in the library with waves of violent inclination suddenly invading my muscles taking some one of their myriad forms such as throwing myself out of the window, or knocking off the head of the benignant pater as he sat with his silver locks, writing at his table, it used to seem to me that the only difference between me and the insane was that I had not only all the horrors and suffering of insanity but the duties of doctor, nurse, and strait-jacket imposed upon me, too. Conceive of never being without the sense that if you let yourself go for a moment your mechanism will fall into pie and that at some given moment you must abandon it all, let the dykes break and the flood sweep in, acknowledging yourself abjectly impotent before the immutable laws. When all one's moral and natural stock in trade is a temperament forbidding the abandonment of an inch or the relaxation of a muscle, 'tis a never-ending fight. When the fancy took me of a morning at school to *study* my lessons by way of variety instead of shirking or wiggling thro' the most impossible sensations of upheaval, violent revolt in my head overtook me so that I had to "abandon" my brain, as it were. So it has always been, anything that sticks of itself is free to do so, but conscious and continuous cerebration is an impossible exercise and from just behind the eyes my head feels like a dense jungle into which no ray of light has ever penetrated. So, with the rest, you abandon the pit of your stomach, the palms of your hands, the soles of your feet, and refuse to keep them sane when you find in turn one moral impression after another producing despair in the one, terror in the other, anxiety in the third and so on until life becomes one long flight from remote suggestion and complicated eluding of the multifold traps set for your undoing.

November 7th

I must "abandon" the rhetorical part of me and forego the eloquent peroration with which I meant to embellish the above on the ignorant asininity of the medical profession in its treatment of nervous disorders. The seething part of me has also given out and had to be abandoned. We were going to pitch our tent with a view to permanence in Tunbridge Wells but I have gone into pie, so remaining here at loose ends seemed the only exit from chaos. We have very good rooms and my bedroom is the only room I have been in [in] England where I have not been tossed and rustled by the wind. It is close to the excellent Henry whose anxious and affect[ionate] mind is gratified by keeping a daily eye upon the fading flower, for our hopes have sprung up again, the folds of flesh which were beginning to drape themselves about the bones having almost vanished. As dissolution advances I am to be carried to H.'s flat it not being æsthetic to die in an hotel, tho' K. says it is conducted with perfect decency, the *residuum* being carried down the back stairs whilst the people are at lunch or dinner so that unless your friends or attendants are afflicted with reverberating sorrow your neighbour never suspects that a little race has been run next door. They have strange ways here, of shutting all the windows and doors as soon as a person dies. Nurse says that the corpses turn black if exposed to the air.

I suppose it is some climatic effect. They don't bury them apparently for four or five days and ice seems to be rarely used, and I am much puzzled to know how they arrange about it for the middle-class English house has the minimum of bedrooms and the maximum of progeny and how they are disposed of during these prolonged and painful periods is a dark problem.

They call water on the knee, fluid on the joint, which for some reason makes one smile.

Middle life brings such interest as we see unfolded gradually the destinies of our friends and they take the stamp given by the end, and it occupies me more than a little to fancy what friend No. 1 can possibly stand for! A life lifted out of all material care or temptation to which all the rudimentary impulses were unknown, a collection simply of fantastic *un*productive emotions enclosed within tissue paper. Walls, rent equally by pleasure as by pain—animated by a never-ceasing belief in and longing for *action*, relentlessly denied, all safety-valves shut down in the way of "the busy ineffectiveness of women." As I look up and find my better half Katharine effectually removing certain streaks of grime from the wall paper with a bit of india rubber my spirits rise in the hope that the unremitting and various nature of her muscular contractions may shed a glamour over her humiliated appendage.

November 8th

Developing the decorative sense in the slums has its drawbacks. An aunt of Nurse's has a "Marchioness" in her service, the hue of whose linen is not what it should be. She told her she ought to boil her things, "Please, ma'am when I scrubs 'em it tears the *lyce!*" These objects were festooned about in all directions with rags of *lace!* It can be bought for ha'penny a yard. 'Tis long since I felt impressive but I confess I never expected to feel as little potent as after this[:] a friend asked Katharine whether I read much and K. said when I was well enough to.

"Oh, yes, I suppose Mrs. Sidgwick gives her lists of books. Imagine being classed among those amorphous creatures to whom a book is a book simply, their reading decided by propinquity, or a title remembered. So revolting to all mankind my dear Briton, is your pervasive "virtuous" pose of rising superior to the normal man with your "brotherly love," "civilizing processes" and the rest of it, that until you do things in the name of the Devil, of Stanley, or of whoever may be the inspiring Brute of the moment, you cannot complain at the manifestation of savage joy on the part of other nations at the unmasking of your supreme genius for canting Humbug. Retribution cometh swiftly! The Emin Pasha Relief Expedition bubble has been pricked. What a stench in the nostrils! What pin-points of *result* from it all save the melting down of 800 Zanzibari porters into 240![14]

November 9th

The Nursling has me more often than not. The other day she said, "You have had a dreary day today, Miss," whereupon I must needs put on a frill and say "Oh, no, it hasn't been dreary it's simply destiny and *as* destiny nothing is dreary, you know." —she said nothing, being skilled in the withering silence. A little while after the Australian children burst forth in their accustomary roar and I said, "What a wretched life that poor nurse must have with those children!" "Yes, it *seems* dreary eno', but, you know, it is her destiny, Miss." The "as" above reminds me of another. K. heard of some mind-curers, Charles and Susan Bowles, who are giving lectures. She went to hear them and found what they said much more coherent than any

[14] Emin Pasha was Eduard Schnitzer (1840–1892), German doctor, traveler, administrator, and naturalist. After service in Turkey and Albania he was raised to the rank of Pasha by the Turks. Later he became governor of an Egyptian province in the Sudan; and while carrying out a colonial expedition on behalf of Germany he was threatened by an uprising of the Mahdists, from which Stanley, the English explorer, rescued him.

of those she had heard at home. I thought it would be "fun"
to see and hear the process so "Susan" was invited to give me
a treatment. She bade me shut my eyes and say over to myself,
"I am a child of God and *as* such pure, perfect and without
flaw!" My mind of course began skipping about the horizon
and every now and then I was recalled by her saying "Now,
rest your mind from the thought," "Now, bring your mind
back to the thought." After it was over she said I was too much
barricaded by my "intellectual friends," I was too intellectual,
etc., which methought a delicious fetch. She nobly declined
remuneration, because it was such a pleasure to meet a "New
England mind," etc. I think she is sincere, but what a revelation
of mental penury in the race that that's the sort of thing that
impresses the mass. K. overheard the man Haweis at one of
the lectures saying, "We have been trying all the time to raise
man up, but you have hit it, for you are bringing the *spirit
down.*" He spake wiser than he knew.

Harry came in the other day quite sickened from a conversation he had been listening to which he said gave him a stronger
impression of the demoralization of English society than anything he had ever heard. He had been calling upon a lady
whom he knows very well and who is very well connected; two
gentlemen were there, one young, the other old; one of them
asked about one of the sons who has just failed in an exam.
for one of the services, when she said he had just had an offer
of a place his opinion of which she would like to have. Pulitzer,[15]
the ex-editor of the *New York World*, had applied to the British
embassy in Paris to recommend him a young man of good family to act as his secretary, write his letters, etc., but chiefly to
be socially useful in attracting people to the house—to act, in
short, evidently, as a decoy duck to Pulitzer's gilded salons. A
young man rejoicing in the name of Claude Ponsonby had
fulfilled the functions for three years, and had just been married
to an American, Pulitzer having given him a "dot" of £30,000

[15] Joseph Pulitzer (1847–1911), American newspaper publisher.

and it was presumable that his successor would fare equally well. The Englishmen both thought it would be "a jolly life." She then turned and asked H. what he thought—"I would rather sweep the dirtiest crossing in London!" At which rejoinder staring amazement! H. asked if she knew Pulitzer's history that he had made his money editing the vulgarest conceivable newspaper, oh, yes, she knew all about him and her only anxiety was that the son who was a complete failure might fail in getting the enviable berth. The snobling, it appears, has a strong taste for medicine but thinks it a social disgrace to be a doctor, conceiving a social tout to a Pulitzer to be a nobler form of man.

In coming home, H. saw tossing about among a lot of photos of actresses and ballet girls in a shop, a photo of the beautiful Lady Helen Duncombe—who has just married some one, lying out on a chair or sofa with her arms crossed over her head—to this have all the fine heredities brought the present generation of the aristocracy—how they are crumbling and mouldering from within! Harry said he entirely disbelieved the story of the £30,000 marriage present. I remember H. telling me some years ago that Pulitzer came to him and asked him to write some stories for the *New York World*, that the only essential quality for them was that they mustn't have "anything literary" about them. Have you ever read them!

Whilst we are upon the scum, this story shows what a very thin surface of prosperity those most *en évidence* must often have to skim over. A certain young man was elected to Parliament by the Gentlemanly Party last year, and hasn't a ragged exterior, but a friend of Harry's told him last winter that she invited him to dinner, she lives in Paris, and that he stayed on trying to sit out, apparently, another gentleman who had lingered after the others. This surprised her as she knew him very slightly, finally he got up and left the drawing-room but she thought she heard him talking to the butler in the ante-chamber for some time. A few days after the butler, an ancient family appendage, came to her and told her that the gentleman had asked him to lend him 200 francs, as he was leaving the house, that he would return them the next day, he had done so happening to have them on hand like a thrifty Frenchman, but they had not as yet been returned. The lady told him to write for them which he did and received an answer that they should be paid in a day or two. Several weeks passed however before the money was paid, which it finally was. Imagine borrowing money of a butler!

I remember in old times, in childhood, how amused I used to be by the Temples[16] and their "pride" and aristocracy and "spirited" nature, etc.,—which, however, didn't seem to prevent their living at the expense of any one who undertook the job—Bob's scorn of the "hatter," as he used to call Mr. Tweedy, and yet perfect willingness to spend his money should it fall in his way. "Noblesse oblige" doesn't seem to be the performance of noble deeds, but the doing of ignoble ones with social impunity and with an increase personally of your snobbish pretensions.

November 23rd

How enriching to the soul at this moment of distended vulgarians, Bismarcks, Williams the Second, Stanley etc., to come upon a modesty like Moltke's![17] The great having fed so exclusively the eye and ear seem so absolutely extinct when their lying in state is done with, while the unheard of are revealed by the great leveller and exalted out of all proportion with their meek and lowly estate.

Kath. smiles indulgently at the manner in which I turn up and rake over the thin soil of Nurse's little substance, but as the gourmet knows none of the satisfaction which bread and

[16] The Temple children were cousins of the Jameses. Catherine Margaret James (1820–1854), sister of the elder Henry James, married Col. Robert Emmet Temple (1808–1854).
[17] Count Helmuth Karl Bernhard von Moltke (1800–1891), Prussian field marshal and at the end of his life head of Germany's council for national defense.

cheese yield to the hungry organism so the well perceive not the tiny flowerets of observation and impression which spring up on the field of restricted vision, full of perfume and colour, however fertilized they may be by intention.

Altho' the soil above referred to is totally without any snobbish germs being more destitute of that fundamental quality than that [of] any one I ever came in contact with, man, woman or child, English or American, rich or poor, she has revealed to me the workings of those hitherto mysterious but powerful factors in life, a "sense of authority," and a "sense of your betters," by bringing it home to me that I stood to her as these two Absolute quantities. Imagine the inflation for my American human accident consciousness in suddenly finding itself a substance apart, a "Better," an "Authority" whose quoted word carries paralysis and finality to the arguments of the Steward's room. There is a certain Stock, a maid, "whom I always feel like contradicting, Miss"—(a case of what Miss Clarke at Leam[ington] used to call "two temperatures coming into contact that never can agree"), with whom we discuss the questions of the moment and annihilate apparently—"Of course I always say that I know nothing about it myself, Miss, but I know some one who says so and so. 'Who is that?' 'My patient, Miss James, and *she* must know.'" And no blasphemy has as yet been reported from Stock!—Let us trust that she breathes a "damn" in her *fer intérieur*. The amazing part of it is that it is in matters of opinion and of her own personality, what is most sacred to us, that she surrenders her individuality completely, while in little trifles about arranging the room, or what not, she is as obstinate as a healthy mule. Last month she went upon her holiday, the day was settled but when the morning came I thought it best as an oculist was coming to see me for her to put off going until the next day. As she was dressing me it suddenly crystallized within me that two of her teeth, they are all at absurd angles, must come out, so K. led her off to the dentist and had the fangs extracted, she meanwhile absolutely passive and unremonstrant under this arbitrary and sanguinary exchange of relaxations.

The landlady at Leam[ington] used to abuse the Radical Mayor simply because he had been a poor boy. "Why, he worked for a builder and can't know anything, now one of the gentlemen would know, Miss, just what we wanted." She despised him simply because he was one of her *own kind* and couldn't perceive that his rise shoved her up a bit, whilst a stodgy foxhunting squire, in virtue of his having been always ignorant, idle and selfish she enthusiastically prostrated herself before. It's this vast class in England, the only nation where it exists, which like the cringing dog is ready to lick the hand that chastises, that gives you in time what you expect so little at first, a sense of unmanliness. It is found in different degrees all through the ascending scale. During the Jubilee months the Prince of Wales drove out of Marl[borough] House one day and came upon a fainting soldier, he stopped and had the man carried into the garden at Marl[borough] H[ouse]. Whereupon a shower of letters descended upon the *Standard* describing this noble feat, from Colonels, Majors, captains, each one with his own version of the cosmic event, what the Prince said, how he stood, whether he sat and all the rest of it until I fairly vomited! And if you only saw the great, handsome God-like creature that officer can be! Harry saw Stanley Clarke once, receiving his "orders" from the Prince, and his manner was precisely that of Smith before him and the manner of the P[rince] just that of a kind master to an upper servant. Col. Clarke remains a lacquey still altho' his wife inherited £70,000 from Sir John Rose.[18] Mrs. Sloane-Stanley thus describes her father, and Julia, Lady Tweeddale,[19] "You can't imagine how

---

[18] Sir John Rose (1820-1888), Canadian statesman and financier. He was remotely connected with the James's Temple relatives, having married Charlotte, a daughter of Robert Temple, of Rutland, Vermont, Lady Rose died in 1883.

[19] Julia Lady Tweeddale, daughter of Keith Stewart Mackenzie of Seaforth, and widow of the 9th Marquess of Tweeddale, married Sir John Rose on January 24, 1887.

strange it was to see Father in love and to see her sitting upon his poor old knee."

November 24th

The ways of Providence *is* peculiar. The substance-full Lady Rosebery[20] dies and a rag-tag like me is left fluttering in the breeze! It must be a strangely muddled moment when it begins to dawn upon the Personage that they are not all there. I trust that matters are conducted humanely, and the poor soul let down easily. Imagine having to begin to learn there that you are simply an atom and not in your essence a future Prime-Ministress of the Great Little Kingdom.

Dr. Ogle tells the following—he once told a story in which he said, "I am in the hands of an unscrupulous Providence." Some half an hour after, a man came up to him and said: "A little while ago you said, 'I am in the hands of an unscrupulous Providence,' you must have meant to say, an inscrutable Providence." The Doctor must have felt himself *then* in the hands of an inscrutable Providence!

November 30th

Could there be a more dramatic irony? Parnell after his years of desperate struggle, within a few months, more or less, of a superb victory, escaping from the huge paraphernalia of the Commission built up so laboriously to crush him, smirched and of necessity to be eclipsed only for a short time by the loathsome divorce-suit, pushed on by relentless fate not only to ruin himself in the present but by a few strokes of his pen to brand himself as infamous for all history. What a heart sickening day was yesterday and how I wept over Parnell's Manifesto with its portent of the possible death and burial of Home Rule,[21]

[20] Hannah de Rothschild (1851–1890) married in 1878 Archibald, 5th Earl of Rosebery.

[21] Parnell refused to resign his seat after having been named co-respondent in the O'Shea divorce suit and accused Gladstone and the Liberal party of betraying the Irish.

for if tomorrow the Irish pronounce for him one's ear must turn itself, one's heart close itself against the woes of that tragic land. No cause is sacred eno' to be fought with such a base tool, the betrayer of his friend, the betrayer of his allies, the betrayer of his country! Alleviations come at unexpected moments and my tears were dryed by another *irony!* Renan was reported in the *Standard* as saying that Parnell should take Gladstone's advice, that he was a great statesman and could by no possibility be influenced by anything but *the political necessities* of the situation so that it was most impolitic to resist him. Oh, the French! their delicious completeness, a moral subtlety worthy surely of the author of *L'Abbesse de Jouarrés.*[22]

I hear that there is one more to be added to the grandchildren! To the virginal bosom 'twould seem as if having entailed human woe upon three hapless souls might have satisfied even a mother's heart, but compassion is, apparently, an impulse unknown to parental bowels. The married, however, thro' their ignoble state are doomed to shatter all the ideals of the soaring spinster. There is an unknown "lady" quantity here, who has only been married a year, and she has already given her wedding-dress to her maid! He is the second venture, to be sure, but wouldn't you have supposed that however indurated a realism he may have invested himself with, some pallid ghost of the bridegroom would have lingered, to be cherished still amid the folds of the gown?

December 7th

What possible connection can there be between music and religion and those doleful chords addressed to the Deity at intervals thro' the Sabbath?

---

[22] This was one of Renan's series of *Drames Philosophiques* published between 1878 and 1886.

December 31st, 1890[23]

Unlike Habakkuk, je suis incapable de tout! Katharine exclaimed in despairing accents yesterday, "for Heaven's sake, don't begin upon a subject which makes you rear up in bed!" She is an excellent, convenient creature, but rarely inspired.

As things are, I am sure that this is altogether the best place for me, but it does violence to a primordial instinct and fills one with a constant sense of shame and weakness to turn one's back and not shape the accidents of nativity to one's purpose, and extract from whatever barrenness the fullest and richest measure of development. It may be primitive, but one seems to have missed what was intended and be so far a failure.

How grateful we ought to be that our excellent parents had threshed out all the ignoble superstitions, and did not feel it to be their duty to fill our minds with the dry husks, leaving them *tabulæ rasæ* to receive whatever stamp our individual experience was to give them, so that we had not the bore of wasting our energy in raking over and sweeping out the rubbish. I used to wonder at Father's fulminations against what seemed so extinct, little dreaming until I came here what vitality the ugly things had. The parson they tell you is a link to soap in the slums; but what flavour of godliness can a cleanliness have which involves mental degradation, and what moral elevation can be brought about by a worship propped up by tortuous verbosity and emasculate evasions. Imagine a religion imposed from without, a virtue taught, not as a measure of self respect, but as a means of propitiating a repulsive, vainglorious, grasping deity, and purchasing from him, at a varying scale of prices, a certain moderation of temperature through the dark mystery of the future.

[23] From this date on the manuscript is in the handwriting of Katharine P. Loring, to whom Alice dictated her diary until the day of her death. Miss Loring's spelling and punctuation often differ from Alice's, and have, as necessary, been harmonized with the rest of the text.

The great family event, over which I have been palpitating for the last 18 months or more has come off: *The American*[24] was acted for the first time at Southport, which they call the Brighton of Liverpool, on January 3rd, and seems to have been, as far as audience, Compton and author were concerned, a brilliant success. H. says that Compton acted admirably, and it was delightful to hear and see him (Harry) flushed with the triumph of his first ovation. At the end, he was called for with great insistence, and pushed onto the stage by the delighted and sympathetic company; at the third bow and round of applause, Compton, who was standing with him, turned and seized both his hands and wrung them; very pretty of him, wasn't it? I am so thankful that the dear being has had such a success. The "first nights" to come, we shall be less quivering about. The Comptons, who are the best judges of the pulse of an audience, are radiant about the prospects of the play.

H. says that at about four o'clock he got so nervous that his knees began almost to knock together, that he couldn't eat any dinner, and went off to the theatre and walked about the stage, dusted the mantel-piece, set the pasteboard vases straight, turned down the corners of the rugs, after his usual manner in my apartments, when lo! as soon as the curtain went up, he became as calm as a clock. If H. should have dramatic success now, it will be a very interesting illustration of the law that you cannot either escape or hasten the moment. Almost two years ago he got a letter from Compton, asking him to dramatize *The American* for him; he was going to answer "no," immediately, when he said to himself "No, I'll think about it

[24] *The American* was produced at the Winter Garden Theatre, Southport, by Edward Compton, and was played in the provinces in England and Ireland until the autumn when it was brought to London. For an account of these productions see *The Complete Plays of Henry James* (ed. Leon Edel), 1949. James's letters to the Comptons were published by the actor's son, Compton Mackenzie, in *My Life and Times: Octave Two, 1891–1900* (London, 1963).

for a week," and the result has been this beautiful play, fo
beautiful it is, with its strongly human quality.

As self-revelations are the supreme interest, the following
anecdote in its rounded completeness is valuable, apart from
its comicality. William Archer,[25] the dramatic critic of the
World who, Harry says, is far and away the best of his kind
in London, wrote to Harry proposing to go to see the play at
Southport. H. discouraged his doing so, on the grounds of the
distance and the cold, but he was there, notwithstanding, on
Saturday night; and Harry, who had never met him before
was introduced to him in one of the entreactes. After the play
was over, he told Balestier[26] to tell Harry that he wished to
speak to him at the hotel. On returning, H. sent a message
inviting him to his sitting-room: upon his entrance, Archer
murmured some words of congratulation upon H's success
adding immediately, "I think it's a play that would be much
more likely to have success in the Provinces than in London,"
and then he began, as by divine mission, to enumerate all it
defects and flaws, and asked why H had done so-and-so, in
stead of just the opposite, etc., etc. To H, of course, heated
from his triumph, these uncalled-for and depressing amenitie
from an entire stranger seemed highly grotesque, none the
less so, that to the eye, by his personal type (that of a dissent
ing minister), the young man seemed by nature, divorced from
all matters theatrical. In spite of the gloom cast over his spirits
H was able to receive it all with perfect urbanity, and the
Comptons etc. coming in to supper before long, he bowed him
out, and served him up as a delectable dish of roast prig, done
to a turn.

But so small is this neat little world of ours, that K picked
up this afternoon a key which fits the Archer lock with exquisite

[25] William Archer (1856–1924), the drama critic and playwright.
[26] Charles Wolcott Balestier (1861–1891), young writer-publisher, had in
terested himself in Henry James's theatricals and acted as his unofficial agent in
promoting them. See James's preface to Balestier's posthumous volume *The
Average Woman* (1892).

precision; she was calling upon a friend who was very much interested about Harry's play, and said that a gentleman dining with them the day before had seen Archer, who said it was a most extraordinary and unheard-of, almost immoral thing, for a tyro to undertake to write a play without consulting a competent dramatic critic! Smile not, but be broadly imaginative and perceive how nobly Archer has really acted: Harry with unparalleled insolence and bravado had dared to write a play without asking him how, but he in the most disinterested manner imaginable, without hope of other reward than the satisfaction of his fabulous fatuity, came notwithstanding, and dealt out for him the full measure of his wisdom; that the play had just been a most brilliant success was, of course, a most trivial detail. How we three laughed and laughed again!

When you come upon these forms of existence, absolutely destitute of imagination and humour, can you wonder at the maddening irritation with which the critic fills the artist soul? who whatever he may not have done has at least *attempted* to create. H replies, "No, but one is so inadequate for it, and would have to be a Frenchman to hate them enough, and to express the irony, scorn and contempt with which one ought to be filled!" H., with his impervious mildness, certainly *is* inadequate to the subject, and remains completely unruffled by the whole fraternity. A propos of literary inclination, Lady Lonsdale,[27] now Lady something else, asked Harry to come to see her at a certain hour one day, as she had something of great importance to consult him about; when H. arrived, she told him that she wanted to write a book about Boucher and Watteau and she wanted him to tell her how to begin a book, to which H. replied "that there is no difficulty in beginning, the trouble is to leave off."

[27] Lady Lonsdale, the former Lady Constance Gladys Herbert, sister of the 13th Earl of Pembroke, was the widow of St. George Henry, 4th Earl of Lonsdale, whom she had married in 1878.

January 10th

The Princess of Monaco told H that Bourget was dining with her one day, when he sat speechless and wrapped in gloom for a long time; suddenly bursting into tears he rushed from the room; on being followed, he was found sobbing with his face in his hands, and on being asked what the matter was, he exclaimed: "La vie! la vie! la vie est si amère!" He is now honeymooning in Algiers, but still in despair.

January 12th

Mrs. Burton,[28] the actress who takes the part of the respectable Mrs. Bread, said, when Harry thanked her after one of the rehearsals, "I *try* and do my best, but you must remember that for the seven years I have acted for Mr. Compton, I have always played the *red-nosed* lady." Picture the obscure tragedy all the hardships and miseries of the lot and no tinsels and spangles, but a red nose simply, for consolation. H. says "Yes she is thrown every night to the jeers of the brutish British public, like a Roman captive into the arena."

Katharine is a most sustaining optimist; she proposed writing for me this morning. I said "Why, you won't have time." "Oh yes, I'm not going until twelve, and by that time you are always back again in bed, fainted."

I read out of the *Standard* that they had finally decided to have a telephone between England and France, when Katharine exclaimed "What courage!—why the French might hurl an epithet at them." The little island cowering between the Channel tunnel on the one side, and the prospective army and navy of poverty stricken "Separated" Ireland on the other penetrates one with a sense of robustness.

---

[28] Alice Burton played the role only while *The American* was on tour.

William says in his *Psychology*: "Genius, in truth, is little more than the faculty of perceiving in an unhabitual way."[29] This seems to the sisterly mind, or heart rather, more felicitous than the long-accustomed "infinite capacity for taking pains," but what length of tether does it allow to our greatly esteemed Cousin for browsing in unaccustomed fields and along the untrodden ways, for *he* only respects himself when he *is* habitual.

This was forcibly impressed upon me by something Mr. Frederick Myers said, in an exceedingly cordial note which he wrote to Harry about *The Tragic Muse*,[30] in which the only sign of Harry's being an alien is that he puts into the mouth of one of his characters, an Englishman, "Never, never," and "Never in the World," "for no Englishman ever said that." This is undoubtedly true, for you *can* absolutely assert what an Englishman never has said, it satisfying his highest craving to crib, cabin and confine his fancies within a dozen or so locutions, as if there were a certain absence of decency in playing with verbal subtleties: "very clever" for example, doing service for the infinite and delicate shades of subdivision to be noted upon the intellectual scale, from Lady Dunlo[31] to Mr. Gladstone; but how could one deny that this or that had been said by a Yankee, for is *his* soul ever more rejoiced than when he has made the next man "sit up" by some start into the open, linguistic or ideal?

[29] The passage occurs in Chapter XIX of William James's *Principles of Psychology*. Alice makes a slight slip in quotation, for her brother wrote "Genius, in truth, means little more . . ." (Not "is little more.")

[30] *The Tragic Muse* had appeared in book form during 1890 after serialization in the *Atlantic Monthly*.

[31] Lady Dunlo, the former Isabel Maude Penrice, had married in 1889 William Frederick Le Poer-Trench, Earl of Clancarty, Viscount Dunlo of Dunlo and Balinasloe, Baron Kilconnel of Garbally, County Galway, in Ireland, who was a peer of the United Kingdom as Viscount Clancarty and Baron Trench of Garbally.

Ellie Emmet,[32] who is staying with her cousins, the Roses, was driving one day with Mrs. Charles; on the carriage turning into Russell Square, Ellie exclaimed "this is where Amelia lived," when a shiver of the unusual brought from Mrs. Rose, "Why, do you take London in that way?" I am as much amused, dear Inconnu (please note the sex! pale shadow of Romance still surviving even in the most rejected and despised by Man) as you can be by these microscopic observations recorded of this mighty race; they are as grotesque as the following, in which the infinitesimal and the colossal were never more happily contrasted. When I was in Leamington, one of my friends asked Harry if I were not coming soon to London: he said "No." "What a loss to London," was the dislocated rejoinder.

The phrase quoted above, "Jamais, jamais de la vie" is taken from the Paris American, and Harry purposely gave it to an Englishman who might be hoped to wander occasionally from the path of rectitude.

A friend said to K. the other day: "You always look so serious; we can never tell whether you are joking or not, I think there ought always to be a twinkle in the eye"—"Yes," said K., "as warning this is a joke." "Is it true that Americans think that we *don't* take jokes?" she pathetically asked.

January 21st

How picturesque and instructive of the Duke of Bedford[33] to commit suicide at this moment of frozen misery, showing his destitution, before the affluence of the slums, of that apparently inextinguishable animal appetite for simple respiration, without which all power and splendour are inoperative against the canker of weariness. It makes it a more perfect whole, that

[32] Ellen James Temple (1850–1920), a cousin of the Jameses, married Christopher Temple Emmet (1822–1884).

[33] Francis Charles Hastings, 9th Duke of Bedford (1819–1891). The obituaries recorded simply that the Duke had been ill and said he died of "a congestion of the lungs."

as his possessions were spoils of the Church, he should outrage the Canon against self slaughter, for the Church may say "Here is our revenge."

The meteorological hysteria which every now and then seizes upon them makes one picture, at last, this Mighty Race which conquers the world in every clime, a huge soft mass of palpitating dread, when confined to its island.

Katharine has all the passion for accuracy of statement characteristic of the child of the "perceiver"; she says her respect for truth is so profound that she rarely ventures to meddle with it.

I told Nurse that when Harry's play came to London, she should go to see it, and have a seat in the stalls. "I think, Miss, I would rather go in the gallery, and then I could get some of the maids to go with me, and I would be sure not to tell them before that it was written by Mr. James, and then if it did not succeed it wouldn't be any matter." This simplifies the complexity of existence!

From the Kensington weekly paper:

"The following postcard reached me on the day after Christmas:—

Civil Service Co-operative Stores.

———

Patrons:
The neighbouring Vicars, Curates,
and
Other Civil Servants.
You are cordially invited to support the above
Stores.

Shares and all particulars may be had in the Vestries of the Churches after Divine Service on Sundays, when the Pew Rents and Subscriptions from Tradespeople and others towards the support of the Clergy and Church will also be received.
Yours faithfully,

A Priest.

The Parson is an unfailing emetic!

From *Truth:*

> Thou shalt Love thy Neighbour as Thyself.
> S. Mark xii. 31.

———

> N. B.—Shopkeepers are affectionately recommended to you as being "a set of people" useful for supplying small articles on credit to suit your convenience. They also exhibit "showbills" in their windows; they help to pay the Rates and Taxes; their competition keeps down prices; they subscribe to the Church; and they always vote for the union of Church and State. But—
> Ye cannot serve God and Mammon.
> S. Matthew vi. 24."

"In constructing the earlier basis of a model, sculptors generally commence by moulding the form without drapery of any sort, and it was the Queen's incessant fear that her subjects should contemplate the Royal forms when undergoing this preliminary, imaginative 'building-up' that led her to insist upon a special studio being reserved exclusively for work connected with the Royal Family." (From *Truth*.)

Isn't she the supreme grocer?

When I was last here, in London, a friend who use[d] very often to come to see me said one day: "I have just been to the 'Wild West,' and I do enjoy your country so, it's so free and fresh." As the female of the Cow Boy, my attractions were explained.

January 23rd

Before the year waxes older, I must recount our novel festivities at Christmas. Little Nurse has an exemplary habit of telling me all her experiences, great and small, and since I have been here, she has afforded me infinite amusement by psychological revelations of the Stewards' Room. She is allowed to report all mental eccentricities of the Lady's Maid, the Chef, the Steward, the Waiter, etc., but the line is supposed to be rigidly drawn at all gossip about the "ladies," though I must confess that curiosity often gets the better of my high tone, and I listen, with great receptivity, to the shortcomings of Mrs. Jones, Brown and Robinson; for alas! I am sorry to say, that the ladies' maid mind, like mine, finds the recital of humanity's shortcomings more succulent than that of its perfections; virtue permitting of little license of treatment more than accounts for our preoccupation with the deviations therefrom.

In this way a wide social range was vicariously opened out to us—beginning by a servants' ball in the hotel on Christmas night, tapering down through a party at "Cousin Val's," a bootmaker, who has been to Marlborough House to measure the illustrious foot of Royalty, and ending on Saturday night with a comprehensive gathering at the Sweep's at Hampstead, where the exalted Assistant from Marshall and Snelgrove's watched from the other side of the room the inspirations of a Carter and a ploughboy.

The Nursling, knowing that she did not shine as a dancer, and being in no way inclined to obscurity, disguised herself for the ball very successfully as an old hag, and sang and acted one of those dreary Compounds of "Charing." "Betsey Waring," "Damp-attics" and "roomatics" known as a Comic song. We have long had it impressed upon us that she "knew" music and Drawing, but her histrionic genius had lain fallow, so we were much surprised and delighted at its unexpected blossoming. One day, when I told her how anxious I was about the first night of *The American,* she asked: "Should you have felt very badly if I had failed on Christmas night?" adding: "I never should have held up my head in this hotel again if I had."

The Ladies and gentlemen being invited to honour the occasion: K. put on her mouse-coloured velvet gown, and went down just before Nurse's song. She was received at the door, by one of the "gentlemen" in the office, who escorted her to a chair. When Jennie, our housemaid, came up with enthusiasm, to greet her and introduced another housemaid, Jessie (our second housemaid) sat beside her, while our three waiters interchanged conversational amenities with her from time to time all as if they were friends and hosts, till one's heart was melted to hear about it. These æsthetic decencies so wrap about the iniquities, and so explain and justify their long continuance, that one has flaccid moments of shivering at the raw edges that will be laid bare as democracy sweeps its pope's-head through the festooning cobwebs, and crumbles the richly hued mould into dust. Jennie said to Nurse, with delight, the next morning "fancy Miss Loring shaking hands with me before the whole room." Let us pray that our unconscious benefactions outweigh our unconscious cruelties!

This by the way allies K. with the Countess of Portsmouth,[84] who says she always shakes hands with the village school mistress, because she thinks "it's the best plan." Think of the swindle of being so placed! rigid with the framework of the Personage, and ne'er a shady corner from the cradle to the grave for the limbering and rejoiceful somersault. But I must get on with my festivities.

Cousin Val's party seemed commonplace with the trail of Royalty and a professional comedian upon it,—Ivan Berlin, more woolly than terrible; but real life was found in perfection at the Sweep's, who lives in a little cottage in one of the hollows of Hampstead Heath.

The party consisted of about 20, 10 having fortunately failed, who were placed, in order to fit in, on stools close together round the walls of the little sitting-room, against which they couldn't lean, however, because they were dripping with wet, there being no fire, for fear of too much heat at this frigid season. Upon her stool, Nurse sat from five in the evening until six the next morning, save at the moments when she burst into song, the essence of the occasion being uninterrupted vocaliza-

---

[84] Lady Eveline Alicia Juliana Herbert, daughter of the 3rd Earl of Carnarvon, had married the 5th Earl of Portsmouth in 1855.

tion and an all night sitting. Nurse at one moment raised the tone, by making to the Marshall and Snelgrove contingent, a literary allusion to the clammy hands of Uriah Heep,—"The others wouldn't have known to what we referred, Miss." They seemed to be differentiated by special songs, one recalcitrant young woman being besought at frequent intervals through the watches of the night to sing "Joanna in her Shroud," which turned out to be "Joe in the Copper," and the Sweep coming to Nurse, to tell her that a young woman was about to sing one of her songs, and what could he do about it, as if there were a vocal copyright. Over the evolutions of the carter and a gallon of beer we must sadly draw a veil, but the plough-boy, pitted with small-pox, with features fashioned in one of the least kindly moods of Providence, seemed the rarest flower of benignancy. So preoccupied was he with the welfare of the guests, and making the occasion "go off," that Nurse thought he must be related to the hosts—the last note of a song had hardly died, before he would exclaim: "If no one else is going to sing, I know another"; and perched on his stool, his eyes tight shut, clenched hands, and heels tucked under him, he would drone out, by the yard, ditties to the refrain of "My Com*ryde* died for me," and the like. Think of the joy in life of this lowly lad, his soul rapturous with song, all instinct and fluid with the grace of hospitality, as compared, for instance, with Lord Wharncliffe,[35] whose ancestral exigencies are such that he turns his back upon his guests however fair they be, and takes his own sister, without a grimace, in to dinner, four days in succession. A lady staying with this unfortunate bond-man, pathetically remarked that "having no title, I had to go in to dinner every day with the same gentleman, and *that* gentleman, Mr. Smalley, too."

---

[35] Edward Montagu Granville Montagu-Stuart-Wortley-Mackenzie, 1st Earl of Wharncliffe (1827–1899).

January 27th

The beloved Katharine is under the weather—looks as meek and mild as a Baptist, and has that touchingness about her, which sickness always brings to the purely normal of the animal kingdom.

January 28th

How surprised and shocked I am to hear that Ellie Emmet, whose heart, I had been led to suppose, was seared by sorrow, is contemplating marriage again, in the lightsome mood of eighteen,[36]—Poor Temple's devotion, his tragic death, his fatherhood of her six children, all forgotten; not even his memory sacred, for she says she "never loved before." What ephemeræ we all are; to be sure, experience leaves no permanent furrow, but like writing on sand is washed out by every advancing ripple of changing circumstance. 'Twould seem to the inexperienced that one happy "go" at marriage would have given the full measure of connubial bliss, and all the chords of maternity have vibrated under the manipulation of six progeny; but man lives not to assimilate knowledge of the eternal essence of things, and only craves a renewal of sensation.

February 6th

K. is booming this week, seventeen "invites!" She greedily accepts all that the limits of the social day permit—and this is the devoted 3,000-mile friend, oh, the poseuse!! I am on my knees to her perpetually not to bewilder the natives with her jokes, when she is let loose; the same entreaty was on the lips of her aunt Mrs. Asa Gray, when she was with her in England 20 years ago. Mrs. Clough[37] asked her last night if she did not think it morally wrong to "take in" *Truth.*

[36] She remarried that autumn George Hunter (1847–1914).
[37] Widow of the poet Arthur Hugh Clough (1819–1861).

What a devil of a bore it must be, to be the superior person! those mental anæmics, who never read about murders, divorces, or whatever their especial squeamishness may be, to which they pin their vanity; as grotesque as going to the play and boasting that you shut your eyes tight whenever the villain walks across.

Àpropos of the opposite tendency, a most unique process is taking place in the race of Cross,—a passionate identification of themselves with the unworthy; all as a protest, as a sign of their not to be measured allegiance to George Eliot. When one thinks of the cruel violence which they must do to the strenuous, strictly moral angles of their osseous conformation, it makes one ache to think of their striving after Bohemia, through the cigarette, and feeling, I suppose, dear souls, as the chokey smoke permeates their being, as if they, too, like the immortal George, had deviated from the straight and narrow path. The good and maternal Mrs. Otter, whose digestive organs forbid the noxious weed, abandons herself to even stronger measures, and permits herself to say: "there is one man who understands a woman's heart more perfectly than any other, a Frenchman, Guy de Maupassant." As she lives in the depths of Lincolnshire, this makes the brave and the fair of the fens seem more sportive than one had pictured. This spiritual adoption is so ardent, it makes one curious to know, if in a generation or so, a Darwinian or Spencerian adaptation may not take place, in the physical woman; their progression is now altogether by jerks, a pulling of the string—how interesting if in time the interrupted current of their speech and motion should take to itself the undulating suppleness and flow, natural to the unmanufactured votary of moral relaxation.

How wild can be the fancies of the unimaginative female! I, even, had exhaled the aromatic perfume of the défendu for the nostrils of a Leamington spinster. She was a refined mortal, and although fifty years of age, embodied still, as K. said, the Wordsworthian maiden, having that wearying quality which always oozes from attenuated purity. It seems that on one

occasion I told her that Father had hated all forms and ceremonies, which she took to be an intimation that I had been born
out of the bonds of holy wedlock. This doubt had devastated
her breast for long, until she was driven to ask K. who with one
burst of laughter restored me to virtue and the commonplace;
but she was not so immoral as to keep the joke to herself, as
she told the poor lady she would.

The first time she entered my Presence, I use the word
advisedly, she said to herself, "They *say* there is no rank in
America, but it is not true, for *this* is rank!" and reconciled
subsequent developments, no doubt, by looking upon me as
a royal bastard. I told Mr. Boott last summer, when he
exclaimed and explained, "You must be a Fitz-James, then,"
and we thought we could hear a spiritual chuckle from on
high.

February 8th

There is a certain mortuary flavour in late messages, so I judge
that my death is booming in the U. S.; I hope Helen Paine
isn't losing it again; I once told her that I had been very ill,
and that it had been thought I was dying, when in grieved
accents she exclaimed, "Oh, why! I lost that!"

To the American born to "rattle round" in space, who can
have no representative value for his own consciousness or that
of any one else, the sense of their place possessed by all sorts
and conditions here is very instructive, and the skill they attain
in keeping the balance of the exact measure of their worth,
as between butler and baron, is most remarkable. There was a
pathetic remnant in Leamington, a decayed gentlewoman, who
gave one such an impression of an indestructible essence in proportion to her being a mere human shadow. Fortune had led
her down the rungs of her ladder, to an income of ten shillings
a week; Mrs. Nickleby was a stern logician as compared to her,
and she had the mental range of an ant,—not a dear little

burnished definite ant, who could tell you, if he only would, with such precision, all the architectural tragedies of his career, but a blurred vague ant, if such a thing is possible. On this little heap of social ruin, however, the *Gentlewoman* was impregnably intrenched, and how often have I gazed sadly through her atmosphere of *inherited* good breeding, and seen unfold itself the endless row of desperate ciphers, by which she is multiplied on this teeming island.

We were talking one day of an American woman who is very good natured and amusing, but of the denuded, distasteful type, so beloved here, when Miss Palmer said: "She once said a most extraordinary thing to me," and she went on to tell me that at one time she had lodged in a house kept by an ex-butler and his wife; the man was very fine looking and used to decorate the Leamington dinner parties in turn, and his name happened to be Palmer. In a misguided moment, the American humorist said: "I should think you wouldn't like to live in the home of that man Palmer, for you might be taken for his sister!" and I am sure every defunct Palmer fortified the accent of the inconceivable, with which she disclaimed the possibility of such an incongruous calamity suggesting itself to her. A few minutes later she described a meeting she had been to, where Miss Kingsley, who is considered very excitable, had been "in such a stew," as the Vicar of Tachbrook[38] said, "that she called out to Lord Leigh,[39] 'Come here!' forgetting in her hurry the respect due to rank." To her, the Butler, the Gentlewoman and the Nobleman, were fixed substances, as little interchangeable as the elements; and to her pale gentility it would have been as much out of nature to have hurried the one as to have played with the thought of being the sister of the other, although the misguided Yankee asked: "Why not, you know he is a very handsome man." Can there *ever* be an international

---

[38] J. T. Hallett had been vicar of Tachbrook, which included the town of Leamington, since 1884.

[39] William Henry, 2nd Baron Leigh (1824–1905).

point of view? Feeling themselves to be, primarily, members of a class, and only secondarily, human beings, they are free from the responsibilities that the floating Yankee is under to his individual dignity; and they are able to accept without a squirm, from their betters, every manner of favour, from the loan of the great house down the infinite degrees to the nimble six pence. À propos, an intimate friend of Matthew Arnold's said to Harry: "You know he is so very clever about getting houses lent to him."

March 4th

If K. knows the blessedness of giving, I certainly know the curse of receiving! No matter how great the iniquity she may commit, if I start up to confront her with it, there suddenly stares me in the face 3000 miles of solid sea-sickness, and my righteous indignation turns to pulp, and I flop back into a tangle of shawls swindled into savourless amiability.

Billy it seems teases little Peggy[40] dreadfully; she bears it usually serenely, but every now and then her indignation breaks forth. The other day she said to her mother, "When I speak so to Billy, it makes my stomach tremble." Heaven forbid that this should be a portent of heredity, and that her innocent framework should be destined to enclose within its depths a cave of emotional borborygmus, as has been known!

What an incongruity to meet in a London drawing room a grand-nephew of old Dr. Channing,[41] with a rich wife, having resigned his nationality, to become a radical M. P. and asking his hostess eager questions as to the confection of a gown for his daughter who is to be presented this season.

A woman was brought to the London hospital the other day with a very bad bite on her arm. The doctor asked her

[40] William (1882–1961) and Mary Margaret James (1887–1952), children of William James.

[41] William Henry Channing (1818–1901), nephew of William Ellery Channing, social reformer and Transcendentalist.

whether she had been bitten by a dog. "No, sir, 'twas another lydy did it!!"

Jennie, the housemaid, has been to see the *Cabinet Minister*,[42] she prefers a deep play with a murder or two in it, and guns going off "something deep, you know." The mind stirred in proportion to the muscular starts. Mrs. John Wood[43] she considers a very good actress "for rough and refined."

Poets have always had a genius beyond their fellows for irritating the feminine devotee by their ineptitude in paring themselves; to judge by the wingless widow, Clough, Arthur Hugh carries off the cake in this respect. Katharine went the other day to see the *Dancing Girl*[44] with Mrs. Clough. In the course of the play, a wicked duke rehearses his villainies, and says how much better are the lower orders than such as he, whereupon Mrs. C. exclaims, "I'm so sorry to hear him say that; it is hard enough as it is to keep people in their place, and it does them a great deal of harm to hear that kind of talk."

[42] *The Cabinet Minister* by Sir Arthur Pinero (1855–1934) had been produced at the Court Theatre the previous year.
[43] Mrs. John Wood (1831–1915), the former Matilda Charlotte Vining, was an actress both in England and the United States. She managed the Court Theatre for ten years.
[44] *The Dancing Girl* by Henry Arthur Jones (1851–1929), had just been produced at the Haymarket.

Kensington

1891-1892

HOW AMUSING it is to see the fixed mosaic of one's little destiny being filled out by the tiny blocks of events, the enchantment of minute consequences with the illusion of choice weathering it all! Through complete physical bankruptcy, I have attained my *"ideel,"* as Nurse calls it, and we are established since March 12th in a little house on Campden Hill (41 Argyll Road). We decided a little while ago that I could not go out of town, or become the prey of the landlady, so that a house to ourselves was a necessity, and a possibility with Katharine at hand, who had only to wave her magic wand, and in three weeks from our decision we found ourselves delightfully settled, she, after her usual manner, having levelled all the rough places and let sunlight into the dark corners of suggestion.

Our "staff" of two consists of a Mrs. Thompson, a cook included in the lease of the house, and the excellent Louisa, who having left Mrs. Clarke, K. transported from Leamington, and is transforming from a Slavey into a House-and-parlour-maid. This domestic exiguity tries Nurse, of course, whose conversation has been greatly decorated this winter, with the "staff of 63 at the Hotel." But the sorest trial for her is the low intellectual level at the dinner-table. The second day, she said: "Mrs. Thompson must be a Wesleyan, Miss, she talks about the Maker, and that is not a High Church expression, and she is always having a 'beautiful dream' in which some one asks her questions, and she says: 'The strangest thing is that I never make any answer, but always simply points upward—to the Saviour.' " Stranger than the dream is the fact that the constancy of this dramatic pose towards the skies has no disastrous result to her sublunary savours which are of a most delectable and body-sustaining description, notwithstanding that her piety is doubled by a most strenuous teetotalism, so that she won't put wine into her sauces, K. says because then she can't eat them herself; it seems to be all there, so that ascending finger, like the electric rod, must conduct some spiritual quickening thereinto. But the truly thrilling thing to see is the simple soul of Louisa shedding the chrysalis of the drudge and learning to flutter her wings in the house-maids' empyrean. The slightest shades of her psychological state are noted with the keenest interest, and the whole household is grouped about her, watching the stages of her development. Her first question was: "Is this the Jack-the-Ripper part?" The first time she went out alone, she, of course, managed to lose herself, but, fortunately, just as she was going to "roar" she was rescued by a constable—"them '*buzzes* frightens me awful"! Nurse and Thompson are contending over her for Church and Chapel; honours are easy so far, and if Louisa is wise, they will remain so.

Was there ever such a repulsive spectacle as those creatures, like spiritual carrion, surrounding the death-bed of Prince Napoleon,[1] and trying to snatch some word from his unprotected weakness, which they may distort into ignoble concession, making capital out of, and greedily feeding upon his unholy career[?]

March 23rd

In arranging and fitting yourself here, you have always to remember and count with the far-backness in which the simplest evolution retroacts, and in the manner of doing, the rigidity imposed by the long burden of Time, whilst in Yankeedom

[1] Napoléon Joseph Charles Paul Bonaparte (1822–1891), commonly called Prince Napoléon or more familiarly Plon-Plon. Son of Jérôme and Catherine of Württemberg, he was named successor to Napoléon III, and remained a pretender to the throne after the death of Napoléon III's only son and the end of the Second Empire.

it is simply tomorrow that you must stretch yourself to. The
continuity and localness is shown by a van to be seen in Kensington Sq[uare], on which is written: "Van to and from London, daily." Before the bad weather began K. was dining out
one evening, and they waited a long time for two of the guests
who were coming from Wimbledon. They finally arrived, having
had numberless adventures on the perilous journey, their cab
losing its way from the station, and they losing their wraps,
and had the lady crossed the plains, she couldn't have taken
longer to thaw out; they were personally conducting a precious
box, as they were going to pass a few days in town with some
friends; it seems a funny thing to bring to a dinner party, but
they were well advised, for Katharine sent one Monday by
the Carrier, her trunk from Fulham, a 35 minute drive, and
it reached Queen's Gate Terrace on the Wednesday.

If the aim of life is the accretion of fat, the consumption of
food unattended by digestive disorganization, and a succession
of pleasureable sensations, there is no doubt that I am a failure,
for as an animal form my insatiable vanity must allow that
my existence doesn't justify itself, but every fibre protests
against being taken simply as a sick carcass, as foolish friends
so flatteringly insist, for what power has dissolving flesh and
aching bones to undermine a satisfaction made of imperishable
things. This winter has been rich beyond compare, the heart all
aglow with the affectionate demonstration of friend and brother,
the mind deeply stirred by most varied and interesting events,
public and private, the spirit broadened and strengthened, let
me hope, by a clearer perception of the significance of experience, whilst from the whole has flowed perpetually those succulent juices which exude at the slightest pressure from the
human comedy.

March 27th

Picture the flutter in the cote, a male introduced in the shape of
an intoxicated gardener, who invited Thompsonia, the tee-

totaller, first to take a drink with him, and then to lead him to the altar; K. most blessedly combines with her petticoats, certain male virtues, and trembleth not before the mouse or the drunken man, so the sinner was evicted with decision, and hysteria cut short.

With what joy I think of the vengeance the non-piano player will have over t'other in Heaven, it can surely be nothing less than a long, long draught of his blood. There were 15 pianos at the South Kensington, and 23 uproarious children, who were allowed to turn the corridors into nurseries, and to scream for hours outside of one's door, so that the old notions about the suppressed British child and the solemn respectability of a London hotel were found to be sadly antiquated. The change that has come even since I have been here is most extraordinary, young girls going to dances alone, and the mothers not even invited: Bessie Clarke, Mrs. Stanley Clarke's charming daughter of twenty, told K. that she rode at eight A.M. in the Park because she had no groom to go with her, and her mother would not allow her to ride alone at twelve, as so many of the girls did, and she and Minnie Emmet[2] seemed to be going about alone, in omnibuses, wherever they wanted to.

This makes it the more natural, of course, that the Misses Chamberlain, not generously endowed by nature or freighted by long descent, should be proportionately hedged about by propriety and not allowed to go out alone, Joseph of many screws and colours out-Torying the Tories even here; but the best of all is that he has a copy of the Endicott ancestor of the fair Mary to decorate his Highbury mansion, Brummagem distilled!

The American has been a great success in Belfast, as well as in Edinburgh; there must be something human, after all, in Ulster! I read a notice from a Belfast paper to the Nurseling,

[2] Mary (Minnie) Temple was the oldest daughter of Ellen Temple Emmet, sister of Alice James's cousin, Minny Temple, commemorated by Henry James in *Notes of a Son and Brother.*

and said: "that's Irish enthusiasm." "Yes, isn't it plainly written, Miss." I felt for the rhetorician. It fills one so, at moments, with gratitude, that fate has placed one just above the line of intellectual penury, for it takes all their little stock to pick out the *objects* in a picture or on a page, and they have no little scraps left over, as we have for a further movement, nothing stored for the new to catch onto and lodge, their minds swept as clean, poor souls, as their denuded cupboards. Think of having to grub and grind all the long days, simply to keep from starving with nothing stirred within but brute sensations, no hallowed memories, no cherished hopes, none of the joys of reflection!

April 5th

When death has come close, how the emptiness seems palpable and to permeate the very atmosphere, making the sounds of life reverberate therein so loud.

This is a delicious feminine muddle at which K. assisted yesterday. Two friends were calling here, one, typical British matron, the other typical Mind-cured Jamaica Plain. She suddenly overheard the latter say, "You call it here hypnotism, we call it *the* Science." "But it must be so very dangerous to manipulate such a delicate organ as the brain," was the rejoinder. K. vainly rushed to the rescue, trying to disentangle them from their respective embroilment, by suggesting that hypnotism was not massage, nor was *the* Science hypnotism, evoking simply from the Yankee, "they mould the brain so wonderfully now." "How is it done, through the skull, by some marvellous instrument, I suppose, and weighing of the brain is so wonderful, too, how do they manage that?" "Post-mortem," murmured K., desiring to throw light upon the dark mysteries of science—but the Yankee only scoffed "With life left out?"

It is certain sure that good manners *are* corrupted by evil communications, to think of my having sent, through Nurse's machinations, an Easter card, a card alone is bad enough, but one with "Easter" appended! Father must have groaned on high, Easter being his special "ab-borrance" as Nurse calls it. She, I gladly have observed, is becoming corrupted by me: she has, however, taken her revenge now: I have found this winter that she actually "celebrates," or "takes celebration" which ever it is called, on a full stomach, having told me in Leamington that it would cause a fatal spiritual indigestion, when I heard myself exclaiming: "Your celebrations and all the rest of it are perfect tom-foolery as long as you prevaricate as you do." The poor little soul has no more conception of what prevarication means than she has of the Cosmos,—'tis only an automatic defensive movement to protect herself against my despotic power,—a few shillings in my pocket to chink whilst she has ne'er a ha'penny!

K. went to Cheltenham this winter to spend a few days with Miss Woolson,[3] she came back in the [railroad] carriage with Sir Michael Hicks Beach,[4] his wife and a friend. The gentlemen had been speaking at a Unionist meeting the night before and they unbosomed themselves after the engaging manner that English gentlemen are so erroneously supposed *not* to do. "You live near the Abercorns, don't you?" "Yes." "Terribly dreary." "Yes, but very good." "I stayed with them once, and they sat in only one room; it was awfully dull." "You know they are very poor" etc., etc. The ducal circle crouching over one fire seems piteous enough, they must be much colder, even than the Bachelers and have but little to save them from depression, but the coarse strain in the fibre that permits of publicly proclaiming the poverty and dreariness of quondam hosts is one of those shocks and surprises to the democratic mind so mistakenly under the illusion of the exigencies of long descended

[3] Constance Fenimore Woolson (1840–1894), American novelist and friend of Henry James.

[4] Sir Michael Edward Hicks Beach (1837–1916), 9th baronet and first Earl St. Aldwyn, a strong opponent of Home Rule, was Irish Secretary, 1886–1887.

delicacies and refinements. Sir Michael asks for nothing more than that his two sons, who are at Eton, should one of them be in the School eleven, and the other in the foot-ball team. One of the Bensons who has been living in Iowa has come back to England to educate his boys, he said he was about sending them to some school in the U[nited] S[tates]; but thought they would get rabbit-shooting in England, so he came back; if they are to be an ornament to their country 'tis surely wise to take measures to develope their instincts for slaughter.

My good Mrs. Bowyer, in Leamington, used to lament to me over the failure of her son to get into Sandhurst: "When he was young, he was an excellent scholar; but his coach writes to me, he hasn't brought away the vices they commonly do from Eton, but that it has wholly destroyed his power of study, as is usual." Having learnt wisdom, I didn't dilate upon the grotesque of sending the young ideas to a seat of learning which acknowledgedly deprives them of what little capacity nature may have endowed them; once in my innocency, before I had learned what *not* to say, lest the Empire totter, I exclaimed, when hearing from a moaning mama how Eton undermined the morals; "Why then, do you send your boys there?" And you could almost hear the reverberation of the mental shock as she gasped: "How can we help it?" But George Bowyer I think must have a special gift of divesting himself of acquired knowledge for he had always been very good in French, and passed very well, until an unlucky inspiration came to send him to Germany for three months to fortify his German; at the next "exam" he had not only not learned any German, but had seemingly amused himself in sweeping clean the hitherto well furnished Gallic cells of his brain.

April 7th

Our old landlady at Leamington said to K. "How do you manage when you are so sea-sick about going off the ship to get your meals?" "I have them in my room." "Oh yes, you always know so well about providing; you're not like ladies, are you? you go into things so—" that is, she grasps, among other trifles, the complications of those cosmic objects to the good old lady, the dust-bin, the copper and the kitchener; she *has* rather been going into things last week. During one 24 hours, she pursued her devious way, in the afternoon, with Doctor Hack Tuke to "Bedlam,"[5] in the evening to a "smart" dinner, and the next morning found her at Clapton, lifting up her voice in prayer as she knelt among the Salvation lassies. It would be curious to know which of these three was the chief centre of lunacy! Her mind may be called "detached" as the *Spectator* Townsend said of Mr. Bryce's:—"Bryce's mind is a good mind, not at all a great one; I should say a *detached* mind"[6] From what Mr. B's mind is detached remains a secret of the Spectatorial oracle, but K.'s is detached from any personal preconception of the situation, and is enabled to "catch on" to the exigency of every passing moment, so that when the Slum-Sister tapped her on the shoulder, instead of striking the customary false note of refusal, she harmoniously addressed herself to the Almighty, without a twinge of conscience. On Easter Monday, Bank-Holiday, she "tended" table at a temperance tea given in the Kensington Town Hall; the Vicar of St. Mary Abbott's, the Hon. and Rev. E. Carr Glynn presided and his wife, Lady Mary, née Campbell "nursed" the various babies in her lap—there was an eccentric specimen, a little girl, who had arrived, through heredity, at the sophistication of not liking seed-cake. "Her mother was the same before her."

Mrs. Shaen, who was a cousin of Thackeray's, and blushingly thinks herself the original of Ethel, is quite a friend of Katharine's, and as she is a poor-law guardian for Kensington, we

[5] Daniel Hack Tuke, M.D. (1835–1913), a pioneer in mental health, president of the Neurological Society of the United Kingdom. "Bedlam" was the Bethlehem Hospital for the Insane.

[6] James Bryce (1838–1922), later viscount, author of *The Holy Roman Empire* (1864) and *The American Commonwealth* (1888).

hear much that is most interesting; she is (as every one must become that works among the poor) a vehement teetotaller, and on several occasions has proved how infinitely more possessed of moral courage women are than men. She finds her fellow guardians and some licensing justices ready to support her, in private encouraging her to propose reformation but at the meetings they don't second her motions, and on one occasion lately, they left her alone, to face the jeers of 400 publicans, she having objected to the renewal of the license of a public, exactly opposite to the gate of the Kensington workhouse, whither three fourths of the inmates are brought by drink. One poor woman said to her of her husband, "I can get him past eight publics, but I can't get him past nine." To reward her for her pluck and to shame craven man, she had a great ovation from the people at the Concert after the tea, on Bank Holiday, when the Vicar said a few words about what she had done. I do wish I had kept an account that was published lately of the proportion of public-house property owned by Dukes and the Church, in some counties, one Duke or two owns them all. Fancy the bestial stupidity of throwing out, year after year, the bill for opening public buildings on Sundays, whilst these infernos are allowed to belch forth their toxic fumes at every corner, and to fulfil the genius of the land, 'tis of course done in the name of Piety!

April 9th

Mrs. Shaen told K. one day that she had just found herself forcing the Marquis of Lorne[7] to declare himself a pauper, by asking him for his vote for her re-election on the board of guardians; when he explained his incompetence, as he was neither a rate payer nor a householder—you see the ignominy of living in a Palace. The story is told, that when he was on his

[7] John, Marquess of Lorne (1845–1914), later Duke of Argyll, married Louise (1848–1939), fourth daughter of Queen Victoria.

honeymoon, he said (in order to make the occasion go off pleasantly) to his bride, "You are nothing but a pauper, supported by the State," which accounts, probably, for subsequent sentiments on her part.

This reminds me that last autumn at the So[uth] K[ensington] Hotel, Nurse told me one day that the Marquis of Lorne had arrived the day before, and that a fine suite had been prepared for him, on the first floor, but that he had taken only one bed-room on the fourth floor, and hadn't brought even a valet with him, and instead of ringing a bell for the housemaid, he went in an ancient dressing gown to a room where they sat, and there gave his orders. When this was told in the Steward's Room, "Mr." Woodford the Butler who presided over the deglutition of the ladies' maids, unctuous of manner, Pickwickian of contour, his legs behind him, "his figure not lost, but gone before," exclaimed "Ah, that's the real kind, you soon tell 'em from the made up ones." How he would despise any one, not a Marquis, who behaved like that! H. says: "It takes a Marquis to make a butler subtle."

While studying the populace in Shoreditch one day, K. beheld a female child therof purchasing a ha'porth of ice cream, which being dabbed upon a bit of newspaper she laid on the palm of her hand and transferred with infinite satisfaction to her alimentary canal by means of lingual gymnastics. In the higher social walks where a glass is provided for the ice you have the choice of a spoon for an extra half penny, but as Nature has been so liberal, in instruments, why indulge in such a reckless superfluity!

Mrs. Shaen tries in every way to save the taxpayers money, so at one of the meetings of the Guardians this winter, when it was proposed that five pounds should be appropriated for Christmas toys for the workhouse children, she suggested that the rich of the Parish should be appealed to, to send last year's toys from their overcrowded nurseries, she was not listened to and the motion was carried. When she got home she found to her satisfaction and surprise, a hamper, containing 60 toys which had been collected by some thoughtful person from the Parochial nurseries. So Mrs. S. thought she had her fellows nicely at the next meeting; but no, the hopeless blunderheads had appropriated the money, so it could not be unappropriated, so they proceeded to vote two pounds more for floral decorations throughout the house.

A little while before Christmas, K. went over the House with her one day, and she spoke to the Master (who after the felicitous English manner, was named Brimblecombe) about her having sixty toys for the children, when he said: "Why, there are the toys and the new sixpences that *Truth* sends every year, and we have only 17 children"; it seems at moments as if they were all simply floundering in a bog of sentimentality, especially when you hear of a silly idle old busy body sending forth strawberries and cream twice a week, to these stalwart pauperized do-nothings. Most of the wrecks are the results of drink: one old man who had sat on the same form at school with Gladstone and Mrs. Shaen's uncle, and one woman who had been governess to one of the princelings.

One hears that it is absolutely impossible for the English working man to put by a penny for his old age, and on the face of it, this seems true, but Mrs. Shaen has made the calculation that by the suppression of the very moderate estimate for the family beer, of six pence a day—the sum of £546 would be saved in a lifetime of 60 years. But then they tell you that the climate "requires" it, whereas, given the climate, beer is simply poison, and I have heard of more "biliousness" since I have been in England than I ever heard in my whole life before.

April 12th

In view of the facts, the remark in *Truth* is very droll, about the introduction that H. wrote for the Catalogue of Alfred Parsons'[8] exhibition of pictures, to the effect that, being a dis-

---

[8] Alfred William Parsons (1847–1920), English landscape painter and illustrator, friend of Henry James.

tinguished member of the Savile Club, Mr. H. J. naturally writes a laudation of his friend's Mr. Parsons' pictures, etc.— the truth being that H. loves not the Savile Club,[9] and goes there about once a year, and Mr. Parsons isn't a member, at all!

H. said one day, that Burne-Jones,[10] Sargent[11] and Alfred Parsons are the most complete artists he knows, in their point of view, and in their natures, the best of men.

It is unusual to see a creature like H. who with so strong, almost complete, artistic inclination, has absolutely a physical repulsion from all personal disorder. 'Tis a sad fate, though, that he should have fastened to him a being like me; and you can't exaggerate the beautiful patience with which he listens to my outpourings on *Questions* (Heaven forbid that I should ever be so base as to descend to *Subjects*) from which he is so detached, and which absorb my rawboned, relentlessly moral organization. I can hear, as of yesterday, the ring of Father's voice, as he anathematized some short-comings of mine in Newport one day: "Oh, Alice, how hard you are!" and I can remember how penetrated I was, not for the first time, b[ut] often, with the truth of it, and saw the repulsion his nature with its ripe kernel of human benignancy felt—alas! through all these years, that hard core confronts me still, though I have moments of indulging myself with the thought that through the heavy hand of Time, the sap of generous and gentle impulse may stir, although it give no sign in the rich blossoms that strewed his path.

This brings back to me one of dear old Wilkins Micawber's favorite jokes: Mr. George Bradford[12] had opened a school in

[9] Henry James was a member of the Savile Club from 1884 to 1899, but rarely went there, preferring the Reform and the Athenaeum.

[10] Sir Edward Burne-Jones (1833–1898), English painter and decorator.

[11] John Singer Sargent (1856–1925), American portrait painter and friend of Henry James.

[12] George Partridge Bradford, a classmate of Emerson and a lifelong friend.

Newport, and one day Mr. Emerson was asking him about it, in the presence of Wilkie who was paying a visit at the Emersons' in Concord. "And what sort of a girl is Alice," asked Mr. E.: "She has a highly moral nature," replied Mr. B. Whereupon, in great amusement, Mr. E. exclaimed: "How in the world does her father get on with her?"—But who shall relate that long alliance, made on one side of all tender affection, solicitous sympathy and paternal indulgence!

April 13th

K. is so excessive in the normal that she seems to me at moments to be barely a rudiment. The Anæmic are so fed by the vanity of emotion and sensation that they become like bloated fungi of the morbid.

April 19th

In the way of the droll could one ask for anything more than to have the Attorney General of a Tory ministry defending Hurlburt[13] in a breach of promise of marriage case, and serenely remarking, that he was a most respectable gentleman, the bloom of whose reputation had never been tarnished by the breath of scandal or libel! Poor Sir Richard Webster, to pass from Piggott to Hurlburt!

The ascendency of the American is emphasized by the

---

[13] W. H. Hurlburt, writer on political and other subjects, and formerly proprietor of the New York *World,* was defendant in a breach-of-promise suit by Miss Gertrude Ellis, known on the stage as Gladys Evelyn. She charged she had been seduced under cover of the promise of marriage by Hurlburt who gave his name as Wilfrid Murray. Hurlburt pleaded that the promise (if any) was conditional upon Miss Ellis's being "a chaste and modest woman, whereas she was a woman of immoral life." It was further claimed during the proceedings that the Wilfrid Murray with whom the actress was allegedly involved was not Hurlburt but his secretary. The verdict was for the defendant, the jury finding there was "no promise of marriage."

fact that a young man from Cambridgeport, I believe named
Fullerton,[14] not more than twenty-five, was sub-editor of the
Times and now is sent to Paris, to, in process of time, undermine
Blowitz,[15] I suppose.

I must congratulate the *Speaker* on having emancipated certain paragraphs, which it entitles "The Week," from the glorious
mission of destroying Howells, all one's admiration for his
special genius, it made him mightier than was justified by reality
to have a London Weekly find him so potent, as to think it
essential to devote paragraph after paragraph to despising
and contemning him; it was a diseased possession for he loomed
so to their imagination, that when the things he *had* said gave
out, they divined what iniquity he *would* commit under given
circumstances. When it was not Howells it was the wisdom of
Jenkins from Tennessee, or Tompkins of *Mizzourah* that was
dragged from its native obscurity to be held up to the repro-
bation of Great Britain; in their wildest dreams, could Tompkins or Jenkins have ever hoped for such glory? The Editor,
too, devoted two wrathful columns—to whom, do you think?
—poor old Marion Harland[16] whose namby pamby tales I
used to read in infancy, in *Godey's Lady's Book*, when I
chanced upon it at the Perrys'[17] in Newport, 30 years ago. How
truly topsy-turvy to have this faint ghost from a long-forgotten
literary! past, suddenly "walk" as a redoubtable quantity to
be crushed by the thunders of a London Weekly, baptised a
"gentleman" too. But finally, the ingenuous editor has discovered that even in the heart of London there is a bibliography

[14] William Morton Fullerton (1865–1952), American journalist who
worked in the Paris bureau of the London *Times* and later became an editorial
writer for the French newspaper, *Le Figaro*.

[15] Henri de Blowitz (1825–1903), chief of the Paris bureau of the *Times*
for many years and an eminent European journalist.

[16] Marion Harland, pseudonym of Mary V. Terhune (1830–1922), writer
of fiction dealing with the South before and after the Civil War.

[17] The Perrys were neighbors of the Jameses at Newport, and Thomas
Sergeant Perry (1845–1928), critic and teacher, was for years a close friend
of Henry James. Margaret Perry, a sister, married John La Farge, the painter.

which 'twere more important to record, so the U[nited]
S[tates] has to take the back seat, and its literary vices appear
no longer as the most central and powerful factors of the
moment.

April 22nd

We have been much interested in the last months in a sad little
story fallen to our knowledge through a nursing friend of little
Nurse's: Lady Alexandra Leveson Gower,[18] the only daughter
of the unspeakable Duke of Sutherland, has been lying very
ill close by, in the house of her uncle, the Duke of Argyll, and
she has just died. Her mother died two or three years ago,
when her father married immediately an abomination in the
shape of woman: the young thing, only 25, was so borne down
by the sorrow of her present and by the memory of her mother's
outraged past, that she went to St. Bartholomew's to try to
distract her mind by nursing.[19] There is something touching
in hearing of the tender soul so artificially reared, stretching
forth its little tendrils to entwine and lose itself in common
things. But she only stayed three months, and left very ill,
and although the Queen has called to ask for her, paternal and
avuncular dukes, fraternal and cousinly marquises, lords and
ladies of all sizes have perturbed themselves about her, the
little maid herself, enlightened by a burden too heavy for her,

[18] George Granville William, 3rd Duke of Sutherland (1828–1892), married Anne Hay-Mackenzie of Newhall and Cromartie in 1849. Her Grace was
sometimes Mistress of Robes to Queen Victoria and was created Countess of
Cromartie. She died November 25, 1888. Princess Alexandra was sponsor for
the Duchess's daughter Alexandra, who died on April 16, 1891. The Duke
remarried in 1889 Mary Caroline, widow of Arthur Kindersley Blair, and
daughter of Rev. Richard Michell, D.D., principal of Hertford College,
Oxford.

[19] Although Henry James entered a similar theme in his notebooks for a
short story in 1888, he seems to have written the tale at this time. His interest
in the subject may have been revived by the history of Lady Alexandra, as re-
counted here by Alice. The tale, "The Marriages," published in the *Atlantic
Monthly* in August 1891, places the daughter, however, in a more unfavorable
light than she appears in Alice's account.

passed with peaceful joy from amidst the vain shadows. Will
there be no stirrings of remorse in her father's bosom for the
brutalities which rent that delicate fibre?

She made a very instructive remark to our differently con-
stituted standard. She said to her nurse that she had had a
great deal of sorrow, and could not live with her father because
he had married some one whom "the Queen would not receive"
—this was, of course, a convenient formula for use to the nurse,
but it was also an absolute standard of the possible and the
impossible bred in her bone. It opened up to one such a new
conception and such an impulse of gratitude that one had con-
genitally escaped from the chance of any such *entravement* of
one's personal prerogative.

But of all the repulsions, the greatest is that of a religion
subscribed to in conformity to an outward standard of respectability, not the spontaneous inspiration of the aspiring soul.
A God with fixed and rigid outlines to be worshipped within a
prescribed and strictly formal ritual, not a Deity that shapes
himself from moment to moment to the need of the votary
whose bosom glows with the living, ever clearer knowledge of
divine things. A faith propped up by a resounding rhetoric
descended from the ages, and by the vain repetitions of men;
not a faith which is the sacred secret of every soul within which
it springs impregnable, whose communion is the common joys
and sorrows, the simple sights and sounds, and whose ritual
shrouds itself from vulgar speculation in the individual mystery.

April 23rd

It has been so thrilling this winter to have that terra incognita,
the stage, opened up to us, and to be able to project ourselves
into the consciousness of the playwright, and learn all the conditions which enchain him. Harry is the most adorable creature
for "telling," and then the things that he sees! Compton told
K. that he had at once told them things about the members

of their company that they themselves, after years, were only beginning to learn. The Comptons also dwelt very much on the fact that, save a little excision, when they came to rehearse *The American*, they had not suggested an alteration; this, it seems, is very unusual. Mrs. Kendal says in her little book, that plays have usually almost to be made over.[20]

When one learns all the cast-iron restrictions within which the poor author has to carry out his purpose, any sort of a play becomes a tour de force; to tell a story within a given number of minutes, so that each syllable has to be measured, is hard enough, and then to tell it so that the commonest mind can understand *au fur et à mesure*; that each act should end with a "curtain"; and of supreme importance that the Actor-Manager and his Wife, if she exists, should have the chief parts, and form a situation at the finale is an Herculean task.[21]

The Actor-Manager *has* to marry his Wife, though as a comedy actress she may have, in order to attain this end, to transform herself into a tragedy queen. And this is Art! Can you imagine anything more ludicrously British than to risk your very salvation rather than break grotesque shackles consecrated by the *far back*, the sacred inherited inanities!

H. came in, a few days ago, all heated from a most sympathetic interview with Hare,[22] who not only accepts play number two, *Mrs. Vibert*, which H. wrote before Christmas for Miss Genevieve Ward,[23] but accepts it with enthusiasm and calls it a "masterpiece of dramatic construction." His talk was most intelligent and his view of the English public all that can be

---

[20] Dame Madge Kendal (1849–1935), the distinguished actress. Actually James's *American* was very considerably revised by him, once the play was brought to London.

[21] Alice is here echoing her brother's continual complaints at being "strait-jacketed" by the exigencies of the stage.

[22] Sir John Hare (1844–1921) had promised to produce James's play *Mrs. Vibert* (later renamed *Tenants*) but never did.

[23] Genevieve Ward (1838–1922), American-born actress, who played both in New York and London.

desired. He talked a great deal about the Cast, and repeated "it is meant for the Français." *Lady Bountiful*[24] which he has just brought out, has unfortunately fallen, and he apparently would bring out H's play now, but that he wants, for a rest, to revive an old play, and he has promised to bring out another new play, next, so H. won't come until the autumn or winter, I am afraid. He seems to be emancipated from the managerial necessity of fitting the play to his company, and is blessedly not possessed of an acting wife.

I was surprised to find that H. didn't seem to see how much more dependent this play will be, for success, upon the actors than *The American*, or The Comedy that he has just written; it depending altogether upon the subtlety and art with which the delicate psychologic situations are introduced, and will only appeal to that limited public which suspects that art and subtlety exist. H. says that *Lady Bountiful* is put on the stage in the most exquisite manner; the English surpass the French so enormously in this way; I suggested that the French substituted the acting—"Yes, of course, here the acting is simply thrown in."—"It adds so much"—as the young Americal girl said to Lizzie Putnam, of the mountains in Switzerland.

H. said, whilst rehearsing with the Compton troupe, that it was all very well to be superior to the *mise-en-scène*, but with such inferior instruments that it was an enormous support, and that he fell back upon, and "clung to every button."

April 24th

Truly nothing is to be expected but the unexpected! Mrs. Chamberlain being out of town, a great box of flowers, which comes to them from Highbury, was forwarded to K. yesterday. Nurse opened it and laid the lovely things across my knees; in the midst I discovered a tidy little parcel which I opened, and lo! I, in my obscurity, found myself suddenly in the exalted

[24] Pinero's *Lady Bountiful* was produced by Hare in March 1891.

presence of two of Joseph's[25] historic "buttonholes." Nurse hastened to decorate my humble person with the ugly things, ugly as orchids only can be, and I felt that life *was* worth living. A few minutes after, I took up the *Standard* and found that the Creature had been making a speech somewhere, the concluding lines of which were to the effect that only a few Irish wanted Home Rule, to make money out of it; how is that for base?

There are rumours of a dissolution; I dread it immensely, the public stagnation of the last months has been such a rest.

One of the things no man can understand in Englishmen is their political relations. They eagerly seize on every occasion, in Parliament and out, to call one another liars, scoundrels, etc., under the thinnest parliamentary disguises, if any; and then they walk off arm-in-arm together, to dine. This excites the loudest national applause and the Standard was lately moved to a leader on the subject—"In what other nation would such a thing be possible etc.?" In none, thank Heaven! Even the French duel with its supremely ludicrous elements makes upon one an impression of manliness, as compared with a lily-livered creature slinking off to dine with the man that has just called him a scoundrel. If it *is* meant, the first movement, one would imagine, would be to knock the man down; if he is simply a liar of degraded sort, making political capital, one's stomach would surely turn at his soup—ah, but the concessions to expediency that are consistent with being "a bold and noble Briton" are manifold and great!

April 25th

How flattening out but useful, when you have complacently taken it for granted that you are having "an influence for good," over a daughter of the people, to find that she all the time was

[25] Joseph Chamberlain (1836–1914) had become leader of the Liberal Unionists in Parliament, and was opposed to Home Rule.

rolling down hill outside the domestic beer-barrel. It is such a shock and outrage to your vanity to find how you have been made game of, until reason shows you that you have endowed the creature out of your own consciousness, with all sorts of qualities and decencies which she never pretended to have, and that, just as the ignorant perceive and observe nothing, because there are no germs within, inherited or acquired, we, with our exotic perceptions, fancy we discover in the coarsest weeds possibilities of the fairest bloom and feel wronged when we are pricked by the thorns and stung by the nettles.

April 26th

We are so absurdly happy in our decidedly silly little house, which 'twould seem as easy to have arrived at, without so many links in the chain, but each one had to be forged at the inexorable smithy of endurance, where no man's measure is ever scamped; I had to get a little worse in order to lose all conscience about absorbing K. as a right, and then I had to get a little more money, which came to the moment in the closing of poor old Cousin Henry Wyckoff's tragic life.[26] I had feared a constant terror of burglars, but ne'er a scare have I had yet. The tone of the household is quite sublimated, full of a serene interchange of amenities, the only contention being over the protoplasmic soul of Louisa; whether at the end of our lease, 'twill have taken a ritualistic or baptismal shape, no sign has yet been vouchsafed—Nurse makes her a bonnet, whereupon Baptisma makes her an apron, etc., whilst the cold blooded Unitarian fish and the impassioned devotee of natural religion upstairs gaze in holy horror(!) at these shameless machinations of ecclesiasticism. K. says I have "the most paying (I suggest bloated) religion of the five, as the three indispensable

[26] See Henry James, *A Small Boy and Others*, Chapter XI, for an account of Wyckoff. James's comedy *The Reprobate* was based in part on this bit of family history.

elements are all united in my own person,—"Allah, the prophet and the votary."

Poor little Nurse is so sunken in her superstition, that although she has heard my scoffs for five years, she can't even yet grasp that the Church has no existence for me, so that when Louisa has been led away to Chapel, she comes and makes some excuse to me, when I most discourageingly exclaim, "An excellent place for her to go."

Given what she is: she is the best little creature in the world, and has fitted herself with most exemplary patience, to all my acute angles, and no groan escaped from her—When all the foundations gave way under me last summer, and I clung to her, as a drowning creature to a straw, I had such an impression of the richness of life, in finding security in anchoring myself to her long narrow Fra Angelico surface, covering simply half a dozen faithful kindly instincts, uniting me with the simple and the good, so that the blessed peace fell upon me which comes from escaping from the fantastic, and burying one's self in the vast ruminating mass. In the old days, when, month after month, and year after year, I used to get my "attacks," and Mother and Father would watch by me through the long nights, I used to cry out to them to know what would become of me when I lost them; and here was the answer to my doubting heart, a little girl then toddling about a Gloucestershire village, was, in a foreign land, to hold out her hand to my necessity, perform all kind offices, and give me an ever deeper sense of the exquisite truth that human good outweighs all human evil, and that only from amidst the clouds shines out the true illumination.

May 3rd

Bob writes that Ned,[27] who is very good about his studies is destined by the good little Mary to be a "ministrant at the

[27] Ned was Edward Holton James (1873–1954), eldest son of the youngest James brother, Robertson.

altar"; given the strain of Father that is inevitable in his blood, this is irresistibly funny: the altar, too, is to be after the episcopal order, that jerry-builder architecture of the soul, with none of the historic splendour of the Catholic Church to lend it romance and authority nor the grim, heroic nudity of austere and masculine Calvinism to brace the mental and moral sinews.

May 7th

K. went on the third of May to the Eight-Hours Demonstration in Hyde Park—she thinks it fortunate that I was not there, as I should have been reduced to a fountain of water, the immensity of it was so overpowering. The whole question is such a turbulent sea of doubt upon which one is tossed without pilot or compass that I have had to close my emotions thereto. The whole system of things is hideous and to be swept away, but just now, the English working man, as some one said of the scenery, "is so petted and pampered" as compared to his fellows in less fortunate lands, and when one needs him for a job, he is so perpetually and exasperatingly seeking relaxation in a whole or half holiday that the "unemployed" become to one's belief a fantastic creation. He seems compact of that quality which continued residence here only forces more and more upon one, the absence of grit in all classes, and the construction and acceptance of life on a weak kneed basis.

H., last summer, gave such an interesting account of the people whom he had seen on the Continent, in Bavaria and Italy chiefly; and one got such an impression of the toiling, unrequited, nameless millions, going silent with unrecorded virtues to their graves, whilst their enduring heroism is the mainspring without which the shrieking irreducent scum would vanish like the morning mist.

What a spectacle, the Anglo-Saxon races addressing remonstrances to the Czar against expelling the Jews from Russia, at the very moment when their own governments are making laws to forbid their immigration.[28]

Nurse took me to the window today, and lo! Spring has been at her tricks! We have a good scraplet of garden which, with those of our neighbours, give us a delightful glimpse of sky and many a feathery bit of green. K. has expended twenty shillings' worth of seeds and twenty pounds worth of energy between our walls, and I dream that, as the season advances, I may occasionally be carried by my slaves through the tangled bloom. How fortunate it is that we have so many æsthetic stomachs, so that when lying in a shaded room, we can chew and re-chew the cud of past contemplations; a slant of light, or a whiff of perfume, or a rustle of wind, and the illusion of the shimmering vista, the murmuring pines, and the damp divine earthiness, is before us in perfection.

May 9th

It is not often that we have the gratification of hearing our theories confirmed and justified out of the mouth of the subject; but an authoritative stamp and seal was given to one by Miss Clough,[29] Mistress of Newnham, when K. was lunching there the other day; what more than anything else makes this estimable race seem so completely foreign, as if we could not have had, possibly, a common descent, is the microscopic subdivision of their knowledge. It is impossible to predicate that supremacy in one accomplishment will shed, not a radiance, but raise to the simplest level of intelligence the whole man, for he carries

---

[28] Alexander III (1845–1894) succeeded his assassinated father as Czar and pursued throughout his reign reactionary policies inspired by fear and ignorance. He sought to Russianize various Russian minorities and enforce old restrictions on the number and occupations of Jews in urban areas. This led to expulsion of large numbers of Jews from Moscow and other cities and their crowding into ghetto areas.

[29] Anne Jemima Clough (1820–1892), sister of the poet, Arthur Hugh Clough, was first principal of Newnham College for women at Cambridge.

his gift which he so often has in great perfection, in an airtight compartment through the walls of which radiates no germinating ardour, and he leaves the rest of himself with a touching, childlike candour, just as Nature made him. One had supposed that he was an unconscious victim; from Miss Cloughs pronouncement, it seems it is what they strive to make 'em, the general intelligence and absence of particular developement which she observes in the American girls that come to her being entirely subversive of the established law, that a child's mind should be dedicated to and perfected in some one study alone, to mathematics, or languages etc., whilst all other fields are left fallow to the seed of accident. This is why things end so short off when you are talking. You ask some question cousin germane to the subject, when all the machinery stops, and they without a squirm proclaim absolute ignorance. Such candour appeals no doubt to the Most High but it discourages and interrupts the social flow to a greater degree than the hit-or-miss flutter and flap we give to the wings of imagination when we feel under foot the distressful ooze of doubt.

It is all very simple, and explains itself, they stand to themselves as "mathematics," not relative, but absolute, and rest placid and content therein, whilst the quivering Yankee catches up, in the ravelled edges of his culture, simply an approximate knowledge of many things. You are so impressed, at first, when you come by the rounded smoothness of intellectual interchange, and are amazed until an illuminating ray is projected, and you see that you can make no call of any sort upon the individual for a movement of inspiration, that his substance, only in exceptional cases, justifies the surface of inherited education and fortunate opportunity that has fallen to his lot—but who, I should like to know, ever saw an over-educated Yankee!— save, always the egregious Norton.[30]

Every spring the first classic or senior wrangler excites in

[30] Charles Eliot Norton (1827–1908), professor of the history of art at Harvard, 1873–1898.

their minds as boyish an enthusiasm as when he was first invented, and all these centuries that they have seen him sink into impotent obscurity don't dim his glory or open their eyes to the fact that an excrescence of one order of knowledge rarely dissolves itself into the practical wisdom of life. Mary Porter told me one day, that, at the other end of the scale, the inability of the people who had been trained to do one thing, never turning their hand to another, complicated the situation so. At the moment she was very much concerned about some men who had been boxmakers; the fluctuations of trade had cut off the work, and all these poor creatures had to sink into dockers, pitiable dregs!

Instances of this sort are infinitely multiplied; one or two more are marked enough to be worthy of mention.—The Estate Agent "off" whom we took this house has a large and important business, but when K. gave for reference Baring Brothers,[31] he knew them not, this winter, when the world has rung with their downfall, makes the cessation of his business consciousness just without their radius the more remarkable.

The Monday after the eight hours demonstration in Hyde Park, K. went to a club in Shoreditch where she goes to amuse the infants of the People, and she asked a Miss Cathcart whose whole life is devoted to the working man and has a great deal to do with organizing their clubs, what she heard the men say about the question and whether she had the impression that the Call for it was genuine or not—she was entirely vague, had never heard it talked of, and apparently had no sort of interest in it—she believed that she had heard there was going to be a meeting in Hyde Park.—

From the vast seething problem of poverty she had fallen upon and made her own the club organizing and amusement department, attaining great success, but no little trickle of

---

[31] The banking firm of Baring Brothers & Co. in London. The senior partner, Russell Sturgis (1805–1887), originally a Boston merchant, was a friend of Henry James, as were his sons Julian and Howard.

interest in the question as a whole oozed into and permeated her mind.

A married lady who is by way of being "very clever" and knowing said one day something that showed such extraordinary ignorance of feminine anatomy, that I exclaimed: "Have you never known any one who has had a child?" "Oh yes, my sister has had about twelve."

Harry, yesterday, was calling at Mrs. Humphry Ward's,[32] who has just moved into a beautiful new house in Grosvenor Place, said to be one of the products of *Robert Elsmere*. Miss Pater was there also, and Harry looking over at the beautiful trees in Buckingham Palace Gardens was moved to address to her a lament over such a lost enjoyment in the heart of London, despised by the Queen and denied to the people; when she timorously said (with her eyes fixed upon them), "Where are they?" H. said, "Why, *there:* before your eyes!" To which she replied, "Oh, yes; I suppose they would be." And this is a lady who is said by her accomplished family to be a "mine of silent learning."

I now bethink myself that all this long preachment might have been epitomized in an utterance which H. made one day, that "the English are the only people who can do great things without being clever."

May 31st

To him who waits, all things come! My aspirations may have been eccentric, but I cannot complain now, that they have not been brilliantly fulfilled. Ever since I have been ill, I have longed and longed for some palpable disease, no matter how conventionally dreadful a label it might have, but I was always driven back to stagger alone under the monstrous mass of subjective sensations, which that sympathetic being "the medical

[32] Mrs. Humphry Ward (1851–1920), English novelist, whose *Robert Elsmere* (1888) was one of the most widely-read late Victorian novels.

man" had no higher inspiration than to assure me I was personally responsible for, washing his hands of me with a graceful complacency under my very nose. Dr. Torry[83] was the only man who ever treated me like a rational being, who did not assume, because I was victim to many pains, that I was, of necessity, an arrested mental development too.

Nothwithstanding all the happiness and comfort here, I have been going downhill at a steady trot; so they sent for Sir Andrew Clark[84] four days ago, and the blessed being has endowed me not only with cardiac complications, but says that a lump that I have had in one of my breasts for three months, which has given me a great deal of pain, is a tumour, that nothing can be done for me but to alleviate pain, that it is only a question of time, etc. This with a delicate embroidery of "the most distressing case of nervous hyperæsthesia" added to a spinal neurosis that has taken me off my legs for seven years; with attacks of rheumatic gout in my stomach for the last twenty, ought to satisfy the most inflated pathologic vanity. It is decidedly indecent to catalogue oneself in this way, but I put it down in a scientific spirit, to show that though I have no productive worth, I have a certain value as an indestructible quantity.

June 1st

To any one who has not been there, it will be hard to understand the enormous relief of Sir A. C.'s uncompromising verdict, lifting us out the formless vague and setting us within the very heart of the sustaining concrete. One would naturally not choose such an ugly and gruesome method of progression down the dark Valley of the Shadow of Death, and of course many of

[83] Dr. John Cooper Torry, member of the Royal College of Physicians, had been practising in London since 1859. He was trained at St. Andrew's.

[84] Sir Andrew Clark, F.R.C.S., (d. 1913) a vice president of the British Medical Association, distinguished Victorian physician and surgeon, was later honorary surgeon to King Edward VII.

the moral sinews will snap by the way, but we shall gird up our loins and the blessed peace of the end will have no shadow cast upon it.

Having it to look forward to for a while seems to double the value of the event, for one becomes suddenly picturesque to oneself, and one's wavering little individuality stands out with a cameo effect and one has the tenderest indulgence for all the abortive little *stretchings out* which crowd in upon the memory. The grief is all for K. and H., who will *see* it all, whilst I shall only *feel* it, but they are taking it, of course, like archangels, and care for me with infinite tenderness and patience. Poor dear William with his exaggerated sympathy for suffering isn't to know anything about it until it is all over.[35]

June 5th

As canker i' the rose, so lurketh disappointment in the tumour! I had always supposed that I could throw myself back upon a tumour with perfect moral security, but lo! I find that the wretched thing is simply absolute as tumour; commonplace and well intentioned as curtailing life, but stirred up to all sorts of unusual discomforts by *my* being brought to bear upon it, so that I am as much tortured as ever to decide as to the degree of anguish as compared to all other tumourous victims I must undergo before I can apply the pacifying anæsthetic.

It seems that Sir A. C. said that although I might die in a week or so, I might also live some months. This is a strain, as Katharine says I have looked "prepared" for a week, and I am sure I shall not be able to keep that up for some months.

I tease the Nurseling to death, to explain to me by what hocus-pocus my unshriven soul is to enter Paradise, as she ardently although inarticulately assumes that it will. I think that it is all covered in her *fer intérieure* by that mystic, but

[35] William James was informed, however, and came to England in the autumn of 1891 to visit Alice.

all-accounting-for word "American." When she says on Sunday: "I shall be late today, Miss, because I want to see the procession," how can her Anglican manœuvres suggest anything but the ordinances of our Fourth of July!

I cannot make out whether it is an entire absence or an excess of humor in Destiny to construct such an elaborate exit for my thistle-down personality, especially at this moment when so many of the great of the earth are gobbled up in a day or two by a microbe. Let Baptisma return from a prayer meeting tipsy, and I should be blown into space; or Louisa be found in dalliance with the post-man, or Nurse insist on hanging her cross *en évidence* outside of her apron, I having sent it to Coventry upon the pretext that it banged my fleshy nose, as she tended the couch of pain, little suspecting that the real offending was to my spiritual nostrils. But life is so hopelessly grotesque with its disproportions and inconsistencies! Could the sham of it all be better expressed than by the fact that the being who presents the *image* of Robert Elsmere has houses and lands heaped upon her by the gaping millions, whilst he that lives the life has that little which he already had, taken from him.

June 6th

Katharine has so strongly the irritating Yankee propensity of doubling up like a jack-knife in your hand when appealed to for moral indignation. She *is* a trial, especially towards 2 A.M.

June 16th

What a cunning trick of Fortune to bring him of Berlin[36] here, at this moment, to enhance the princely pose of "Uncle Wales" thro' the Baccarat Scandal[37]; for however little one may admire

[36] Alice's way of alluding to the German Kaiser, Wilhelm II (1859–1942), familiarly called *Der Reise-Kaiser* because of his constant travels.

[37] The "Baccarat Scandal" came into the open when a lieutenant colonel in the Scot's Guards, Sir William Gordon-Cumming, lost a slander suit against a

that Imperial Barnum, he wallows not in the ignoble. Such an exhibition of sordid greed as it has all been isn't lessened by hearing incidentally that the Prince never pays except when he is asked, and that the Princess plays very high and never pays at all, because she can't be asked. Some diplomatist, I have forgotten who, told H. that the Prince was very much disliked in Paris, in Society, because he was so fierce about being instantly paid, and that lately, he had taken every sou from some young French nobleman, so that he was utterly ruined.

I see a new volume of Anatole France[38] out, which will never be read by me! For a long time past, I have only read what reads with the eyelashes, anything that stirs interest or reflection letting loose the fountain of tears. Sir A. Clarke asked K., when she saw him after his pronunciamento, if I did anything; she said I went on just as usual, and did whatever little thing I could in the way of reading or dictating. "That's right, don't induce her to give up anything; even if she is to die next week, why shouldn't she go on just as usual?" I suppose he imagined that we had entered into an elaborate system of "preparation." What a job it would be for any one who undertook it though!

I have always been greatly struck and disgusted with the nagging little method that Providence uses for our spiritual evolution. To think of grudging me the spectacle of the development of H.'s dramatic genius by hastening it a year or two; that supreme interest might have lightened those unspeakable years in Leamington, which have honeycombed all my moral being with their weary strain of the long desolate "keeping up."

The difficulty with H.'s plays is going to be, according to Hare, the absence of actors for them, their natural home

group of well-known figures in society who had accused him of cheating at cards. The case aroused wide attention when it was learned that Edward Prince of Wales (the future Edward VII) had been among the gamblers. Called to testify, he told the court he found the strongly-supported evidence that there had been cheating to be beyond question.

[38] His new work was probably *Thaïs*, which appeared in 1890.

being the Français. I asked him how he explained his suddenly finding himself in possession of a dramatic construction so perfect, he said that he had always felt sure he could write plays, but hated so the process of hawking them about.

Within the last year he has published *The Tragic Muse*, brought out *The American*, and written a play, *Mrs. Vibert* (which Have has accepted) and his admirable comedy; combined with William's *Psychology*, not a bad show for one family! especially if I get myself dead, the hardest job of all. This playing business is going to multiply H.'s benevolent entanglements in a sad way—besides the people from home whom he visits, the sick and bereft, perpetually renewed, whose hands he holds; now all the dishevelled ladies come to him to set their halting plays upon their legs, which amounts to his rewriting them. À propos of actresses, he says Miss Robins[39] is the most intelligent creature, next to Coquelin[40] with whom he ever talked about her art.

June 17th

We were quite grateful for the Englishry of this: K saw the other day a very smart lady in a victoria driving in the crowd at the canonical hour, down Piccadilly to the Park, and so far carrying out to perfection the lesson of the day, but with that homely burst of nature to which the most encrusted here are subject, she was satisfying the cravings of the stomach by eating, with the utmost complacency, in the eye of man, a huge, stodgy penny bun. The perfection in all her appointments in the way of carriage, etc—with the absence of subtlety in her palate as shown by the placid consumption of the bun, and complete

[39] Elizabeth Robins (1865–1957), American-born Ibsen actress, played the role of Claire de Cintré in the London production of *The American*.
[40] Benoît Constant Coquelin (1841–1909), creator of *Cyrano de Bergerac*, one of France's most celebrated actors of the nineteenth century.

indifference, at this very visible moment, at exhibiting her
features distorted by the ugly process of masticating such an
adhesive substance, had an incongruity very characteristic of
the soil. They seem in matters of taste to have no sense of
gradations. H. is always saying this, but it jumped at my eye
from the first, and is therefore an original if not unique utterance. H., by the way, has embedded in his pages many pearls
fallen from my lips, which he steals in the most unblushing
way, saying, simply, that he knew they had been said by the
family, so it did not matter.

I remember when I was at H.'s during the Jubilee Year, having one of those longings to commit sin that come over us every
now and then. All but gastronomic vice being denied by my
miserable sex, I sent Nurse to Gunter's for some *éclairs*, and
word was sent back that "they were a kind of *biscuit* that had
to be eaten fresh, so they had to be ordered the day before!" I
laughed and thought of little MacElroy's in Harvard Sq[uare]
20 years ago. They now have arrived at the sophistication you
can often find them here; but our cousins are not *previous!*
One might say that they were pre-historic, or, at least, mediæval,
in the perfect absence of modulation of the sleeping arrangements, the knowledge of which has unfolded itself gradually
with increasingly repulsive details. The first summer we were
here (1885), we had a tiny cottage, in the most beautiful situation at the top of Hampstead Heath; besides the servants'
department, it consisted simply of four very small rooms: into
which we (K. and I) squeezed for two months: as it was such
early days with us, we were quite overwhelmed by surprise
to learn that before the Toynbee Hall Barnetts (who were our
landlords) had hired it, it had been occupied by a gentleman
blessed with a wife and five children; our wonder didn't naturally diminish, when we found that his predecessor had possessed nine olive-branches: I suppose there was standing room
in the house for them, but we were perfectly certain that they
were laid away in tiers at night, each with its [his] little

drapery neatly folded up beneath him. These people were highly respectable and educated, and were, I believe, artists. But we long ago abandoned the attempt to solve the problem of how the multifold offspring was disposed of through the watches of the night; but we have been simply appalled by having more and more light thrown in upon the loathsome sleeping arrangements of their servants! I am, of course, speaking only of "middle-class" houses. They live in such comfort and luxury, indulge and feed their servants to the last degree, but give them nowhere to lay their head, for the butler and footmen actually sleep in pantry and scullery, where the china and glass you eat off is washed every day. In large houses the butler does it in order to protect the plate: conceive of having plate with nowhere to put it, except in the butler's bed-room! The visions which the dullest imagination calls up at these thoughts are too horrible to be hinted.

Dr. Ogle, the Registrar General, told K. that the rich people subscribed to build St. George's Hospital in their neighborhood, as they had to have a place to send their footmen, when they were laid up with scarlet fever in the scullery. When the servant is fortunate enough to have a bed-room, it seems to be immersed in the bosom of the family. Constantly in reading police reports, which to a foreigner are so seductive and instructive, the most curious domestic arrangements are revealed: The other day, a Mr. Antrobus, whose father, I think, is a very rich banker, was found shot in his room, and the evidence brought out that the valet and the butler slept in the next room, which communicated by a door, with his. They seem to be sprinkled about, anywhere. K. had strange experiences in looking for this house; out of the 30 she saw, this was the only attractive one, and there was only one other possible. The absence of cleanliness and the smallness and disproportion of the bed-rooms to the reception rooms were universal. She saw a largish house in Palace Gardens Terrace with four reception rooms and eight masters' bedrooms; when she asked the "lady-housekeeper" where the servants' rooms were, she said: "downstairs next the kitchen"—"How many?" "One"—at K.'s exclamation of horror, she replied: "It is large enough for three"—maids: of course there was the pantry and the scullery for butler and footman. This cutting from the *P.M.G.* only confirms the impression:

"To-day Mr. Gilbert's famous house, 39 Harrington Gardens, will be sold by auction by Messrs. Fox and Bousfield, at Token-house-yard. It was built in 1883, by Messrs. George and Peto, and is a palace in miniature. From the porch to the roof everything is sumptuous. The outer hall is lined with oak, and looks like a Baron's. The inner hall is used as a reception-saloon, and has high oak panelled dado, with walls of gold Japanese paper. The ingle-nook is lined with curious old Dutch tiles of the seventeenth century; the hearth is mosaic; and the dog fireplace is of red brick. The dining-room, too, is lined with a carved oak dado, each panel being treated in allegorical subjects. On the first floor is Mr. Gilbert's library, in which he has written many of his plays and operas. To give some idea of the size of the house we give a list of the rooms:—

Halls and vestibule	. . .	3	Dressing-rooms	3
Entertainment rooms	. .	5	Bath-rooms	4
Billiard-room		1	Secondary bedchambers .	5
Best bed-rooms		4	Servants' rooms	3

The whole is lighted with electricity. Great is comic opera!"

The Clarkes' house in which I lived in Leamington, where there were only three bed-rooms of any size (and they were small enough), had been rented, shortly before I went there, to the Hon. Somebody—among other large families—for a year, who brought with him five children, his wife, governess, butler, nurse and maids. Then the complete absence (except in the fine old houses, where I believe they exist) of closets and places for putting away things not in use, is most bewildering to us poor Yankees, although we are so relatively destitute of heirlooms; I

have been told that they lay clothes in piles on the chairs, and
have rows of boots around the edges of their bed-rooms. The
dumb patience of the creature is shown in their having sub-
mitted so long to the wretched system of land tenure, which
has allowed the Jerry-builder to wantonly destroy all domestic
privacy: the generality of middle class houses having the con-
sistency of a band-box, they rock and quake when one walks
across the floor, and you hear the voices of your next door
neighbours as plainly as in a summer hotel, at home. Mrs. Lang
told me that there was a hole in the front wall of her house,
through which she could see the sky. The Ashburners, after a
nine years' search, took a large and good house and had it
thoroughly "done up," and then for weeks vainly tried to
warm the drawing-room sufficiently to sit in it; then they were
told by the people who had the house before them, that the
room could never be used in cold weather: George was then
inspired to climb up on a ladder and look at the top of the
windows, which had all been examined by the British workman,
who had carefully left in the setting of them, several inches
of ventilation into the open street.

The immensity of London is so overpowering that a superficial impression of solidity goes with it, and it makes one rather
heartsick to learn by degrees that it is simply miles of card-
board houses, compared to which our wooden houses are like
mediæval fortresses. It is not only in this region, but in May-
fair where I lived formerly, and where the houses are oldish—
I must add that these are the houses not of people of limited
means only, but of people to whom belong smart broughams
and victorias, high stepping horses, first and second coachmen,
butler and footmen, etc.

June 24th

I suppose we are perpetually coaling up, as it were, and taking
in unconsciously information for future application. Half a dozen

times a day I find myself saying, "I must ask K. about that," or "I must find out about this," with the idea that some day I may need the knowledge, when suddenly I am stopped off by the thought that the "some days" are over for me; a thought natural and simple, and of a most desirable complexion. It seems more like the gentle dropping of natural things, than the taking up of spiritual ones; as it comes nearer, it will doubtless seem more positive. Owing to my curious, given my inheritance and surroundings, complete absence of intellectual curiosity—philosophies and systems, theologies and sciences having ever been as dry husks to the living emotions and moralities—these last possess me with such an unquestioned and sustaining force, that they function unconsciously, I suppose, and I don't have to pick them up now, with the parson and prayer-book.

This turning away one's mind so persistently from what bores it, and allowing one's being to absorb itself in one motive, the active principle conceived in youth and never modified, show a restricted nature, not admirable or generous in its impulses, but highly practical and time saving, in so far that it never runs you off the track, and one soon learns the bearings of one's little compass. So many seem to pass their lives starting afresh on every side track.

As one's inconsistencies, or rather those of one's brother, lend to life its chief charm, I should, if not so obscure, give a handful of people a rejoiceful occasion to scoff, as in all probability an Anglican priest will supervise my obsequies. I am to be taken to Woking, and if Harry were only like his French confrères, he could easily record the sublimity of my past and save me from the humiliation of admitting that the parson has some raison d'être after all, and that however superior one may be, raw edges grate upon one sadly. Having been denied baptism by my parents, marriage by obtuse and imperceptive man, it seems too bad not to assist myself at this first and last ceremony; perhaps the impish part of me will hover about, and enjoy the fine and highly decorative rhetoric, to say nothing of the joke against the "Not as other men" part of me. When Mother and Father died, we fell back upon the uncompromising and amorphous Unitarian shepherd, for whom no sheep has too varied a fleece, but he is hard to find in these pastures.

A week before Father died, I asked him one day, whether he had thought what he should like to have done about his funeral. He was immediately very much interested, not having apparently thought of it before; he reflected for some time, and then said, with the greatest solemnity and looking so majestic: "Tell him to say only this, 'here lies a man who has thought all his life, that the ceremonies attending birth, marriage and death were all damned nonsense,' don't let him say a word more." But there was no Unitarian, even, elastic enough for this: what a washed out, cowering mess humanity seems beside a creature such as that.

July 15th

I have a delicious consciousness of wide spaces close at hand, and this morning a letter came from Harry who is in Ireland recruiting[41] from influenza, bringing such a foretaste of Heaven from amid the divine absence of the Respectable in that inspired and inspiring race! Imagine the emancipation that it will be, after seven years of this stifling land, where "form" is the god of gods!

One day, talking about some good reviews of William's *Psychology*, which reprobate his mental pirouettes and squirm at his daring to go lightly amid the solemnities, H. said, "Yes; they can't understand intellectual larking"—I remember the *Spectator* once describing some of Father's flights from the Commonplace as "coarse."

William has had four requests already to translate his book

---

[41] Alice here uses the word in its rare sense, that of replenishment or renewal.

into German. There is a review, of reviews, in the *Nation,* written apparently by a district school boy or a minister in the Green Mountains, which makes Father out such a double-dyed materialist that it is astonishing that a son of his could have any spiritual glimpses.

The Comic and the tragic alternate; picture my hearing that Jules Lemaître is not only vicious and repulsive in his ways, which one had taken for granted, but is so base and degraded in his life, that my feminine construction would prevent my ever having offered him again mental hospitality.

September 3rd

It is very gratifying at this mortuary moment to learn how many people have been "struck and *impressed*"! But I can't help thinking how cheered and sustained I should have been had they only been inspired to bare their indented bosoms in the earlier stages of the weary journey.

These long pauses don't point to any mental aridity, my "roomy forehead" is as full as ever of germinating thoughts, but alas the machinery is more and more out of kilter. I am sorry for you all, for I feel as if I hadn't even yet given my message. I would there were more bursts of enthusiasm, less of the carping tone, through this, but I fear it comes by nature, and after all, the excellent Islander will ne'er be crushed by the knowledge of the eye that was upon him, through the long length of years, and the monotone of the enthusiast is more wearisome to sustain than a dyspeptic note.

Like a sheep to the shambles, I have been led by K. to the camera! Owing to some curious cerebral condition, Annie Richards was heard to say, "Alice has fine features": K. seized the "psychologic moment" of titillated vanity and brought the one eyed monster to bear upon me; such can be woman's inhumanity to woman.

I sha'n't be able to enjoy quite as much martyrdom as I

expected, for a I shall, after all, have seen a bit of *The American*; for Harry brought a sample of Madame de Cintré's ball dress the other day, he having been to choose it, with Mrs. Compton.

September 7th

Mes beaux restes have returned from the photographer in refulgent beauty! so very much flattered that my heart now overflows with mansuetude for that admirable Katharine, so wise of counsel, so firm of purpose, so gentle in action!

September 18th

It was very interesting the other day to have K. come across a young American girl who is studying at one of the Colleges here, and to have her confirm, in every respect, Miss Clough's opinion of the unspecialized, unprepared, intelligent American student. She had done very well indeed at home, but found herself overwhelmed with mortification at her ignorance of what she had supposed her chosen branch of knowledge. She found her fellow students kind and friendly and desirous to help her, but the dullest companions, for outside of their special interests, their minds were perfectly blank and indifferent, and absolutely without any general curiosity; one of them recommending as a novelty of which she had probably not heard, and by which she might be shocked, *Jane Eyre* to read; another, whose name is known in two hemispheres, asked her what she spoke when she went to Paris, English or American; and whether New York is a seaport. All the American girls find the climate and the food terribly trying for the first year or two. She confirmed our impression of the necessity which the Briton is under, to eat *immediately*; that he can't feel a pang without complete collapse. She also said, that there is no need to make rules regulating the walking together of male and female students, for as almost all the latter would presumably be governesses or teachers, any man student would rather throw himself into the Cam than be guilty of the bad form of walking with any one of them, however pretty or attractive she might be, and desirable as a companion outside University recognition. Such things illustrate why every American, the longer he stays in England, feels himself more and more completely a foreigner, for what American young man could enslave himself to a consideration born of such unmanly snobbery?

"Nurse, I don't think that cook Henderson can be a good friend for Louisa, if she talks about followers, as you say she does, all the time." "It's the housemaid, Miss, who is her chief friend." "Is she a good girl?" "Oh, yes, Miss, she seems very nice, only she's very dressy, she's downstairs now, in a heliotrope gown trimmed with gold braid." "How dreadful, Nurse!" "But you know, Miss, we can't protect Louisa from everything."

Louisa went to a Band-of-Hope beanfeast (picnic) on the "Ups and Downs" (Epsom Downs), fortunately the day *after* a bad head-ache, for as she said, she "could never carry such agony with her, to a place where she expected such enjoyment." She told us, afterwards, that she rode the donkeys with great perfection, because she was used to riding in processions: this amazing accomplishment proved to be taking part in the Lady Godiva processions in Coventry as a child, "dressed up in colours"—"Lady Godiva used to ride with nothing on, but now she wears tights, and Peeping Tom is there too"—"Oh, yes, it is the real Lady Godiva, and always has been the same."

September 20th

A letter from dear old Mr Child[42] is good to get, as coming from him, but how little all assurances of one's own immortality

[42] Francis James Child (1825–1896), professor of English literature at Harvard and a friend of Alice's parents. See Henry James's tribute to him in *Notes of a Son and Brothers* (1914), Chapter X.

seem to concern one, now, and how little to have gained from the experience of life, if one's thoughts are lingering still upon personal fulfilments and not rooted in the knowledge that the great Immortalities, Love, Goodness and Truth include all others; and one need pray for no lesser survivals! References to those whom we shall meet again make me shiver, as such an invasion of their sanctity, gone so far beyond, for ever since the night that Mother died, and the depth of filial tenderness was revealed to me, all personal claim upon her vanished, and she has dwelt in my mind a beautiful illumined memory, the essence of divine maternity from which I was to learn great things, give all, but ask nothing.

October 31st

A dreary letter to Harry from Mr. Godkin, set to the futile tune of which the old cow died so many centuries ago—"everything going to the dogs here." How humiliated one would be to come to the end confessing one's vision so feeble that the mists of evil were impenetrable! But an impossible strain upon humanity is the asking that it should reflect any illumination other than the individual or personal one.

Hold up a minute and let us ponder whether Edwin's dreariness isn't heightened by a too clear perception of an absence of grace in his acceptance of my photo! A personal reflection indeed.

I came across this: "Since drink fell away from me"; such a perfect example of the squashy evasion of "Sin" characteristic of the contemporary mystic; "chromo" mystic, as the jargon goes.

December 1st

It is psychologically interesting to see anyone so humorous as Labouchere, revealing such an infantile simplicity by the length to which he pushes the wingless pose, and so nullifies completely his Idol, effectiveness.

It is curious to see "subjects" and "questions" slipping from out of the mental grasp, as the physical degeneracy advances; one lays them aside and turns from them as naturally as from any muscular exertion, so that the General Election, the "Race," etc., those slight topics to which I felt myself so adequate, and tossed about so lightly, lie dormant under their present colossal expansion.

December 4th

If it were possible, with Death so close at hand, to take anything which concerns one's ephemeral personality, with seriousness, I might pose to myself before the footlights of my last obscure little scene, as a delectably pathetic figure, for I have come to the knowledge within the last week or so that I was simply born a few years too soon; as however this discovery in no way dims to my imagination the glorious possibilities of my immortal being, I shall keep the occasion cheerful by contemplating simply the truly human and topsy-turvy aspect of the situation.

Three or four weeks ago, the treacherous fiend Morphia, which while murdering pain, destroys sleep and opens the door to all hideous nervous distresses, disclosed its iniquities to us, and K. and I touched bottom more nearly than ever before. K. under the suggestion of William, turned on the hypnotic Tuckey,[43] the mild radiance of whose moonbeam personality has penetrated with a little hope the black mists that enveloped us. And now, this vast field of therapeutic possibilities is opened up to me, just at the moment when I have passed far beyond the workings of their beneficent laws, save most superficially, and the "aggravating" quality of this retarded discovery is

---

[43] Dr. Charles Lloyd Tuckey, a graduate of Aberdeen, was an early pioneer in hypnosis therapy, author of *Psycho-Therapeutics: or Treatment by Hypnotism and Suggestion.*

made the more complete and "this-worldly" by the agent taking to itself the form and direction which, from experience, I learned, twenty-four years ago was the some-day-to-be-revealed secret, of suspending for the time from his duties, the individual watch dog, worn out with his ceaseless vigil to maintain the sanity of the modern complicated mechanism. That the golden solution of the complex riddle should be a mechanical process of inconceivable simplicity, is only another of the myriad beautiful illustrations that the highest Divine order is brought about by the humblest means.

December 11th

The young Balestier,[44] the effective and the indispensable is dead! swept away like a cobweb, of which gossamer substance he seems to have been himself compounded, simply spirit and energy, with the slightest of fleshly wrapping: we are sorry indeed for the far reaching loss; and the irritating sense of waste pursues us. Rarely, I suppose, has a life so short, only of twenty-eight years, touched so many others for good. Poor Harry has gone to Dresden to see what he can do for the mother and sisters. I was so happy in the thought that this was going to be a life-long companionship for him, and secure in his having, at last, a business friend, whom he sadly needs. I ne'er saw the youth, but I wonder if we sha'n't soon meet in that "twilight land," swooping past each other like Vedder's[45] ghosts. Will he pause and ask: "What is your name?" And shall I say, "I do not know, I only died last night"—à l'Aldrich?[46]

The difficulty about all this dying is that you can't tell a fellow anything about it, so where does the fun come in?

[44] Balestier had died of typhoid fever in Dresden, and Henry James attended the funeral there. Balestier's sister, Caroline, married Rudyard Kipling.

[45] Elihu Vedder (1836–1923), American illustrator and author.

[46] Thomas Bailey Aldrich (1836–1907), American poet and novelist, editor of the *Atlantic Monthly* in the 1880's.

The American died an honourable death, on the 76th night.
It seemed, as far as the interest and enthusiasm of the audience
went, a great success, but owing to a disastrous season for all
the theatres, and Compton being new and impecunious, the run
was shorter than we hoped. I have to thank the beautiful play
for all the interest and expectancy with which it has filled the
last two years. The excitement and brilliant success of the first
night, then, the subsequent anxiety for a week or two about
the "run," when failure brushed us as she flitted past, seemed
too heavy a load of emotion and impressions for my weakness
to profit from, but as I have lived on, have had time to assimilate
the apparently indigestible mass and see all in its right proportions, it has explained so many hidden mysterious impulses,
putting one in touch for the first time (and quadrupling one's
indulgence) with the huge mass of strugglers after the concrete,
that one seems to have added a new story to one's worldly
store-house. Then the whole episode was so shot thro' with the
golden thread of Comedy, that we grew fat with laughter. The
best moment was one afternoon when H. came in, with the
strangest, amused, amazed, disgusted-with-himself expression
and said that he had just got a telegram from Compton, telling
him that the Prince of Wales was coming to the theatre that
night and wanting him to "dress" a couple of boxes with "smart
people;" and in the most pathetic voice H. exclaimed: "here I
am, having put away my self-respecting papers, come out to do
it!" I'd do anything for the good Comptons, but it will make me
charitable to the end of my days." We stared at ourselves in our
nakedness, and wonderingly found satisfaction within the germ
at our core of the basest Tranby Crofter, moved to a common
impulse of prostration before his tawdry Idol! 'Twas truly an
instructively blushful moment. Another fortunate accident was
Harry's arriving at the theatre, at the nick of time to hear the

accomplished artist that acted the Marquis[47] ask Compton, on his seventieth night of acting, "why he was so anxious to give the letter to Madame de Cintré, in the Fourth Act." This is the sort of material H. has had to work over, and he has toiled like a galley slave. He has been so manly, generous and unirritated by all the little petty incidents and exhibitions, so entirely occupied with the instructive side, that one has had infinite satisfaction in him. He has had the most delightful relations with all the Company and he says the Comptons are of an inconceivable respectability, he has never even heard Compton say "damn," at the most exasperating crisis.

January 1st, 1892

As the ugliest things go to the making of the fairest, it is not wonderful that this unholy granite substance in my breast should be the soil propitious for the perfect flowering of Katharine's unexampled genius for friendship and devotion. The story of her watchfulness, patience and untiring resource cannot be told by my feeble pen, but all the pain and discomfort seem a slender price to pay for all the happiness and peace with which she fills my days.

It must be allowed, however, that she has one most serious defect; she is most unbecoming to the race of man, and when he takes the shape of the British Doctor, the spectacle of impotent paralysis that he presents is truly pitiful. Baldwin did keep his shape and colour, but even the great Sir Andrew Clark faded visibly to the eyes.

When will men pass from the illusion of the intellectual, limited to sapless reason, and bow to the intelligent, juicy with the succulent science of life.

[47] Sydney Paxton (1860–1930) played the Marquis.

The gain isn't counted to the recluse and inactive, that having nothing to measure themselves by, and never being tested by failure, they simmer and soak perpetually in conscious complacency. Although Sir Andrew Clark, like Professor Haagan, is "all fair and blooming without," there's a skeleton within, and we saw its ghastly grin!

When we were in Bournemouth, eight years ago, there was a young American who went up to London to consult him; Sir Andrew was a couple of hours after his appointed time; as he entered the room and was announced, he immediately added "the *late* Sir Andrew Clark!" During *our* wait, I said to K., "You bet" (as Mary Cross says in every one of her notes, to make us feel at home, and encouraged) "he will make the same exclamation when he comes into this room." When hark! the door opens, and a florid gentleman enters, and "the *late* Sir Andrew" falls upon our ears, followed by the self same burst of hilarity, rippling down to us, thro' all these years. Imagine the martyrdom of a pun which has become an integral portion of one's organism to be lugged through life like the convict's ball and chain. Do you suppose he vainly tries to escape it, or is he passive in its clutches or can it be possible that some memory of the joy still survives which irradiated his being, the first time he heard it fall from his lips in the spring-time of his practice?

Sir Andrew is doubtless good and kind at bottom, but they are all terrible, with that globular manner, talking by the hour without *saying* anything, while the longing pallid victim stretches out a sickly tendril, hoping for some excrescence, a human wart, to catch on to, but it vainly slips off the polished surface, as comforting and nourishing as that of a billiard ball. In order to show K. how *en rapport* and sympathetic he was with my nervous state, he described his own sufferings in that way, and gave an account of his own pathetic youth, which never knew a woman's kiss "until I was married," this shows a rare ante-nuptial delicacy in the chaste Andrew.

Mr. John Cross told K. a curious fact, that numbers of ladies come to Sir Andrew, and never pay a fee—In answer to Mr. Cross' objection that perhaps they were nervous and forgot it, Sir Andrew said: "I should think so, if it happened the first time only, but it occurs again and again; and it is only *rich* ladies that do it, the poor ones always pay." Etiquette prevents his sending any bill, and he is too shy to ask for his fee, so in this respect as in many others the poor pay for the rich.

January 6th

It is reassuring to hear the English pronouncement that Emily Dickinson is fifth-rate, they have such a capacity for missing quality; the robust evades them equally with the subtle. Her being sicklied o'er with T. W. Higginson[48] makes one quake lest there be a latent flaw which escapes one's vision—but what tomes of philosophy *resumes* the cheap farce or expresses the highest point of view of the aspiring soul more completely than the following—

> How dreary to be somebody
> How public, like a frog
> To tell your name the livelong day
> To an admiring bog![49]

Dr. Tuckey asked me the other day whether I had ever written for the press. I vehemently disclaimed the imputation. How sad it is that the purely innocuous should always be supposed to have the trail of the family serpent upon them. The domestic

---

[48] Thomas Wentworth Higginson (1823–1911), writer, teacher, social reformer, was the first to encourage Emily Dickinson (1830–1886), editing two volumes of her verse with Mabel L. Todd (1890–1891).

[49] The poem from which Alice quotes has been included as No. 288 in *The Poems of Emily Dickinson* (ed. Johnson), 1958.

muse isn't considered very original; Mr. Cross[50] the Georgian widower asking K. whether William got his psychology from Mr. Frederick Myers, and Mrs. Lichfield (née Darwin) speaking of having just read Miss Burney's letters,[51] asked whether "Mr. Henry James had read them, and was it out of those books that he got the characters for his novels." When I held my "salon" in Bolton Row, she came to see me and asked what was the matter with me, I said: "they call it latent gout:" "Oh! that's what we have, does it come from drink in your parents?" It occurred to me that the Darwinian mind must be greater in science than in society.

January 30

Some friend was gushing to K. over Mrs Charles Kingsley's devotion to the memory of her husband, and gave in proof of it, that she always sat beside his bust and had his photo pinned to the adjoining pillow; as the last expression of refined spiritualized sentiment, could anything be more grotesquely loathsome.

On Friday, K. said to the band-master: "Why do you come back every week when you know you are never allowed to play?" "How should we know that the lady wasn't dead yet?" was the propitiatory reply. We have five braying torments every Friday.

Mr. Henry Adams[52] said to K. the other day, in discussing the ignorance of the English doctor with regard to the American invalid—"The English doctor before a New England organization is like a pink faced boy with an apple in his hand."

February 1st

I am politically quite degenerate, I couldn't even faint over the great victory at Rossendale; it stirs the blood a bit, however, and

[50] John Cross, George Eliot's husband.
[51] Fanny Burney, Mme. d'Arblay (1752–1840), novelist and diarist.
[52] Henry Adams (1838–1918), historian, was visiting in England at this time.

casts a faint shadow of regret not to be in at the fun of seeing
the poor dear, "respectable" Liberals dashed against their
scruples and floating helpless spars upon the tidal wave of
labour which will flood in as soon as the Irish question takes a
back seat.[53]

It isn't in the sorrows and the pains, but in the inexorable
inadequacy for happiness that the tragedy lies.

A lady told K. with perfect solemnity the other day that she
had cured her liver by Theosophy, and removed a tumour by
Mind Cure, pretty good for the Briton; but the gem of the first
water comes from Boston Highlands. K. told her the other day
that I had dreadful pain lately; "It is caused by London in
mourning," quoth she; "but she hasn't been out of bed for
months—and hasn't seen London in mourning, and her spirits
are perfectly cheerful." "That doesn't make any matter, it tells
upon her body and produces pain." Some one suggested that
the proper name is, "Mind Disease."

The success or failure of a life, as far as posterity goes, seems to
lie in the more or less luck of seizing the right moment of
eclipse. Poor "Collars and Cuffs" has had that chance, his
diaphanous and vapid personality will be draped about for men,
by the film of romance arising from the dramatic contrast of the
moment; in the tender feeling roused by his days of suffering,
the poor vacuous soul took on quite a human shape.

February 2nd

This long slow dying is no doubt instructive, but it is disappoint-
ingly free from excitements: "naturalness" being carried to its
supreme expression. One sloughs off the activities one by one,
and never knows that they're gone, until one suddenly finds that

[53] The by-election January 23, 1892, in Rossendale (Lancashire) was one
of the most interesting in the struggle for Home Rule. John Henry Maden,
a manufacturer and a Gladstone Liberal, won over the Liberal Unionist, Sir
Thomas Brooks.

the months have slipped away and the sofa will never more be laid upon, the morning paper read, or the loss of the new book regretted; one revolves with equal content within the narrowing circle until the vanishing point is reached, I suppose.

Vanity, however, maintains its undisputed sway, and I take satisfaction in feeling as much myself as ever, perhaps simply a more concentrated essence in this curtailment. If I could concern myself about the fate of my soul, it would give doubtless a savor of uncertainty to the fleeting moments, but I never felt so absolutely uninterested in the poor, shabby, old thing. The fact is, I have been dead so long and it has been simply such a grim shoving of the hours behind me as I faced a ceaseless possible horror, since that hideous summer of '78, when I went down to the deep sea, its dark waters closed over me and I knew neither hope nor peace; that now it's only the shrivelling of an empty pea pod that has to be completed.

A little while ago we had rather an amusing episode with the kind and usually understanding Tuckey, who was led away into assuring me that I should live a good bit still—I was terribly shocked and when he saw the havoc that he wrought, he re-assuringly said: "but you'll be comfortable, too," at which I exclaimed: "Oh I don't care about that, but boo-hoo, it's so *inconvenient!*" and the poor man burst into a roar of laughter. I was glad afterwards that it happened, as I was taken quite by surprise, and was able to test the sincerity of my mortuary inclinations. I have always *thought* that I wanted to die, but I felt quite uncertain as to what my muscular demonstrations might be at the moment of transition, for I occasionally have a quiver as of an expected dentistical wrench when I fancy the actual moment. But my substance seemed equally outraged with my mind at Tuckey's dictum, so mayhap I shall be able to maintain a calm befitting so sublimated a spirit!—at any rate there is no humbuggy "strength of mind" about it, 'tis simply physical debility, 'twould be such a bore to be perturbed.

February 28th

It is taken for granted apparently that I shall be spiritualized into a "district messenger," for here comes another message for Father and Mother; imagine my dragging them, of whom I can only think as a sublimation of their qualities, into gossip about the little more or the little less faith of Tom, Dick or Harry. I do pray to Heaven that the dreadful Mrs. Piper[54] won't be let loose upon my defenceless soul. I suppose the thing "medium" has done more to degrade spiritual conception than the grossest forms of materialism or idolatry: was there ever anything transmitted but the pettiest, meanest, coarsest facts and details: anything rising above the squalid intestines of human affairs? And oh, the curious spongy minds that sop it all up and lose all sense of taste and humour!

February 29th

A young woman in a confectioner's shop in Geneva, tells a friend of some perambulating potentate that had come into the shop in the morning and she had fed him with cakes: "How did you feel?" said the friend. "I blush to say, I felt an emotion." Nurse tells of a navvy who was once in hospital of a most foul-mouthed description. He was to go under chloroform, and she and the assistant nurse were very much perturbed as to what he might say—so one of them stood by his head to cover his mouth with a handkerchief should he curse, when to their amazement he began to babble of Jesus.

How wearing to the substance and exasperating to the nerves is the perpetual bewailing, wondering at and wishing to alter things happened, as if all personal concern didn't vanish as the "happened" crystallizes into history. Of what matter can it be

[54] Mrs. L. E. Piper, the famous Boston medium, whom William James discovered in 1885.

whether pain or pleasure has shaped and stamped the pulp within, as one is absorbed in the supreme interest of watching the outline and the tracery as the lines broaden for eternity.

March 4th

I am being ground slowly on the grim grindstone of physical pain, and on two nights I had almost asked for K.'s lethal dose, but one steps hesitantly along such unaccustomed ways and endures from second to second; and I feel sure that it can't be possible but what the bewildered little hammer that keeps me going will very shortly see the decency of ending his distracted career; however this may be, physical pain however great ends in itself and falls away like dry husks from the mind, whilst moral discords and nervous horrors sear the soul. These last, Katharine has completely under the control of her rhythmic hand, so I go no longer in dread. Oh the wonderful moment when I felt myself floated for the first time into the deep sea of divine *cessation*, and saw all the dear old mysteries and miracles vanish into vapour! That first experience doesn't repeat itself, fortunately, for it might become a seduction.

Katharine can't help it, she's made that way, a simple embodiment of Health, as Baldwin called her, "the New England Professor of doing things."

FINAL ENTRY BY KATHARINE P. LORING

All through Saturday the 5th and even in the night, Alice was making sentences. One of the last things she said to me was to make a correction in the sentence of March 4th "moral discords and nervous horrors."

This dictation of March 4th was rushing about in her brain all day, and although she was very weak and it tired her much to dictate, she could not get her head quiet until she had had it written: then she was relieved and I finished Miss Woolson's story of "Dorothy"[55] to her.

K. P. L.

[55] Miss Woolson's story was published posthumously in *Dorothy and Other Italian Stories*, 1896.

A Selected Bibliography

Allen, Gay Wilson. *William James.* New York: Viking Press, 1967.

Burr, Anna Dobson. *Alice James, Her Brothers, Her Journal.* New York: Dodd, Mead, 1934.

Dupee, F. W., ed. *Henry James: Autobiography.* New York: Criterion, 1956. (Contains *A Small Boy and Others* and *Notes of a Son and Brother.*)

Edel, Leon. *The Life of Henry James,* 5 vols. Philadelphia: J. B. Lippincott, 1953–1972; also paperback, 5 vols. New York: Avon Books, 1978. In England, 2 vols. London: Penguin, Peregrine Books, 1977.

———, ed. *Henry James: Letters,* 3 vols. Cambridge, Mass.: Harvard University Press, Belknap Press, 1974, 1975, and 1980.

James, Henry. *The Bostonians: a novel.* New York: Random House, Modern Library, 1956.

Matthiessen, F. O. *The James Family.* New York: Alfred A. Knopf, 1947.

——— and Murdock, Kenneth B., eds. *The Notebooks of Henry James.* New York: Oxford University Press, 1947.

James, William. *The Letters of William James: edited by his son Henry James,* 2 vols. Boston: Atlantic Monthly Press, 1920.

Perry, Ralph Barton. *The Thought and Character of William James,* 2 vols. Boston: Little, Brown, 1936.

Strouse, Jean. *Alice James: A Biography.* Boston: Houghton Mifflin, 1980.

Yeazell, Ruth Bernard. *The Death and Letters of Alice James.* Berkeley: University of California Press, 1981.

Index